He Had No Idea What She Was Really Like.

"Slade, you startled me."

He walked slowly into the room. "Who were you expecting?"

"No one. That's why I was so frightened. I . . . I think I'd better go up to my room."

"Stay and have a nightcap with me."

"No, I . . . I don't have my robe," she said desperately.

"It's strange how seductive women are when they're only lightly clothed," he said, eyeing her deliberately.

"I'm sure you're an expert on the subject, but I'd rather not hear about it," Holly said, turning away.

"Does it bother you that I'm as much of an expert on women as you are on men?"

TRACY SINCLAIR
has traveled extensively throughout the continental United States as well as Alaska, the Hawaiian Islands, and Canada. She currently resides in San Francisco.

Dear Reader,

Silhouette Special Editions are an exciting new line of contemporary romances from Silhouette Books. Special Editions are written specifically for our readers who want a story with heightened romantic tension.

Special Editions have all the elements you've enjoyed in Silhouette Romances and *more*. These stories concentrate on romance in a longer, more realistic and sophisticated way, and they feature greater sensual detail.

I hope you enjoy this book and all the wonderful romances from Silhouette. We welcome any suggestions or comments and invite you to write to us at the address below.

Karen Solem
Editor-in-Chief
Silhouette Books
P.O. Box 769
New York, N. Y. 10019

TRACY SINCLAIR

Mixed Blessing

Other Silhouette Books by Tracy Sinclair

Paradise Island
Holiday in Jamaica
Never Give Your Heart

SILHOUETTE BOOKS, a Simon & Schuster Division of
GULF & WESTERN CORPORATION
1230 Avenue of the Americas, New York, N.Y. 10020

Distributed by Pocket Books

ISBN: 0-671-53534-X

First Silhouette Books printing July, 1982

10 9 8 7 6 5 4 3 2 1

Map by Tony Ferrara

America's Publisher of Contemporary Romance

Printed in the U.S.A.

Mixed Blessing

ANGEL ISLAND STATE PARK
Sausalito
GOLDEN GATE NATIONAL RECREATION AREA
N
W
E
S
SAN FRANCISCO BAY
Alcatraz
Fisherman's Wharf
GOLDEN GATE BRIDGE
Telegraph Hill
Lombard St.
Chinatown
Embarcadero Center
PACIFIC OCEAN
Nob Hill
Japan Center
SAN FRANCISCO
Mission Dolores
GOLDEN GATE PARK
SAN FRANCISCO AREAS
Twin Peaks
San Francisco Zoo

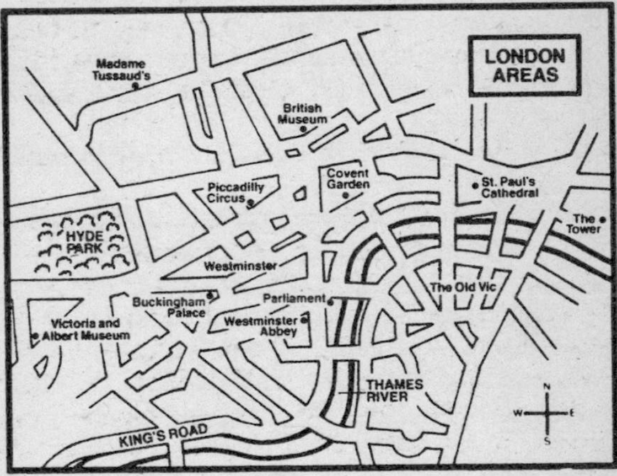
Madame Tussaud's
LONDON AREAS
British Museum
Covent Garden
St. Paul's Cathedral
Piccadilly Circus
The Tower
HYDE PARK
Westminster
The Old Vic
Buckingham Palace
Parliament
Victoria and Albert Museum
Westminster Abbey
THAMES RIVER
N
W
E
S
KING'S ROAD

Chapter One

"What are we having around here, a wake?" Holly Holbrooke demanded, surveying the other three people in the large newsroom.

"We didn't think a celebration was called for," Tim Griffith answered sarcastically, stretching his long legs out and crossing them at the ankles. With his head resting on the back of the chair, he was a picture of dejection.

"Well, I don't think we need to throw in the towel yet."

"Maybe not, but I wouldn't put a down payment on a yacht if I were you," he replied cynically.

Thrusting her hands in the back pockets of her jeans, Holly stuck her small chin out. "I don't know what's the matter with you people. We don't know for certain that we're going to get the ax, but if we do so what? You act like this was the only newspaper in San Francisco. If the worst does happen, we'll get *better* jobs that's all."

The others lounging apathetically around the city room regarded her with various degrees of bitterness. "Sure, that's fine for you," Ed Smalley said. "You're what—twenty-three, twenty-four?"

She looked half of that in her jeans and checked shirt, especially since her long mane of black hair was tucked under an old baseball cap. From the back Holly looked like a young boy, but nobody could make that mistake when she turned around. Those small rounded breasts could only belong to a very delectable female.

"I'm fifty-one," Ed told her. "Who wants to hire a fifty-one-year-old rewrite man?"

Holly's blue-green eyes sparkled angrily. There were times when they were a clear aquamarine, but in the grip of emotion they tended to turn a deep turquoise. "You've been with the *Bulletin* for fifteen years, Ed. Loyalty has to count for something and if this Rockwell hotshot has the sense he was born with, he'll keep you on."

The older man shrugged. "Sentimentality has no place in business and from what I hear about Slade Rockwell, he's a pretty ruthless man. He didn't build a publishing empire by being Mr. Nice Guy."

"I don't know what he wants with the *Bulletin* anyway," Holly said impatiently. "It's been losing money for a year."

"That's the way he operates," Cynthia Gordon told her. "He likes to take over ailing publications and shake them up like a dog worrying a bone. I suppose when you have all the money in the world the only thing left is the challenge." She sighed and drummed long red fingernails on the desk.

The gloom was palpable but Holly tried to rally their spirits. "Why expect the worst? So what if he has a reputation for swallowing up little companies? He has to have someone to run them doesn't he?"

"Sure—his own people," Tim said. This was his first reporter's job and he was especially bitter over the prospect of losing it. "He brings in a team of efficiency experts to cut expenses to the bone and then installs his own men to preside over what's left."

"Or else he merges the paper with one of his other publications," Ed chimed in. "Either way we get lost in the shuffle. People are only chess pieces to men like that."

Holly was opening her mouth to express her contempt for this kind of behavior when a deep masculine voice in back of her said, "Good morning, I'm Slade Rockwell." Before she could turn around, a strong hand gripped her shoulder. "Would you mind telling Mr. Farnsworth that Mr. Rockwell is here to see him, sonny?"

She whirled around, pulling off her cap so the gleaming hair spilled over her slender shoulders, but the angry words she was about to deliver died on her lips. The broad shouldered man towering over her was enough to take any woman's breath away.

There were laughter lines around the clear gray eyes that were fringed with thick black lashes, but the firm mouth warned that this was a man to be reckoned with—in more ways than one. The full lower lip hinted at a dormant sensuality that, under the right circumstances, could be dangerously compelling. His lean muscular frame belonged on a professional athlete rather than a businessman and the deep suntan spoke of hours spent outdoors instead of in stuffy offices.

But it wasn't his blatant masculinity that made Holly's breath catch in her throat. It was a sense of déjà vu—a feeling that she knew this man intimately. But she had never seen him before surely? And then it came to her! He was the shadowy figure in her recurring dreams, the man who came to her in the night and lifted her in his arms, his dark head bending over her as he claimed her willing mouth. She knew every contour of that hard body but his face had always eluded her—until now.

Holly's lips parted in wonder and she drank in every detail of his appearance, staring at him as if mesmerized. He seemed equally taken by surprise but for a different reason.

One dark eyebrow rose sardonically as his eyes swept over her slender curved figure. "It seems I've made a serious error. Please forgive me."

His lips twitched with the amusement he was trying to suppress and the romantic illusion was abruptly shattered. Holly's spine stiffened as she realized what an insane trick her mind had played on her. This was Slade Rockwell, the enemy, the unprincipled man who was going to disrupt her whole life. How could she ever have confused him with that supremely tender lover who cradled her so protectively in her dreams? Disappointment coursed through her followed by scalding anger. Not only was he an imposter, he had insultingly mistaken her for a little boy and now he was *laughing* at her!

She had to tilt her head back to look up at him but there was outrage in every inch of her slight body. "Can we print that in the paper? It must be a scoop when the famous Mr. Rockwell admits to making a mistake."

She heard Cynthia gasp and Holly experienced a moment of discomfort herself. Had that childish insult really come out of her mouth? She was an experienced professional reporter, used to dealing with all kinds of difficult people and situations. Why was she letting her personal feeling for this man dictate such churlish behavior?

Everyone was looking at her with shocked disapproval and it banished the fleeting guilt, making Holly stubbornly defiant. Slade Rockwell had probably decided their fate already and even if she had been all girlish smiles, it wouldn't have changed the result. One glimpse of that hard handsome face had told her that it wouldn't have made any difference if they had all strewn rose petals in his path. So much for her earlier optimism. This was a man who couldn't be influenced and Holly was glad she had spoken her mind.

Ed's quiet voice broke the tension. "I'll show you to Mr. Farnsworth's office."

"Thank you," Slade Rockwell answered absently, his eyes holding Holly's appraisingly.

Hers were the first to waver and she looked away, noticing for the first time the platoon of silent men in back of him. They were all young, neatly dressed and studiously inconspicuous, each armed with a black briefcase. Hatchet men, she thought scornfully as they disappeared into the managing editor's office. Well, they all knew whose name would be first on the list didn't they?

"Were you out of your mind, Holly, saying a thing like that to him?" Cynthia asked as soon as she was sure they were out of hearing.

"I don't care, he deserved it," she muttered, "calling me sonny in that patronizing manner."

"What did you expect with that stupid baseball cap on your head?" Tim asked disgustedly. "You sure gave him some first impression of this paper. He probably thinks we're a bunch of hippies."

"What difference does it make what he thinks?" Holly answered. "We could all be up for the Pulitzer Prize and it wouldn't influence his decision."

"You're sure changing your tune. What happened to that pep talk you were giving us a minute ago?"

"That was before I met him," Holly said somberly. "I don't trust that man."

"Because he took you for a boy and your feelings are hurt?"

"Of course not. It's . . . I don't know . . . it's just something about him."

Tim shook his head. "You're really amazing! Do you honestly think you can judge a man after one brief glimpse?"

"This one I can," Holly said stubbornly.

"You're crazy," Cynthia said. "I thought he was perfectly charming. Under great provocation, I might add."

Holly ignored the last part. "The Medici were also considered charming and Henry VIII was supposed to have been a barrel of laughs—when he wasn't chopping off heads."

"Only his wives'," Tim said mockingly, "and you aren't apt to be one of those."

"Unfortunately, none of us are," Cynthia sighed. "What a waste of such a handsome hunk. It's no secret that Monique Duvall has been after him for years and if she can't get him to the altar no woman can."

Tim's eyes gleamed at the mention of the famous actress. "Who could turn down Monique Duvall? The guy must be an oddball after all."

"I didn't say he turned her down." Cynthia gave him a knowing look out of the corner of her eye. "He just doesn't want to get married. There's a delicious story about him that's going around the party circuit. Our Mr. Rockwell is supposed to have told somebody that falling in love is enough of an aberration without compounding it by getting married. It isn't anything one can print though of course."

"Why not?" Holly demanded. "It's the kind of thing you would slaver over if one of your precious socialites said it."

Cynthia regarded her dispassionately. "My dear girl, I enjoy my job as society editor and, unlike you, I have no death wish. I don't want to go back to the want ads. You're the only one around here who bites the hand that feeds you."

"I wouldn't dare. Anyone who bit Slade Rockwell would be asking for blood poisoning!"

"Oh, come on, Holly, you have to admit he's gorgeous," Cynthia urged.

"And about as principled as one of those Grandees at the Spanish Inquisition," Holly remarked coldly.

That's what he looked like too, she thought, autocratic and imposing. His self-confidence in that impeccably tailored suit infuriated her. Even his thick black hair was expensively cut and faultless. There wasn't a chink in his armor anywhere. An unaccustomed feeling of helplessness threatened to overwhelm Holly and she grabbed her denim jacket and stalked toward the door.

"Where are you going?" Tim asked.

"To City Hall. Chief Kelley is giving a briefing on the hunt for those service station killers."

"I thought that wasn't until two o'clock."

"I'll be back later," she evaded.

Wheeling her car out of the parking lot a few moments later, Holly breathed a sigh of relief. She knew she had made a fool of herself by her childish behavior and if the reason for it were known, she would appear even more ridiculous.

Fortunately, it was only a momentary aberration and she had seen through the man almost immediately. He was ruthless and arrogant and overbearing and

. . . Holly searched wildly for other derogatory adjectives. All of the romantic illusions he inspired so briefly had been transformed into a tremendous dislike.

Logically, of course, he wasn't responsible for her fantasies but Holly was beyond logic. He had made her feel young and tremulous, like Cinderella at her first glimpse of Prince Charming and she would never forgive him for that. Prince Charming? Hah! Make that Blackbeard the pirate!

After driving aimlessly for a few blocks, Holly decided to work at her own apartment finishing an article she was doing on sweatshops in Chinatown. It might never see print but she was still on the *Bulletin*'s payroll and they were entitled to her services until those were discontinued.

Pounding the familiar keys of her battered portable temporarily banished all thoughts of the unsettling conditions at the newspaper, but when a glance at the clock showed that it was almost time to go downtown, they returned in force.

On an impulse, Holly decided to change clothes. San Francisco was a casual town but maybe Tim was right. Perhaps she had gotten a little *too* casual lately. It certainly didn't have anything to do with that Rockwell character. He would be gone by the time she got back anyway and good riddance to him!

It was getting late so Holly grabbed the first thing that came to hand, a gray and lavender tweed dirndl skirt. She pulled a white lamb's wool sweater over her head and ran a comb through her silky swinging hair. Shrugging into the matching tweed jacket, Holly spared one swift look in the mirror and then paused, frowning. The softly feminine reflection that stared back should have pleased her but it didn't.

Her colleagues were used to seeing her in jeans and Holly was proud of the fact that even seasoned pros treated her like one of the guys. She had never asked for any quarter on grounds of being a woman and they hadn't given any. How would they react to her new image? But there was no time now to change. Grabbing the obligatory roomy shoulder bag that was large enough to hold a notebook and pencils, she sped out the door.

It was late afternoon when she returned to the office and the big newsroom was empty. Had the ax fallen already? It was a sobering thought but out of habit, she sat down to write her story. As soon as the typewriter began to chatter, Mac Farnsworth appeared in the doorway.

"Where the hell have you been all day, Holly?"

"Working," she answered shortly without elaborating.

He looked tired and Holly felt suddenly contrite. None of this was really his fault. It was the economy and the fierce competition that existed in publishing plus a number of other things. Poor Mac was a minnow in a pool of sharks.

"Slade Rockwell wants to talk to you," he said. "He hung around for a while waiting and I gathered it was a new experience for him." Holly was sure of that but his next words cancelled her small victory. "He wants to see you at his hotel suite as soon as possible," Mac informed her. "You better get up there on the double."

The Huntington Hotel was small but exclusive, with a green and white canopy stretching from the entry to the curb and a portly uniformed doorman who was straight out of *The Merry Widow*. It had been an elegant apartment house at one time and now catered to a transient but moneyed clientele. Located on top of Nob Hill, it faced a carefully manicured little park.

The living room of Slade's suite was furnished with all the style of a private home, but he and his staff had made somewhat of a shambles of it. A young woman was utilizing the graceful French desk as a highly unsuitable typewriter table and papers and manila envelopes had descended like a blizzard on every available surface including some of the chairs.

"Can I help you?" The attractive young man who had answered the door was looking at Holly appreciatively. He was tall and thin with light brown hair falling across a high forehead and there was a pleasant twinkle in his hazel eyes.

"I've come to see Mr. Rockwell," she said distantly. His admiration was evident but she was determined not to give an inch.

He turned slightly and she could see through the living room to the open door of the bedroom beyond. Slade Rockwell was lying on the bed propped up against the headboard, his long legs outstretched. He had the telephone receiver cradled on one shoulder and was barking orders into it while rapidly making notes on a pad.

"I'm afraid he's kind of busy right now. I hope there's something I can do for you. I'm Alan Beale."

"No. He sent for me but it probably isn't important. Just tell him Holly Holbrooke was here." It was only a reprieve but she was willing to settle for small favors.

"Wait!" His urgent voice stopped her as she turned toward the elevator. "If he wants to see you it probably *is* important and I don't want to be responsible for letting you get away." A winning smile accompanied the confession and Holly couldn't help smiling back. "Won't you come in and wait?"

She entered the suite reluctantly and Alan went to tell Slade she was here. He glanced up and frowned at her but made no move to cut short his conversation. Holly frowned back and seated herself stiffly on the couch.

Alan came back and said, "I hope it won't be too long. Can I get you something to read in the meantime?" When she shook her head, he disappeared back into the bedroom.

Holly was furious at being kept waiting like a naughty pupil in the principal's office, but the activity around her was engrossing. In a way it was like a city room when a deadline approaches. Extra telephones had been installed and they rang incessantly. A thin faced older man sitting behind an improvised desk, sometimes talked on two of them simultaneously. He had looked up when she entered and nodded vaguely in her direction, but his attention was immediately reclaimed by the importance of the calls.

Holly couldn't help overhearing the conversations and she was impressed in spite of herself. The scope of the Rockwell empire was even more awesome than she had guessed. He controlled publications all over the world and her glimpse into the international world of publishing was both impressive and frightening.

It was like a giant Monopoly game with the commodity being communications instead of real estate. In just the time that she sat there, properties were bought and sold and merged and buried. It was a sobering thought to realize how much power this man wielded.

Holly's resentment at being kept waiting had long since faded into fascination at what was going on around her, but about seven o'clock her stomach began to remind her that she had skipped lunch. Didn't these people even stop for meals? At that moment, Alan came out of the bedroom shrugging on his jacket.

"I'm sorry it's taking so long, Miss Holbrooke." He smiled wryly at her. "Every day brings crises but some days more than others. Mr. Rockwell says he will be with you soon." He turned to the man on the telephone. "Time to leave, Victor. We have to make that plane for Las Vegas."

The older man murmured a few last words into the phone before hanging up. Pushing back his chair, he stretched tired muscles before coming toward Holly to extend his hand. "I'm Victor Cranston, Slade's attorney. Didn't mean to ignore you that way."

Alan threw her a charming smile. "Me either, Miss Holbrooke. I'm sorry we have to rush off like this but I hope we'll be seeing a lot of you."

Holly didn't have time to voice her doubts before the two men hustled out the door. The girl at the desk put a cover on the typewriter and followed them out with a vague smile in Holly's direction.

Suddenly the room was very quiet. Holly's heart started to race and her palms were damp with perspiration. The meeting with Slade couldn't be delayed much longer. What on earth is the matter with you she chided herself sharply, all he can do is fire you and that won't mean the end of the world. But something inexplicable was making her stomach muscles tighten.

"Come in here, Miss Holbrooke." Slade's deep musical voice sounded so suddenly that she jumped.

She approached the bedroom with trepidation and stopped abruptly in the doorway, her eyes widening incredulously. He was unbuttoning his shirt and as she watched, he pulled it out of his waistband and shrugged it off completely. Powerful muscles rippled over his shoulders and she couldn't drag her eyes away from the broad tanned chest with its mat of black curly hair.

To her utter dismay, her voice came out in a small croak. "What . . . what do you think you're doing?"

"I *thought* I was removing my shirt, what does it look like to you?" he mocked, his gray eyes filled with suppressed merriment.

Holly recovered, although a wave of color suffused her face. Ignoring the taunting question she snapped, "Well, you can just put it back on."

He looked at the offending garment critically. "Are you that fond of it? Personally, I thought those green stripes clashed with my eyes."

"You know perfectly well what I meant," she said stormily, "and the answer is no, Mr. Rockwell."

He sauntered across the room and came to stand very close to her. Holly was overwhelmed by the sheer masculinity of that long, lithe body and danger signals started clamoring in her brain. There was a feeling of leashed power that frightened, yet fascinated her. He was like a jungle animal poised to spring and she had to force herself not to turn and run. Holly dug her nails into her palms and raised her small chin defiantly. That was one satisfaction he wasn't going to have.

"I don't recall asking you anything, Miss Holbrooke," he said softly.

His insolent glance traveled from her face down over her slender figure, lingering on the soft curve of her breasts revealed by the clinging sweater and she drew a sharp breath. If anyone could actually undress you with his eyes, this man was doing it. She actually *felt* naked—and terribly vulnerable. Sudden apprehension filled Holly as the blood thundered in her veins and she turned to leave, no longer caring that he had won another round.

"Wait a minute, where are you going?"

She didn't trust herself to answer, quickening her steps toward the safety of the front door, but a long arm shot out and a large hand fastened like a handcuff around her slim wrist.

Unreasoning panic set in and she pounded against his bare chest with her free hand. "Let me go! If you don't let go of me this instant I'm going to scream the house down, I warn you!" Even as she said it, Holly realized that there was no one to hear. When her frantic struggles were futile, she tried to kick his shins and only succeeded in hurting her foot since she had on open-toed shoes.

He captured the hand she was pummeling him with so ineffectually and held both of them behind her back, jerking her body against his so she couldn't fight any longer. "What the devil is wrong with you?" he scowled. "All I want to do is talk to you."

She was painfully aware of being crushed tightly in his arms, the dark hair on his chest tickling her cheek. She was molded to the length of his body, his muscled thighs digging into hers. The male smell and feel of him was doing strange things to her pulse rate, but Holly would have died sooner than admit it.

Raising blazing blue eyes she said, "I don't think that's what it would look like to a casual bystander."

"You are the most exasperating child I've ever come across," he ground out. "Will you tell me why we always get off on the wrong foot at every meeting?"

"Perhaps it's because every time we get within shouting distance of each other you insult me," she glared. "And for your information, I'm not a child."

Some of the anger left his face and his grip loosened but it didn't add to Holly's peace of mind. In a subtle way, his hold on her became an embrace instead of a restraint. "Perhaps that was the wrong word." There was a smile in his voice. "But for *your* information, I have no designs on your delectable body. I wasn't preparing for . . . action. I was merely changing my shirt so that we can go downstairs and have dinner."

His explanation and her own overreaction made Holly feel like a fool and she lowered her lashes in a flushed embarrassment. "I'm not hungry," she muttered.

"Too bad," he drawled, "I'm starving. I guess you'll just have to sit there and watch me eat." His arms loosened tentatively. "I meant what I said though, I do want to talk to you. If I let you go will you behave yourself?"

"That's what I should be asking you!" she exclaimed indignantly, wriggling out of his grasp.

"Don't you think it's time you dropped the act, Miss Holbrooke?" His firm mouth curled in scorn. "I've already told you that I'm not going to assault your virtue," the last was said sneeringly, "but even if I were, what's the big deal? I'm well aware of how permissive your generation is."

Holly had taken a great deal of ribbing over what was considered her prudishness. It was true that most of the girls she knew had had at least one affair and they scornfully asked if she was saving herself for marriage. It wasn't that but how could she explain to them that she had never met a man she wanted to go to bed with—until now. No! Her face flamed at the ridiculous thought. She hated this man! He was insulting and domineering and everything she despised.

She wanted to lash out and tell him just how wide of

the mark he was, but instead she took a perverse delight in saying coolly, "Oh, we are, Mr. Rockwell, we certainly believe in taking our pleasure where we find it the same as men but we like to be *asked* not coerced."

His look of contempt scorched her but she forced herself to endure his glare and return it. "I'm sorry I didn't say 'may I,' we would have been in bed by now," he said glacially.

"Don't count on it, Mr. Rockwell. I don't need the job that badly!"

Comprehension lit his face and some of the harshness went out of it. "You thought I . . . oh, Holly, you're even younger than I thought. Never mind for now but I can see that you and I have some talking to do." He gave her a gentle push toward the bar. "Go make us a drink while I get cleaned up."

He was freshly shaven when he reappeared in a dark suit that emphasized his broad shoulders, although Holly knew their width needed no padding. The clean white shirt accentuated his tan and everything about him was big and male and overpowering. She resolutely tried to ignore his indisputable magnetism, but it was a relief when they finished their drinks and left the suite to go downstairs.

Many heads followed their progress through the elegant dining room, especially the female ones and Holly felt an unwilling pleasure in having this man as her escort. Especially since Slade had surprised her by making a complete turnabout and was exerting himself to be charming. It would have taken someone a lot more experienced than Holly to resist him and she allowed herself a tentative truce.

She had eaten her way through oysters on the half shell, caesar salad, a steak and asparagus hollandaise and was now attacking a chocolate mousse. Slade was drinking black coffee and he regarded her with amusement.

"I thought you said you weren't hungry. I'd hate to feed you when you are."

She grinned cheerfully. "It isn't often I get taken out this fancy."

"Do you kids still exist on pizza and hamburgers?"

"I wish you would stop calling me a kid, Mr. Rockwell. I'm twenty-three years old and I have been self-supporting since I got out of college."

"Sorry. I'm afraid we're victims of the generation gap," he said sardonically.

She put her spoon down and studied his strong face, carefully appraising the straight nose, the high cheekbones and the thick dark hair that didn't show even a trace of gray. "I wish you would stop talking like my father because you aren't old enough. I know this is going to come as a great shock but you and I are the same generation."

His raised eyebrows denoted incredulity. "I suppose at thirty-seven I'm *not* old enough to be your father, but you're right it's frightening to think we're contemporaries."

"What do you have against my—*our* generation?" she demanded.

He shook his head. "We've been getting along famously—for the first time since we met, I might add. I don't want to rouse that fiery temper of yours again."

"I promise not to get angry. Please, just tell me what your objections are."

He hesitated for a moment and then said, "All right, if you're sure that's what you want." Slade's narrowed eyes were no longer indulgent. "Well, in the first place, I can't help but object to any group of people who call themselves the 'me' generation. Thinking only of yourself in our world today is a very unpalatable form of narcissism."

"Are you any different?" she challenged. "You seem to be pretty single-minded yourself. Aren't you really just out to make the almighty buck?"

He looked at her somberly. "Is that what you think motivates me? My dear girl, I have already made enough money to last several lifetimes but money carries responsibility—or should. A great many people are dependent on me. If I closed up shop tomorrow I would survive famously, but do you know how many lives would be disrupted?"

Holly's eyes fell as she remembered some of the conversations she had overheard in his suite that afternoon. A portion of them had concerned relocating people and much thought was going into the decisions. If he were really as ruthless as she had accused him of being, would he have bothered?

"I . . . it's possible I may have misjudged you," she faltered.

His smile was grim. "Save your apology until you hear the rest of my critique. It isn't just your hedonism that annoys me. I also disapprove strongly of your morals. It is incomprehensible to me how you kids can fall in and out of bed so easily."

Holly's temper rose in spite of her promise. "Don't you think that's rather hypocritical in view of your own rather notorious reputation?"

The smile he gave her was cynical this time. "If you can't see the difference then I'm sorry for you."

"I don't want your pity, I want equality," she flared. "If we slept together tonight, why would it make you any better than me?"

"I sincerely hope that's not what you have in mind

because I'm not going to oblige you," he mocked. Holly's cheeks flamed but before she could explode, he held up a cautioning hand. "Allow me to answer your question. If I took you to bed I would be considered a dashing fellow. You would be considered—something else."

"It was just an example," she said stiffly. Seeking wildly for a way to get back at him she said, "You're too old for me anyway."

His mouth curved cynically. "Am I really?"

To her dismay, his hand went to the nape of her neck under the long tumbling hair and strong fingers stroked the tense muscles slowly. She tried to move away but the fingers tightened, turning her face toward him. He was so close that she could feel the heat of his body and her heart began a tattoo that was almost audible. Her lips parted involuntarily, drawing his attention to her mouth, and he gently traced the shape of it, pulling down the lower lip slightly and running a long forefinger just inside.

A sensation she had never experienced gripped Holly. She was drowning in his sensuous touch, unable to move, and her wide aquamarine eyes never left his face.

Slade drew a sharp breath and abruptly released her. "You're right, I am too old for you," he said grimly. "That was entirely too easy. Lucky for you I don't seduce little girls no matter how willing they are. What you need is a chastity belt, young lady."

Holly was crimson with embarrassment and rage. After finding that coherent speech was beyond her, she started to get up. Even ignominious flight was preferable to remaining here with this destructive man. But Slade pinned her arms to her sides and pushed her back against the leather booth.

"You were the one who insisted on the truth. You also promised you wouldn't get angry," he reminded her.

"I'm not angry, I'm bloody well furious!" she raged. "I asked for a general opinion, I didn't expect you to get so blasted personal."

"It was an object lesson, my dear," he said grimly. "But at least you've answered my question. It's just pure sex with you kids isn't it? Didn't your parents ever teach you anything about love?" Holly's expression changed and long eyelashes swept her flushed cheeks. When she didn't answer, he shook her slightly. "Well, didn't they?"

"If they did I was too young to remember," she said dully. "My parents died when I was eight."

His punishing grip loosened and he looked at her searchingly. "I'm sorry, that was thoughtless of me."

She accepted his apology with a slight shrug. "You couldn't know."

"Who raised you?" he asked quietly. "Were you brought up in an orphanage?"

"No." Her mouth curled in a bitter little smile. "I would probably have been better off in one but it wouldn't have looked right to all the friends and neighbors. I lived with a succession of reluctant relatives who fed and clothed me adequately, but you're right they didn't teach me much about love."

His warm hand covered hers and when she curled her fingers into a fist, he straightened them out one by one. "Now I understand all those thorns and prickles," he said softly. "But it isn't necessary to bristle at the whole world, little one."

His voice was so gentle that it brought a lump to her throat which for some obscure reason made her very angry. "Save your pity, I don't need it. I can fend for myself."

A smile curved his firm lips and laughter lit his gray eyes. "I've already found that out. And while we're still speaking to each other, maybe we'd better get back on neutral ground and talk business. Suppose you start by telling me about the people in your office."

Some of the tension left her taut body and Holly welcomed the suggestion. Her emotions felt like they had been put through a food processor. "What do you want to know?"

"Start with Mac Farnsworth. Is he happy as managing editor or would he rather be in a job that has less pressures?"

Comprehension swept over Holly leaving her even angrier than before. "So that's it! That's what this whole evening has been leading up to—you want me to be a spy! Well, let me tell you this, Mr. Rockwell—"

His hard palm covered her mouth and she almost choked at the amusement on his face. "I hate to cut off your undoubtedly eloquent condemnation of me, but to save time let me set the record straight. I don't use spies. I merely wanted your opinion on the capabilities of the people you work with."

"And you don't call that spying?" she asked scornfully.

"No, I don't. Use your head, Holly. The *Bulletin* is losing money in spite of the fact that it's a good newspaper so there's something wrong somewhere. If Mac Farnsworth isn't right for the job, chances are he isn't happy doing it."

"And if I told you that then you'd fire him."

He sighed. "You really don't trust me do you? I'm not going to fire Mac. From the little I've seen of him I know he's a good man, but not necessarily a good managing editor. I think he might be happier heading up a monthly publication where there isn't the grinding pressure of a newspaper. I have a number of slots where I could place him."

Holly was amazed at his insight on such short acquaintance with her boss. Mac had often expressed a wistful desire to have more time and space to do stories in greater depth than a paper allowed. Now it looked like he might get his wish. "I'm glad to hear Mac isn't on your hit list," she said slowly, "but how about the others? Ed Smalley has been with the *Bulletin* for fifteen years and he's fantastic at what he does."

"That's exactly the sort of thing I want to know."

Holly ducked her head and fiddled with her dessert spoon, the dark curtain of her hair partly shielding her delicate face. "I hope I really *have* misjudged you, but I still can't tell you the things you want to know because I don't want to sit in judgment on my friends. Maybe some of us do our jobs a little better than others but you can't ask me to flunk anyone."

A long forefinger tipped her chin up so that she had to look at him. "I don't expect front page scoops from everyone and the only reason I ever fire anybody is for downright incompetence or disloyalty. If I tell you that none of your friends are going to lose their jobs will you believe me?"

Searching his strong face anxiously, Holly was finally convinced. "How about me?" she faltered.

He gave her a broad grin. "You're something else entirely."

"What does that mean?" she demanded.

"We'll talk about it in a little while. First tell me about the people in the newsroom—this young fellow, Tim Griffith for instance."

They talked and Holly gave her opinions succinctly, her trust completely won by this complex man. She still sensed that he could be deadly under certain circumstances and it was a sobering thought, but Holly knew with an inner certainty that anyone he turned his back on had probably earned the punishment.

After they had covered everyone in the office she looked at him tentatively, "I guess that only leaves me. Would you like my qualifications?"

His savoring glance swept over her and then returned to her full mouth. "I think most of them are evident."

She stiffened angrily. "I suppose that answers my question but you might as well know right now that in spite of your low opinion of my morals, I don't intend sleeping with you just to hold my job."

"As I told you before, it's polite to wait until you're asked. Delicious though you may be, Angel Eyes, I have something entirely different in mind for you."

"I can just imagine!"

"I don't think you can. What I'm offering you is a job as my personal assistant."

Holly gasped. "You have to be joking!" When assured that he was not, she said, "But why? You don't approve of a single thing about me!"

"I wouldn't say that. You have many excellent qualities that appeal to me."

"Name one," she said shortly.

"Among other things, you have leadership ability, a keen mind and you're very conscientious. How is that for starters?"

"Very flattering but what makes you think so when you don't really know me?" she asked suspiciously, sure that there must be an ulterior motive here somewhere.

"I spent quite a lot of time around the *Bulletin* offices

waiting for you to return," he said dryly, "but at least it wasn't wasted. Farnsworth and your co-workers were very complimentary."

"That's nice," she said uncertainly.

"You have a knack of getting along with people—everyone except me that is." He smiled derisively. "But perhaps that will come in time."

Considering how rocky their relationship had been in the short space of one day, Holly wasn't that certain. "I'm not so sure it will," she murmured doubtfully.

"Would you be willing to try?"

"I have tried," she said indignantly. "You're the one who is difficult. One minute you're nice to me and the next you're insufferably insulting."

"I know you won't believe this but I never meant to be. However, I'll stop badgering you if you'll stop playing games with me."

"I wasn't aware that I had been."

"You don't call it devious when you act like a liberated woman one minute and a coy maiden the next?" he demanded.

"I have never acted coy in my whole life!" she denied hotly.

His raised eyebrows were skeptical. "Oh, no? How about this evening in my bedroom? Although all of your statements have been designed to make me think differently, you blushed like a little virgin when you watched me take off my shirt. If I didn't know better, I would almost have believed you were inexperienced."

Holly's cheeks flamed and she looked away. "I was just giving you what I thought you wanted," she lied.

"Well, don't do it anymore," he said curtly. "Just be yourself and we'll do fine together. Now, let's get back to business. We're engaged in a massive reorganization campaign and I need someone to assist in evaluating the capabilities of our employees. You have a knack for sizing people up and I think you would enjoy the job. It will mean almost constant travel, but since you have no ties that shouldn't pose any problem."

"N . . . no," she said faintly.

"As soon as we are finished here we go to London and then Rome. You will have to be ready to leave within a week." He named a salary that made Holly gasp. "Well, what's your answer?"

"I . . . I don't know what to say. Suppose . . . suppose it doesn't work out and you're not happy with me?"

"Then I'll give you a ticket home and your old job back or a comparable one anywhere else in the world."

There could be no refusal to an offer like that and Holly knew it but a strange reluctance gripped her. From the moment she had met this man the sparks had flown. Granted her original appraisal of him had been wrong but that didn't make their relationship any more palatable. She trusted him now but she didn't really like him. In fact, Holly disapproved of Slade as much as he did of her. He was forever putting her in the wrong and his derogatory opinion of her was galling even though that was entirely her own fault, Holly admitted. She could have set him straight a dozen times but perversely, had chosen not to.

What would happen if he ever found out how wrong he was about her morals? Not that it was likely to happen. Even though they would be working closely together, it would be strictly business. On her part certainly but would Slade change his mind and prove to be difficult? Even if he did, what was there to worry about? He could be very disarming as she had witnessed this evening, but surely she was impervious to that phony charm.

He watched the play of emotions over her troubled face. "There is a whole world out there, Holly. Can you turn your back on it?" he asked softly.

She gave a deep shuddering sigh, knowing that she couldn't. It was an opportunity that came only once in a lifetime. A chance to see foreign countries and gain experience that would be priceless. It would change her whole life—but for better or worse?

"If I take the job I'm going to tell you exactly what I think," she said slowly, almost hoping he wouldn't agree. "No soft pedaling it because you're the boss."

He ran his finger lightly down her tilted nose. "My dear child, I didn't doubt it for a minute."

Chapter Two

The week that followed was unlike anything Holly had ever experienced. It was something like being in the eye of a hurricane, but although she had never worked harder there was a feeling of heady excitement that kept her constantly keyed up.

Alan Beale was in charge of showing her the ropes and after a very short time, she felt as though she had known him all her life. Perhaps because he was only five years older than she, they discovered that they had so much in common. His admiration was evident but never intrusive. Holly felt relaxed and comfortable around him, a state she never achieved with Slade, although she had to admit her new boss was a genius.

The atmosphere around the *Bulletin* went from apprehension to relief as Slade listened attentively to suggestions and when necessary, switched people around so unobtrusively that it almost seemed as though the changes had been their own idea. Reorganization went smoothly, the only problem child being Cynthia, the society editor, but since she was out of town on assignment the resolution of her job hadn't been made.

The week was drawing to a close when Alan suggested they take the afternoon off. "We'll be leaving for London soon and I haven't seen anything of San Francisco. How about giving me the grand tour?" he asked.

Holly was dubious. "How will the boss feel about that?"

"Slade? He won't mind. He knows we're just about finished and as a matter of fact, he flew down to Hollywood for the day."

The information annoyed Holly because Slade had been driving them to finish up this week so they could leave on Sunday. Now he wouldn't be available in case anything came up that needed his attention. Well, that wouldn't be their fault. His personal life didn't interest her and if he thought it was more important to cavort with a sexy movie star that was his business.

Giving Alan a brilliant smile she said, "I think that's a smashing idea. We'll do the whole tourist bit."

They started at Fisherman's Wharf and then rapidly toured some other notable spots, including Chinatown, the museums and Cliff House where they watched hundreds of seals climbing over a mammoth rock that jutted out of the sea. It was a lot to cram into such a short time, but their ultimate destination was the wine country of the Napa valley.

The crisp sunny day seemed made to order and a flotilla of little white sailboats chased each other through the choppy waters of the bay as they drove over the Golden Gate Bridge.

The picturesque town of Sausalito greeted them at the other end and Alan looked with interest at the houses clinging to the steep cliffs that surrounded the small business section and waterfront. They were terraced all the way to the top and crowded together with no sense of order.

"It looks like a town in Italy," he commented.

"A lot of people have said that but I wouldn't know. I've never been to Italy."

"You'll love it," Alan assured her, "especially traveling with Slade. He goes strictly first class all the way." There was admiration in his voice and Holly had already discovered how fiercely loyal he was. In Alan's eyes, Slade could do not wrong.

"He's a strange man," she said slowly. "We didn't hit it off at all in the beginning. In fact, I detested him."

Alan looked at her with surprise. "That isn't the usual reaction. He has to fight women off with a stick."

"Maybe our chemistry is wrong," she shrugged. "Or maybe I'm just wary of handsome men who use their looks to get what they want."

"It's more than looks with Slade. He can charm the birds out of the trees when he wants to."

"An apt analogy," she said dryly. "Isn't that what the British call girls?"

Alan grinned. "True."

Holly hesitated a moment, caught between curiosity and a strange reluctance to have it satisfied, but curiosity won out. In an elaborately casual voice she remarked, "I understand he has quite a thing going with Monique Duvall."

"She's just his Hollywood connection, wait until we get to London and you see Lady Dillingham. Now there's a dish."

"Slade sounds like a sailor with a girl in every port," Holly remarked acidly.

Alan shrugged. "Maybe it's the old safety in numbers theory."

"It's a good thing he doesn't plan on getting married. It would be a shame to deprive that large a segment of the female population," she said stiffly.

Alan's eyes glinted with amusement as he registered her disapproval and deftly changed the subject.

The broad highway led through the Valley of the Moon where gently rolling hills were cloaked in deep green. Cows dotted broad pastures and there were horse barns and acre after acre of grape vines.

They stopped at one of the big wineries and toured the ivy covered building, shivering in the sudden coolness of the stone vaults and marveling at huge oaken casks that reached almost to the lofty ceilings. Afterward, they sipped several different wines in the tasting room. Then they wandered outside in the beautiful garden where roses of every variety filled the air with perfume.

On the way home they stopped at a small Italian restaurant that had crimson tablecloths and fat candles flickering in hurricane lamps. It was a random choice that turned out to be a happy one. The veal *piccata* was done to a turn with just the right tang of lemon and the *torta Margherita con pescas* melted in the mouth.

Holly put her fork down with a sigh of repletion. "This has been the most heavenly day, Alan."

"The first of many I hope," he told her fondly.

Holly expected to drop Alan in front of the hotel when they got back but he motioned to the doorman to take the car. "I have to go to the airport to pick up a package first thing tomorrow morning so Slade wants you to take that revised project list to Farnsworth. Come up to the suite with me and we'll go over it together in case there is anything you don't understand."

The suite was deserted when they got there although it was quite late. Slade is making a real night of it, Holly thought waspishly and then forced herself to put him out of her mind. If women wanted to make fools of themselves over him that was their business. It was just irksome to her pride as a member of the sex.

They were seated close together on the couch when a key sounded in the lock. Alan had his arm thrown casually around her shoulders as he bent over to point out something and he looked up and smiled over her head.

"Hi, Chief, I was wondering if you would make it back tonight."

There was an enigmatic look in Slade's gray eyes as his glance encompassed the two on the couch. "I always leave a trail of bread crumbs," he drawled.

"How was Los Angeles?" Alan asked.

"Very enjoyable," he said reminiscently and Holly ached to wipe the smug smile off his face. "How was everything in San Francisco today?"

"Very enjoyable," Holly said before Alan could answer.

"You sound like you're enjoying your work."

"I did today," she answered demurely, "but it wasn't work. Alan and I played hookey."

There was a short silence. "I didn't think you would mind, Slade," Alan said a trifle uncomfortably and Holly suffered a momentary guilt pang. She might have phrased it better. Out of an obscure desire to get back at Slade, she had made them both sound like irresponsible children.

Slade fixed her with an expressionless look and shrugged off his jacket. "Why don't you fix us all a nightcap, Alan? I've had a long day." He took off his tie and unbuttoned the first few buttons of his shirt.

Holly stared in fascination as the strong brown column of his neck came into view, remembering their encounter the first time she had come to the suite. Wrenching her eyes away, she met Slade's sardonic gaze and blushed. He gave a low chuckle and flung himself into a chair, stretching his long legs out.

Alan had moved to the bar and was pouring ice cubes into a bucket with a noisy clatter as he enlarged on his explanation. "We didn't leave till afternoon and there really wasn't much to do today. Farnsworth was over at the magazine and the *Bulletin* personnel is pretty well straightened out. The new managing editor isn't due until tomorrow."

Slade nodded noncommittally. "Were did you two go?"

"All over. This is beautiful country, you ought to see it," Alan said enthusiastically. "Holly is a terrific tour guide."

"I'm sure she is but I haven't been offered her services." He gave her a slow smile and Holly's pulses quickened.

To her horror, she heard herself saying, "Would you like to compare them to the ones you received in Los Angeles?"

Slade's firm mouth thinned but whatever he was going to say was interrupted by the pealing telephone and Alan went into the bedroom to answer it. Slade rose from the chair in one lithe movement like a supple jungle cat going into action.

He slung his jacket over one shoulder and came to stand very close to Holly. She had risen when he did, intending to beat a hasty retreat, but Slade captured her chin in his free hand forcing it up so she had to look at him.

There was a warning light in his gray eyes but his voice was very soft as he said, "I suggest you start behaving yourself, Angel Eyes, or I might decide to find out if you're bluffing. It isn't wise to start something with me that you don't intend finishing."

"It's your overseas call to London," Alan called from the bedroom. "Bosley is on the line."

Holly tried to pull away but his fingers tightened on her chin. "I don't know what you're talking about," she said breathlessly.

"Don't you?" His grip loosened and he rubbed his thumb gently across her mouth, pulling the lower lip down slightly so the edge of her small white teeth gleamed evenly. "You liberated ladies use very provocative language. That usually turns me off because I like to do the pursuing, but in your case I just might make an exception."

He was standing so close that she could sense the leashed power of his body and smell the heady male scent that was exclusively his own. Holly's legs began to tremble but she forced her voice to remain cool. "Don't compromise your principles for me, Mr. Rockwell. I dislike being part of a crowd."

His lips curled cruelly. "Play your cards right and I might move you to the head of the line."

"Slade," Alan's voice floated plaintively from the bedroom, "Bosley has those figures for you."

"Think about it, Angel." Slade's arm curved around her waist pulling her against his lean body and his mouth covered hers in a hard possession that held no tenderness. When she began to struggle frantically, his arms tightened like steel bands and his mouth bore down, bruising her lips and forcing them to open. It was an assured male invasion that played on her senses, leaving her completely vulnerable. Her head was pillowed on his shoulder and a creeping warmth began to envelop Holly's lower limbs. But when her hands went to the open front of his shirt, spreading out searchingly over the hair roughened skin, he abruptly released his hold.

Her jewellike eyes were confused and she would have fallen if he hadn't steadied her with his hands on her shoulders. Slade surveyed her with an amused look of understanding and then he was gone.

Holly drove home in a daze, powerful emotions warring within her. Her first impression had been right, she thought grimly. Slade Rockwell was a treacherous, terrible man, about as trustworthy as a pit viper! Although he disapproved of the permissiveness of her generation, he wasn't above seducing a member of it just to show his contempt. That was what rankled. If he had been attracted to her it would have been a different story, but he never made a pretense of even liking her.

Holly's cheeks burned and she gritted her teeth until they ached, remembering that inadvertent moment of response. It was only because he had caught her by surprise, but he must have thought she was enjoying his hateful attentions. The colossal conceit of the man was what infuriated her. He actually thought all he had to do was quirk a little finger and she would fall like a ripe plum. Well, she had a flash for him—he might be catnip to other women but he was definitely ragweed to her!

For a brief instant she considered quitting and then rejected the idea. That was probably what he was expecting her to do and she wouldn't give him the satisfaction. Holly's eyes widened suddenly at the implications of that thought. Could he be regretting his job offer and this was his way of harassing her into quitting? That would explain a lot. Why else would he have acted in that disgusting manner?

Righteous indignation engulfed her and Holly's rounded chin set determinedly. If that were the case, she wasn't going to make it easy for him. He would have to fire her and do it to her face. In fact, she would confront him in the morning.

Holly showed up at Slade's suite ready for battle the next morning but he wasn't there. Since Alan had already left for the airport and couldn't tell her Slade's whereabouts, she deduced that he was probably at *Pleasure* Magazine, one of the many publications he owned and the one that Mac Farnsworth was being moved to. Slade had expressed concern about Mac and would undoubtedly want to check on his progress before leaving for London. But no one there had seen Slade that morning.

Holly found it difficult to concentrate on anything while her own job was in limbo, but Mac was waiting for the editorial list and she had to spend precious time going over it with him.

By the time she finished their business and got over to the *Bulletin* offices, her nerves were wound tighter than a watch spring. There were voices coming from the managing editor's office and it was evident that Slade wasn't alone but she headed in that direction anyway. His low soothing tones were audible along with Cynthia's quavering ones and Holly halted in the doorway.

Cynthia was seated in a chair in front of the desk, her taut body bent forward beseechingly. There was polite interest on Slade's face, but when he looked up and saw Holly his eyes became murderous.

"Come in, Miss Holbrooke, I was wondering where the . . . where you'd gotten to."

Cynthia swiveled around and her face lit up. "Holly,

you're just the one I want to see! Tell Mr. Rockwell how successful my column has been. Tell him that I know every important hostess in San Francisco. Tell him—"

"I don't need Miss Holbrooke to tell me any of those things," Slade cut in smoothly. "I'm already aware of your considerable talents."

"Then why are you taking away my column?" Cynthia's voice rose in pitch.

The glance that he shot at Holly was savage, but when he turned back to the other woman Slade was all urbanity. "I'm switching you to a *new* column. You will actually be broadening your base of experience."

"But my column is *important.* It's the first thing the really elite women in this town turn to. They like to read about themselves and I give them what they want."

"I don't doubt it for a moment but that's part of the trouble," Slade explained gently. "The *Bulletin* used to be one of the high circulation papers in the country mainly because it was read by all the outlying communities. We've lost those people because they really don't care about what goes on solely in San Francisco. Helen Selkirk," he named one of the leading syndicated columnists, "has an appeal that is far-reaching. Now if you don't care to take over the household hints department, I'll be happy to listen to any other ideas you might entertain. Your salary, I might add, will remain the same."

Cynthia bristled with outrage. "You're demoting me aren't you? Why don't you come right out and say so?"

He remained unruffled. "That's entirely in your own mind but if you are that unhappy, if you don't feel you can give it your best shot, then I can move you to another publication entirely—or I can give you a good recommendation at one of the other local papers."

It wasn't exactly a threat but there was a hint of steel in his voice and Cynthia paled. She knew there was validity in his argument because circulation had fallen off alarmingly in the past year. The fact that her salary would remain the same made up for a great deal, but pride dictated that she argue the point at length. In the end, she capitulated as they both knew she would.

Holly had been hovering near the door and when the interview was over, she turned to follow Cynthia. But before she had taken more than one step, Slade's roar halted her.

"Miss Holbrooke, close the door and come here!"

Slade was standing up and bending over the desk, his full weight resting on his knuckles. It had to be a trick of her imagination, Holly told herself, but it seemed that there was smoke coming out of his nostrils.

"Will you tell me where the hell you've been this morning?" he demanded.

"I was . . . I was over at *Pleasure* Magazine looking for you," she faltered.

"You were not hired to follow me around like a little toy dog. I know what *my* functions are, you are supposed to be explaining theirs to our employees." Each word came out as a small cube of ice. "This interview with Miss Gordon was your hot potato not mine."

"But I didn't expect her back so soon. Cynthia went down to the celebrity tournament in Carmel. A lot of San Francisco people have houses down there and it's one big social event. She wasn't supposed to be back until tomorrow."

"Spare me your excuses, I've heard them all. This is

exactly the kind of situation I want to avoid. You are being paid a handsome salary to handle these hysterical females."

"I wouldn't say Cynthia was being exactly hysterical," Holly said tightly.

He moved swiftly around the desk and came to stand in front of her, taking unfair advantage of his height. "Of course not! To another woman her behavior must have seemed perfectly reasonable."

Holly was smoldering but she made an effort to check her temper. "You can hardly blame her for trying to hang on to her column. Cynthia loves the party circuit and all the perks that go with it."

"Exactly. And I'm running a newspaper not a country club bulletin for a bunch of idle women whose only concern is what to wear to the next social gathering."

Holly agreed with him about the triviality of the society column, but thumbscrews wouldn't have dragged the admission out of her. "I don't know what your sudden bias is against parties. I seem to remember reading that you have attended a few in your day."

Slade looked up at the ceiling. "Dear Lord, must women reduce everything to a personal level?"

"That is your least endearing quality, Mr. Rockwell, turning every discussion into a battle of the sexes," Holly flared.

"My dear Miss Holbrooke, your opinion of my qualities, endearing or otherwise, doesn't interest me. All I require of you is a little devotion to your job and so far you have shown precious little of it. To quote a famous president, if you can't stand the heat, get out of the kitchen."

She drew herself up to her full height. "Are you asking for my resignation?"

"Are you tendering it?" His face looked like it was carved out of stone.

Holly felt almost physically bruised. He seemed nine feet tall and made out of tempered steel but she stiffened her spine and faced him defiantly, her eyes the deep blue color of a stormy sea. "No, damn you, I'm not! If you want to get rid of me you'll have to fire me."

Some of the tension left his body and he looked at her appraisingly. "I don't remember mentioning that."

"But you *are* trying to get rid of me aren't you?" Holly demanded.

He lounged against the desk, folding his arms over his chest. "What gave you that idea?"

"That elaborate performance in your suite last night." Her hands curled into tight little fists. "Wasn't it designed to make me angry enough to quit?"

Amusement washed over his face. "I've had women question my intentions before but they never thought I was trying to get rid of them because I kissed them."

"That wasn't a kiss it was a punishment!"

"Which you deserved, although I'm sorry to hear you regard my caresses in that fashion." He seemed to be enjoying himself. "I must be losing my touch."

She could have told him differently. Her mouth still remembered the demanding way he had taken possession of it, forcing entry with a male dominance that had seduced her into responding. "You only did it because you were angry that Alan and I took the afternoon off."

"You have a convenient memory. The way I remember it is that you went out of your way to provoke me with that sharp little tongue of yours."

Holly had to admit that was true but it didn't make her feel any kindlier toward him. Lowering her eyelashes protectively, she stuck out her lower lip. "Well, you didn't have to retaliate in that . . . that manner."

"You're right. I should have turned you over my knee instead."

His supreme male confidence drove her wild. "I'd like to see you try it!"

"Is that an invitation?" he asked softly.

There was hard purpose in the glance that took in her slight, defiant figure and Holly knew she was balanced on a precarious edge. "N . . . no, of course not," she stammered, regaining caution.

"That's good because I don't think you would enjoy it nearly as much as my other . . . punishment."

"What makes you think I enjoyed *that?*"

His raised eyebrows were mocking. "Surely I didn't imagine that warm response?"

Holly's cheeks flamed and she ignored the question. "Just what are you trying to prove? You're about a foot taller than I and at least ten times stronger. I'll admit you can dominate me physically but you're never going to break my spirit."

"Would you believe that isn't my intent?"

"How can I?" she cried.

His eyes softened as they rested on the delicate troubled face. "We've had a rather stormy beginning haven't we, little one? But hang in there, it's bound to get better."

She looked at him doubtfully. "Is it Slade? Do you think it's going to work out?"

"It will work, honey, trust me."

Her smile was tentative. "Is that a two-way street?"

"Absolutely! As long as you don't stick me with another one of those emotional females."

Holly had forgotten the origin of their argument but she had to acknowledge that in this instance he was dead right. "I'm sorry about today, Slade. I should have been here to handle it, but I honestly thought Cynthia wouldn't show up till tomorrow. It won't happen again though, I promise you."

He smiled and put his arm around her shoulders, walking her to the door. "Okay, let's start from there. Come on, I'll take you to lunch."

Chapter Three

Holly looked around the first-class cabin of the airplane on Sunday morning and wriggled with pleasure. She had been up before the alarm rang which made the wait until flight time seem endless, but now that takeoff was imminent, excitement was coursing through her veins like vintage wine.

Alan was leaning over the high back of the chair in front of Holly and his disappointed face reflected his opinion of the seating arrangements. Slade had put Holly next to the window, taking the seat beside her and Victor and Alan were in the row ahead.

As soon as they were airborne, the stewardess came around with a tray of champagne cocktails and Holly accepted one eagerly, although she didn't usually care much for champagne. Today it provided the proper festive touch.

"I've always wanted to have champagne for breakfast," she confided happily to Slade who had refused his.

He watched her with amusement. "Haven't you ever?"

The cloud of dark hair swung against her cheek as

she shook her head. "Only on birthdays and New Year's Eve."

"This is scarcely in the same category."

"On the contrary, today is every holiday rolled into one—my very first trip to Europe."

The champagne had gone straight to the bottom of her empty stomach and everything was taking on a rosy glow. When the stewardess came around again, Holly held out her empty glass for a refill.

"Are you sure you won't have any, Mr. Rockwell?" the girl asked, bestowing a special smile on him, Holly noted acidly. "Or can I bring you something else?"

Slade returned her smile. "Perhaps I'll have a Bloody Mary."

"Maybe I'll have one of those too instead of this," Holly declared.

But Slade shook his head. "You will stick to wine."

Holly felt mortified in front of the stewardess. "I wish you would stop treating me like a child," she hissed.

"Someone has to take care of you."

"I'm not going to get sick if that's what you're worried about," she said with injured dignity.

"I certainly hope not." He regarded her flushed face and bright eyes with amusement. "What you need is some breakfast. It should be here soon. In the meantime, be a good girl and look out the window, I have work to do."

He put his tray table down, placing his attaché case on it and Holly resentfully did as she was told. But her pique soon vanished as she looked down at the wide expanse of ocean, following the progress of a freighter that looked incredibly tiny from this height.

After breakfast her eyelids began to droop. She

didn't want to miss one moment of the flight but her sleepless night began to take its toll. Putting her head back, Holly closed her eyes for just a minute and fell fast asleep. The steady drone of the engines was soothing, but the headrest was designed for someone taller and she couldn't get comfortable. Every time her head rolled sideways she frowned and struggled up through the mists of sleep only to sink back into discomfort.

Then strong arms lifted her with an arm around her shoulders and one under her legs and Holly was cradled against a firm shoulder that offered blissful support. Deep in slumber, she flexed her knees and cuddled into Slade's lap, her fingers slipping inside his jacket. She burrowed her head into the curve of his neck and gave a sigh of satisfaction.

When she awoke some time later, Holly felt disoriented. She was warm and comfortable and disinclined to move a muscle, but the unfamiliar scent of aftershave mixed with tobacco was vaguely disturbing. Lifting her head, Holly's wide startled eyes met Slade's.

"Did you have a nice sleep?" he smiled. His arms tightened as she started to scramble up. "Lie still, you aren't fully awake yet."

Maybe he was right. It had to be a dream that Slade was holding her so gently and looking at her with that strange expression. And then common sense took over.

"How did . . . I. . . . Oh, I'm so sorry!" She was almost stuttering with embarrassment. "You must have been terribly uncomfortable. Why didn't you push me away?"

"That wouldn't have been very chivalrous." He reached up to smooth her hair back and then his fingers trailed down her cheek, leaving a tingling sensation.

Holly struggled to sit up. "How could you let me do that and what did everyone think?" She looked furtively around the plane but the other passengers were either reading or sleeping.

"I imagine all the men envied me."

Holly slipped back into her own seat, discovering that the armrest had been raised to allow her to stretch her legs out. "I'm sure they didn't. Who would want a dead weight sprawled all over them?"

"Fortunately, you weigh about as much as a dandelion and I rather enjoyed it. You sleep very quietly except for your eyelashes. They flutter very intriguingly."

"I wouldn't know," she murmured.

He watched her intently. "Didn't anyone ever tell you?"

Holly stood up abruptly. "If you'll excuse me, I'm going to the ladies' room to comb my hair."

Victor was in her seat when she returned and Holly took the empty one next to Alan, grateful that she didn't have to make small talk with Slade. Awakening in his arms had been a shattering experience and it was going to take her some time to calm down. Why on earth hadn't he just propped her back up in her chair instead of enduring what must have been an hour of discomfort? The more she found out about this contradictory man, the more he baffled her. Sighing in perplexity, she turned her attention to a delighted Alan.

When they finally landed at Heathrow Airport, Holly could barely wait to step out onto foreign soil. It seemed to take forever until the hydraulic steps were maneuvered into place. When the heavy door swung back she had to force herself to walk through decorously, instead of dancing down the ramp. Going through customs was another experience and then they were in a limousine driving toward London.

Holly's head swiveled back and forth so rapidly that Slade finally caught her chin in his hand. "Slow down, youngster, you're going to dislocate something."

"I don't want to miss anything," she protested.

"You won't," Alan reassured her. "I owe you one from San Francisco and one day soon we'll do the town."

He was sitting on the jump seat facing her and she leaned forward impulsively and put her hand on his arm. "Really? Do you promise?"

"Sit back," Slade frowned, "we're in heavy traffic."

The long black car pulled up in front of the Hyde Park Hotel and a uniformed doorman helped Holly out. She followed Slade up the broad stone steps to the impressive lobby and looked around appreciatively while he registered. Luxury was evident in the rich red patterned carpet and crystal chandeliers and the employees were exquisitely polite without being obsequious.

As soon as the formalities were over, they were escorted to a suite that mirrored the opulence of the lobby. A long sitting room looked out on Hyde Park across the street and the tall draped windows opened onto a curved balcony that ran the length of the three rooms. Deep couches and chairs were covered in muted damask and fresh flowers provided a welcoming touch. Through doors at opposite ends of the living room, two bedrooms faced each other.

Several bellmen bustled about bringing in the luggage and Holly was reveling in the unaccustomed luxury until Slade said carelessly, "Take whichever one you want."

"What do you mean?"

"Your bedroom. I think they're the same but you can look at both and then make up your mind. It doesn't matter to me."

Holly couldn't believe what she was hearing. "Do you mean to say you expect me to stay here with you?" she demanded.

"Of course. Why not?" He seemed surprised.

"Because I'm not going to."

He put his hands on his hips and looked at her in annoyance. "What's the matter now?"

"If you don't know then I can't explain it to you. Just take my word for it, I'm not sharing this suite with you."

"I can't see what possible difference it can make unless you sleep in the nude and walk in your sleep."

"I don't do either but I want my own room. A *separate* room," she added before he could point out the obvious.

He looked at her with exasperation. "My dear Holly, it never occurred to me that you would object but in any case, these suites were already reserved before I even knew you were coming."

"Then keep them and get me a single room," she said stubbornly.

"I'm afraid that isn't possible. The hotel is fully booked months in advance."

The idea of sharing quarters with Slade, just the two of them alone all night, didn't bear thinking about. Even though they would each be in their own bedrooms, she would never be able to relax with him so close. Slade was just too masculine to ignore.

"How about the other suite? Why can't I stay there?" she asked desperately.

His firm mouth curved cynically. "I don't think

Victor's wife would appreciate you bunking with him, innocent though it might be, and if I put you and Alan together, I might not get any work out of either of you."

"Oh!" she gasped. "You are despicable!"

"But practical. You won't get into any trouble here where I can keep my eye on you. And I promise not to come crawling into your bed in the middle of the night. Does that make you feel better?"

The cynicism in his voice infuriated her. Slade's attitude gave the impression that *he* was the one who needed protection. She lifted her chin and sparks flew out of her wide aquamarine eyes. "*Infinitely* better. But for your information, I'm going to lock my door!"

She wheeled around and stalked out of the room, ignoring his soft chuckle. The bedroom she picked arbitrarily turned out to be a good choice. One long wall contained mirrored closets—much more storage space than she had had in her small apartment, and the lovely brass bed was reflected over and over again in the long panels. A small chaise, a desk and a down-cushioned chair completed the furnishings.

It didn't take long to unpack and by the time Holly had put her cosmetic articles in the large adjoining bathroom, her resentment faded. It was impossible to stay angry when it occurred to her that she was actually in London and by the time Slade knocked on the door to collect her for dinner, Holly was bubbling with anticipation for whatever came next.

During dinner in the hotel, Slade invited Alan and Victor to join him as he took Holly for a short spin around the city.

"I think I'll take a rain check," Victor yawned. "It's been a long day and I don't have the stamina you kids do."

Slade chuckled. "I'm afraid I don't qualify for that category."

"I'll be happy to take Holly if you're tired also, Slade," Alan offered hopefully.

Slade's smile was sardonic. "Thanks, but I think I can manage to stay up for another hour or so."

They drove along the broad Thames with its low bridges spaced at regular intervals and she saw Cleopatra's Needle pointing up at the stars like a slender ancient finger. Then past the imposing bulk of Westminster Abbey where all but two of England's kings and queens have been crowned. Across the square in the vaulted tower of the Palace of Westminster, Holly got her first delighted look at Big Ben, perhaps the most famous clock in the world.

After these brief glimpses into antiquity, Piccadilly Circus with its blazing lights and hectic activity was a startling change. Neon lights flickered garishly in this equivalent of New York's Times Square and crowds of people jammed the streets on their way to theaters and nightclubs. They were back in the twentieth century with a vengeance, but a quick view of Lord Nelson's statue atop its tall fluted column was a tie to the past.

When Slade decided it was time to return to the hotel, Holly tried to hide her disappointment. It was thoughtful of him to take her on what he must have considered a boring ride and she was grateful. He had been remarkably kind during the short tour, smiling indulgently at her eager enjoyment and she had forgotten their past differences, feeling completely at ease with him. But when Alan said good night and she and Slade entered the suite together, a paralyzing shyness gripped her.

"I want to thank you for the . . . the ride," she managed.

For once there was no mockery in the gray eyes as he viewed her hesitancy. "It was a pleasure. Your enthusiasm makes the same old sights seem special."

"Yes . . . well . . . uh, good night."

"Are you very tired?" he asked suddenly.

Holly was much too keyed up to sleep and she said, "No, not at all. I had a nap on the plane."

She turned scarlet, remembering the circumstances but he tactfully ignored it. "Then have a nightcap with me, it will relax you."

It didn't seem possible that she would ever relax again. The intimate atmosphere was sending little shivers of apprehension up her spine, although Slade's behavior was impeccable—so far. Then he took off his tie and unbuttoned the top button of his shirt and she looked doubtfully toward her bedroom as tiny beads of perspiration freckled her tilted nose.

"Would you like water or soda in your drink?" Slade's voice from the portable bar across the room made her jump nervously.

"Plain . . . plain water will be fine, thank you."

He handed her a glass and she reached gingerly for it, taking great care that their fingers didn't touch. He gave her a slow smile and Holly's heart started to thump. He was so devastatingly masculine and much too experienced for her. She wished now that she had refused a drink.

Slade sprawled lazily in a chair with one leg flung casually over the arm. He took a sip of his drink and looked up at Holly poised uncertainly over him. "Why don't you go sit on the couch and take your shoes off. I'm much too tired to attack you tonight and besides," he grinned wickedly, "you can run faster that way."

Holly stiffened defensively. "Don't be ridiculous, I'm not afraid of you."

"Then prove it by sitting down and talking to me rationally for a change."

She seated herself primly. "What do you want to talk about?"

"You."

"You know everything about me already."

He gave her an intent look. "I'm beginning to think I only know the things you want me to know. Tell me how you got into this business, for instance."

Holly thought about it for a moment. "It's funny but I can't give you a sensible answer. Maybe it was my inborn curiosity. I've always wanted to know about everything and everybody. I guess you could say I'm just nosy but in this business it's an asset," she laughed.

"But why the newspaper business?" he persisted. "It isn't the easiest field you could have chosen."

"That's for sure," she groaned. "It's still a hard way to go for a woman. Every time a farmer grew a tomato that looked like Popeye or an inventor developed a surefire formula to fuel automobiles with chicken soup, guess who drew the assignment? But if there was a bomb threat or an ax murder, I was the invisible woman."

She had taken Slade's suggestion and curled up in a corner of the couch, completely relaxed now that the conversation was impersonal. Slade looked at the slender, vulnerable figure and said, "I can't really fault your city editors. I'm afraid I wouldn't send you out on any story where there might be danger either."

"But that's all wrong! I want to be treated the same as a man. I'm a reporter first and foremost, why should I receive special consideration?"

Slade looked at the long silky hair spilling over the slim shoulders and the creamy skin of her lovely neck. His eyes lowered to the firm rounded breasts and he said, "I'm afraid any answer to that would provoke an argument."

"That's exactly the mentality that made it so difficult," Holly frowned. "But I did it in spite of all of you."

"And now what new worlds are there left to conquer?" he teased. "Marriage? Or would you rather subjugate a whole newsroom full of men instead of just one captive victim?"

"With that attitude, I'm not surprised that you don't ever intend getting married," she said tartly.

A peaked eyebrow rose mockingly. "You sound as though you know that for a fact."

"Your views on the subject are well publicized."

"Like everything else about me," he said dryly.

"What can you expect if you run around with movie stars and countesses?" At his blank look she said impatiently, "Lady what's-her-name, isn't she the one you're having an affair with over here?"

"Holly, you never cease to shock me," he chuckled. "Are you honestly suggesting we discuss my love life?"

"Certainly not!" She blushed and changed the subject. "But I *would* like to know some other things about you. You're always asking me questions but I don't know a single thing about you."

"What would you like to know?"

"Well, to start with, how did *you* get into the newspaper business?"

"Accidentally, you might say. My father owned a weekly paper in a little town in Michigan. He was a great editor but a lousy businessman. The paper was going under through poor management and my dad worked so hard trying to save it that he ended up with a heart attack." He raised an eyebrow. "Are you sure you want to hear all this?" When she nodded vigorously, Slade continued with obvious reluctance. "I was a business major in college so I took over and put the paper back on its feet." He shrugged. "It wasn't that difficult."

"You mean all of this," Holly waved an arm at the lavish suite, "began with a small town newspaper? How did you manage to build it into an empire?"

"Oh, that," he said negligently. "Well, after the *Gazette* began to make money, I bought a daily and then a magazine. After that I just acquired more publications."

She gave him a level look. "I know newspaper writing is supposed to be sparse, but if you ever turned in a bare bones story like that you would be fired off of even the *Hicktown Weekly.*"

Slade laughed. "I'll give you a little lesson in economics, Angel Eyes. If you have several thousand dollars to invest, making a profit is problematical. But if you have several million dollars to play with, making a fortune is inevitable."

Holly digested this in silence, finding it difficult even to envision that kind of money. But while Slade made light of his accomplishments, he was undoubtedly a genius and her admiration was undisguised.

He leaned forward and took the glass gently from her hand, putting it on the table next to the couch. Something glowed deep in the gray eyes and his voice was throaty as he said, "Do I detect the first sign of approval from my sternest critic?"

Holly's breath caught in her throat, every nerve end aware of this compelling male. It was happening again. Her body was responding to his blatant masculinity and it was difficult to remember that he was a man without scruples where women were concerned. How many of them had curled up in his arms, surrendering ecstatically to those hard loins? Holly only knew the persuasiveness of his mouth but that was potent enough. Remembering his warm invasion and the complete surrender of all her inhibitions, a shudder passed through Holly warning her it was time to leave. But she was caught in his net, waiting as if hypnotized, for what would inevitably come next.

The shrilling telephone suddenly ripped the fabric of silence. Holly jumped nervously, snapped out of her strange lethargy and Slade exhaled a sigh of exasperation. But when he picked up the receiver, his irritation vanished.

"Marsha, my dear, how are you? How did you know I had arrived?"

Holly stood up swiftly. It hadn't taken Lady what's-her-name long to get on the trail. Not that he seemed to mind being stalked. Holly started toward her room to give him the privacy she was sure he wanted. He motioned her back out of politeness but she waggled her fingers at him and closed the door.

Her heart was still beating irregularly and Holly forced herself to examine the tiny incident that had taken place before the phone rang. What had happened actually? Slade had leaned toward her and they had both stopped talking at the same time. It happens. He certainly had not been about to kiss her and she assuredly wouldn't have wanted him to. It was the unaccustomed intimacy of sharing this suite with a man that was making her imagine things and it had to stop.

Holly unzipped her dress and stepped out of it impatiently. If Slade wanted a woman, all he had to do was answer his phone. He was in there talking to one of them right now—his local favorite. One of many. She flounced into bed and punched the pillow savagely before turning out the light.

* * *

Their conversation on Sunday night proved to be the last real one they would have for awhile. Work started in earnest on Monday and Holly was thrown in to sink or swim. Slade was only an occasionally glimpsed figure in the *Metro* offices, moving in and out of meetings too swiftly to be waylaid.

"I don't even get a chance to ask him if I'm doing all right," Holly complained to Alan.

"Don't worry about it." He squeezed her hand reassuringly. "Slade is paying you a compliment. If he didn't think you could handle it, you wouldn't be here in the first place."

She had to be satisfied with that and things did seem to be proceeding smoothly. The first week was almost over before Holly even realized it. She worked long hours, often going back to the office at night to run microfilmed articles in order to assess recent editorial content. Evaluating employees meant reviewing their work and it was most tactfully done when they were absent.

Sometimes after a quick dinner with Alan or Victor, Holly allowed herself the luxury of a shower and a change of clothes before going back to the office. Slade was never around but his phone rang constantly. At first, Holly used to answer it but as the list of female callers grew, her temper rose. Let the switchboard do it, she wasn't hired to be his social secretary!

It was an especially lovely afternoon for London when Alan came into the office set aside for Holly's use. "Do you realize we've been here almost a week and all you have seen is the inside of this office?" he demanded.

She looked ruefully out of the grimy window at the

ancient spires glimpsed so tantalizingly in the distance. "Please don't rub it in. I have the feeling that I'm going to have to buy some picture postcards to see where I've been."

"Do you think I'd go back on my promise? Grab your purse, the grand tour starts now."

"Oh, Alan, do you think we should?" Eagerness struggled with uncertainty.

"Of course we should. You've been working like a beaver, you deserve a breather."

"But how about Slade? Maybe we should ask him first."

"He's in a meeting with the bankers and it's apt to go on until all hours. Poor Slade, he's due to break out too. The guy has been working night and day."

The information brought a curious sense of pleasure. Was that why all those women called so ceaselessly? Because he was working nights like the rest of them instead of playing? It might even account for the fact that Holly hadn't seen him either. "Well, if you're sure he won't mind."

"Just pick your spots. What do you want to see?"

Her eyes were shining as she capitulated. "How about the Tower of London and the pandas at the zoo and the flea market in Portobello Road and—"

Alan held up a defensive hand. "I had an afternoon in mind not a week," he laughed.

In the end they settled on her first two choices and after just a short time, Holly saw the wisdom in it. The Tower of London alone deserved a full day. Its turreted battlements dated back to the eleventh century and entering it was like stepping back in time.

Even the blue-black ravens strutting around the entry had their origins in history. According to tradition, the governor drew an allowance of one shilling and sixpence a week for each bird. They were given names and identity cards and one handsome specimen that flourished between the wars was named James Crow and had his profession listed as "thief."

It was damp inside the four-foot-thick walls that sunshine couldn't penetrate and Holly shivered in the somber dungeons. The atmosphere changed drastically when they climbed the worn stone steps to the jewel room where the Crown jewels are kept. Like every tourist, Holly caught her breath at the magnificent display of sparkling gems that blazed such multicolored fire that they almost seemed alive. A fortune in rubies, emeralds, diamonds and sapphires dazzled the eye, while huge pearls glowed with an inner radiance.

The three royal crowns were perhaps the most magnificent but there were also scepters and swords and smaller jeweled pieces. Objects that were priceless for their history as well as their intrinsic value. They were well guarded from theft but Holly learned with amazement that both the beautiful Scepter with the Dove and also the gem encrusted State Sword, used only at coronations, had been casually mislaid for years like a pair of glasses or an extra set of car keys.

Alan had trouble dragging Holly away but threat of the zoo closing did the trick.

On the way across town, she touched his arm. "That was wonderful, Alan. How can I ever thank you?"

He captured her hand and held it. "Would you like me to think of a way?"

She ignored that, perhaps not even hearing it in her exuberance. "I wish we could stay here for a month."

"And I wish I could spend it all with you, playing," he agreed softly.

That did register and Holly gently disengaged her hand. "I don't think that would go over very big with our boss," she said lightly. "He's a demon for work isn't he?"

Alan accepted his rejection in good humor. "Whatever Slade does, he does full tilt. He works hard and he plays hard."

Holly made a face. "Too bad he doesn't fall in love. That's supposed to mellow people isn't it?"

"Most people, but not Slade."

"Has he . . . how does he act when he's in love?" she asked offhandedly.

"I wouldn't know, I don't think he has ever been."

"Impossible," Holly scoffed. "Look at all the gorgeous women he goes with."

"Diversions, honey. Slade is a very virile gent and they satisfy his . . ." he paused delicately.

"Appetites," she supplied grimly.

"You said it, I didn't," Alan grinned. Then he sobered. "I've always wondered about the girl Slade will marry."

"She doesn't exist."

He shook his head thoughtfully. "I don't agree with you. He's been very restless lately and I think he's really ready to settle down even though he may not know it yet. But it has to be someone very special."

"Obviously," Holly said acidly. "Someone as rich and famous as he is."

"Not at all. Just somebody . . . wonderful." He smiled at her. "Like you."

Holly's heart lurched and she said crossly, "Me? I wouldn't have Slade Rockwell tied up in blue ribbons."

"That's good." Alan's hazel eyes held laughter. "I wasn't playing John Alden."

The taxi arrived at the zoo, fortunately putting an end to the conversation and by the time he had purchased tickets and they were walking through the spacious park, it was forgotten.

The panda bears were in a large enclosure and Holly promptly went into ecstasies. The large male was lying in full view, sprawled contentedly on the ground with a sprig of bamboo clutched between his toes. Leisurely plucking off leaves and munching happily, he turned his head occasionally to stare comically at them out of his clown's face. His roly-poly white body and the big black circles around his eyes made him look like a giant stuffed toy.

"Look, Alan, isn't he adorable?"

He gazed at her curved mouth and concurred. "Utterly adorable."

They wandered through the park eating popcorn and looking at the other animals and Alan bought Holly a red balloon which she tied to her wrist. It was very casual and relaxed and when he reached for her hand it seemed completely natural.

They were laughing together as Alan opened the door of the suite with Holly's key but the laughter died abruptly. Slade was sitting on the couch surrounded by papers and an open briefcase and his expression was forbidding.

"Oh . . . Slade . . . I didn't expect you to be here," Holly faltered.

His mouth was a grim line. "That much is evident."

Alan tried to ignore the charged atmosphere. "I took Holly out for a little sight-seeing today. She hasn't seen anything of London since the night we arrived and I didn't think you would mind."

"But you didn't bother asking me." Slade's narrowed eyes were hard.

"Alan said you were with the bankers and we didn't

expect . . . I mean we didn't think . . ." her voice trailed off.

"How inconvenient of me to get through early."

In the face of his inexplicable wrath, Holly's fingers had unconsciously sought Alan's and they stood like two guilty children. But when Slade's wintery gaze fastened on their linked hands, she dropped his guiltily.

"I'm sorry if you—oh, Alan, my balloon!" The string had loosened from Holly's wrist and the red balloon promptly floated toward the ceiling.

Glad of the diversion, Alan hopped on the arm of a chair. "Fear not, fair maiden, at great peril to life and limb, I'll rescue it for you."

As he reached for the dangling string, Alan teetered precariously and Holly threw her arms around his waist to steady him. "Be careful," she laughed, "I don't want you incapacitated."

Her eyes met Slade's and the look of contempt he gave her was scorching. What had they done that was so terrible, she wondered in bewilderment? Surely a few hours didn't warrant this condemnation and it wasn't as though they hadn't been putting in ten and eleven hour days.

The phone rang in Slade's room and he stood up. "Don't disappear, I want to talk to both of you," he warned, stalking into the bedroom.

"What on earth is the matter with him?" Holly whispered.

"I don't know," Alan said slowly. "I've never seen him get this upset over something so trivial."

When Slade returned they were still staring at each other wide eyed.

"Perhaps it's just as well this happened," he said without preamble, "because it gives me a chance to tell you that I don't expect it to reoccur. I don't want the two of you to disappear again without a trace, is that clear?"

The injustice of it was making Holly's temper rise. "Perfectly clear. I'll figure up how much time I owe you and you can take it out of my salary. I'll pay for Alan's time too," she added recklessly. "It was worth it."

Alan put his arm protectively around her rigid shoulders and said quietly, "Don't blame Holly, Slade, it was strictly my fault."

Slade eyed them enigmatically. "I think this is getting out of hand and I have a dinner date. Suppose we all cool it for now. Do you have plans for this evening?"

Alan looked at Slade diffidently. "Holly and I were going to the theater." It was as much a question as a statement.

"Good, but don't make any plans for tomorrow night. Marsha is having a party and I thought Holly might enjoy seeing her house."

Holly looked at him in amazement. Did he think this made up for his temper? Promising her a party as though she were a child!

Before she could splutter into speech, Alan squeezed her hand warningly. "You'll enjoy that. Lady Dillingham's house is one of the show places of London."

It might be but Holly decided that wild horses wouldn't drag her to it. Why would Slade want to take her there of all places? And then the answer presented itself and made her even angrier. There would be eligible men at the party and she was being pointed in their direction. Slade thought she and Alan were having an affair and he wanted to break it up. He didn't consider her good enough for his trusted lieutenant!

Her eyes flashed turquoise fire as she turned to tell him exactly what she thought of him but Slade had vanished into his room.

Chapter Four

Whatever had bothered Slade the night before was evidently forgotten the next day. He remained closeted in his office all morning and Holly didn't see him until eleven o'clock. A meeting was called for that hour and she went to it reluctantly.

She met Alan coming out of the office and he gave her the thumbs up signal which made her feel a little better, but she didn't have a chance to speak to him. Slade was waiting for her and he indicated a chair.

"Sit down and tell me how it's going with Delia Thomas." His manner was businesslike but pleasant.

Holly put aside her personal feelings about this unpredictable man, recognizing that this was no place for them, and gave her report.

"I'm having a little trouble with her. She's a really super reporter and she ought to be out in the field instead of behind the feature editor's desk. Delia doesn't have much organizational ability and I think she secretly hates being stuck in the office, but she feels it would be a demotion to go back to being a reporter. I tried to reason with her but I'm afraid she's becoming pretty hostile," Holly admitted ruefully.

"Let's have her in here," Slade suggested.

Delia Thomas was a tall woman with short brown hair and a normally friendly face. Her lips were compressed in a straight line now though and she came in exuding belligerence.

Slade met her at the door and escorted her to a seat, but the stiff set of her shoulders told that she wasn't about to be taken in by this carpetbagger.

Instead of taking his customary chair behind the desk, Slade lounged in front of it in a relaxed manner. "I understand you're not happy about the proposed changes, Miss Thomas. Suppose we talk about it."

Delia jumped at the chance. She launched into a tirade which included a eulogy to Slade's predecessor, her opinion of the new management and a defense of her own qualifications. "In spite of Miss Holbrooke's criticism, I'm completely capable of handling this job," she finished, with a face flushed with anger.

Slade heard her out, shaking his head imperceptibly when Holly trembled on speech. "I'm sure you misunderstood Miss Holbrooke's comments," he said when the woman had paused for air. "She appreciates your talents more than any of us because she came up the same way. You two have a lot in common."

Delia Thomas looked at Holly scornfully but before she could disclaim the notion, Slade continued in his low, magnetic voice. "Miss Holbrooke can sympathize with you. She knows how frustrating it is to women, knowing they're as capable as men or more so, and still seeing the plum assignments going to the male reporters." He shook his head. "Holly told me how it was in the beginning—all those flower shows she had to cover and the charity bazaars. But when there was a murder or a hijacking, it was always a man who got the nod."

"Amen," Holly murmured.

Delia looked at her with raised eyebrows as though seeing her for the first time.

"Do you remember your first big story?" Slade asked Holly.

"Do I ever!" Her eyes shone with blue fire. "It was a fluke really. There was a jumper on top of a bank building, a young man—just a kid really, I think he was nineteen. He wanted to talk to the press but he specified that it had to be a woman. They didn't have any choice so they rushed me over there and put a rope around my waist and I sat out on the ledge with him." She closed her eyes briefly. "I was never so scared in my life but I talked him back in and went back and wrote the story. That was my first byline."

Delia was listening with interest, her anger momentarily forgotten, and Slade murmured, "I suppose you had many similar experiences, Miss Thomas."

"I did actually. Perhaps not that dramtic but equally fascinating." A reflective smile played over her mouth. "There was the jewel thief who had been plaguing the top hotels all over the Continent. They finally caught him but he refused to divulge where he had hidden the loot. I managed to locate his girl friend and arrange a meeting and between us we persuaded him to tell us where it was in exchange for a lighter sentence. She led me to the hiding place but I had a terrible time convincing her that she wasn't entitled to one of the diamond rings as a finder's fee," she laughed.

"You sound like you enjoyed that life very much," Slade said quietly and in a flash, she recognized the trap. The softness left her face but before she could speak he said, "As feature editor, your name is on the masthead true, but how many people read the masthead, Miss Thomas? You could be the top reporter on the *Metro* with your byline on the front page every day. There would be a lot more recognition, plus the satisfaction of doing what you really love."

His shrewd words hit their target and her confusion was evident in the way she looked at him uncertainly. "I don't know. . . ."

"Think about it, Miss Thomas," Slade said softly.

After the woman had left, Slade found Holly looking at him with a troubled expression. "What's the matter?" he asked.

She hesitated before answering. "You handled that so beautifully and you're absolutely right about Delia."

His brow creased quizzically. "If you agree, why the doubtful look?"

"It's just that . . . well, it was really my job."

"Do you feel that I usurped your duties?"

"No, oh no, that wasn't what I meant at all! I meant I should have been able to do it without your help but I bungled it. If you have to keep bailing me out then I'm not pulling my weight."

"You're being too hard on yourself. I have a few years experience on you, remember." He gave her a friendly smile. "I'm not noted for being a patient man, Holly, and if I have any complaints you will be the first to hear them. So relax, you're doing a splendid job."

Praise from Slade wasn't that forthcoming and Holly glowed at the compliment. Even though their personal relations were sometimes rocky, her admiration for his business acumen was boundless and she valued his good opinion.

That evening after work, they went back to the hotel together which was unusual. Slade's hours were erratic since he was answerable to no one. They were having a very amicable drink in the suite and Holly was enjoying their unaccustomed rapport until he said, "You'd better start getting ready, I told Marsha we would be there around eight."

Holly was reminded of the way Slade had tendered the invitation the night before—and the reason—but he was being so pleasant to her that she decided perhaps she was wrong. "It's very nice of you to ask me but if you don't mind, I'll pass."

"But I do mind. I told Marsha I was bringing you."

Her suspicions returned in force. "And we mustn't hurt the lady's feelings must we?" she asked cuttingly.

"That wouldn't be polite," he agreed.

"I don't think good manners has anything to do with your wanting to take me there."

"What is going through that suspicious little mind of yours now?"

"I don't wish to discuss it, I'm just not going." When he looked at her impassively, her resentment overflowed. "It isn't as though I had a real escort. I wouldn't know a single person there except you and I doubt if you would have much time for me."

His expression was chilling. "It would be different if Alan were going is that it?"

"Certainly!" That didn't have anything to do with it but Holly wasn't going to give him the satisfaction of knowing it. If she had had any doubts about Slade's motives, his curt question answered it.

"Well, I'm afraid you will have to settle for my company tonight—or as much of it as I can spare," he added cruelly.

"You won't have to bother. Just plan on spending all your time with Lady what's-her-name."

"Her name is Marsha or Lady Dillingham and perhaps I'll do that." He stood up and looked at his watch. "You have one hour."

"I told you—"

He cut through her impassioned words. "It's a formal party and I think you would be rather uncomfortable in your present outfit, but if you aren't ready in an hour you will go like that."

Slade's eyes were gray chips of ice in his granite face and Holly knew he meant every word.

Slamming her bedroom door gave her a childish satisfaction, but after that she raced into the shower and then hurried to dress.

The gown she chose was a short turquoise chiffon that matched her eyes. The plunging neckline and empire waist were edged in a band of white and silver pavé bugle beads and the full skirt emphasized the figure molding bodice.

Her thick spicky black lashes needed no mascara and the angry flush on her cheeks made blusher unnecessary, but she added a touch of soft coral lipstick. Then she ran a comb through the long midnight-hued hair that brushed her shoulders.

The dress was one of her favorites, but even if she had known how enchanting she looked it wouldn't have given her confidence. Holly was as nervous as a teenager going to her first dancing party. *I won't know a soul and Slade will probably leave me in a corner all night*, she thought rebelliously.

When she joined him in the living room, the sullen words she had intended to deliver died on her lips. He was wearing a dinner jacket and the finely pleated white shirt under it accentuated his tan. He looked sleek and sophisticated and omnipotent—as indeed he was. He could bend anyone to his will. As angry as she had been a moment ago, Holly knew that if he opened his arms she would walk into them willingly, such was the charisma of this man.

Lowering her head quickly, she made a pretense of looking for something in her evening bag and missed the avid expression that flickered briefly in his eyes. It was gone by the time she glanced up.

Lady Dillingham's home was indeed a show place, a Georgian mansion with big spacious rooms packed now with people. Music was coming from somewhere but the crowds of elegantly dressed guests ignored it, chatting together in tightly knit groups.

Holly's dazzled eyes saw what looked like hundreds of strangers and her fingers were icy cold. She took an inadvertent step backward but Slade captured her hand and smiled at her.

"I'll introduce you to our hostess and then we'll dance," he said gently.

She clung blindly to his hand as he led her through the throng, most of whom greeted him warmly. Holly was too nervous to be aware of the many admiring glances cast in her own direction and Slade didn't stop to introduce her.

"Slade, you darling, I thought you would never get here!" A tall gorgeous blonde in a tight fitting long black velvet gown materialized out of the throng and threw her arms around him. Taking his face in her palms, she kissed him lingeringly on the mouth.

After a moment, Slade removed her hands and held them in both of his. "Marsha, my dear, you look beautiful as always. Let me introduce Holly Holbrooke."

Lady Dillingham turned to Holly and her eyes narrowed in a swift appraisal which Holly returned. The Englishwoman was as beautiful as Alan had described, with a magnificent figure and gleaming silvery blonde curls framing perfect features and flawless skin. Her eyes were cool though as she said, "Oh, yes, the little American that you picked up in the States."

She was quite tall and Holly felt at a distinct disadvantage but she drew herself up to her full height. "I think a more accurate way of putting it is, he *hired* me in San Francisco."

"Oh dear, did I say something wrong? I'm most frightfully sorry." Her perfectly arched eyebrows rose derisively. "Just what services do you perform, Miss Holbrooke?"

"I'm a journalist. What kind of services do *you* provide, Lady Dillingham?"

Slade uttered a strangled sound but what her hostess would have answered, Holly never discovered because another guest approached and Slade hustled her off with a firm hand on her arm. Leading her onto a dance floor that had been improvised in one of the drawing rooms, he folded her stiff body in his arms.

She leaned back and looked up at him defiantly. "All right, get it over with."

"Get what over with?"

"The lecture about how I was rude to your girl friend!" Before he could answer she said, "I suppose it doesn't mean anything that she was horrid to me first?"

His gray eyes were brimming with merriment, much to her surprise. "Have you ever heard of Ivan the Terrible? I think I'm going to call you Holly the Hellion."

"That isn't fair! She was the one who started it. She might be a Lady but she's no *lady!*"

Slade chuckled. "Where did I ever get the idea that you needed protection?"

His fingertips were gently stroking the soft skin in

back of her ear and Holly suddenly became aware of it. "Stop that. What do you think you're doing?"

His fingers trailed down her neck to the pulse that was now beating wildly at the base of her throat. "I never knew a girl with such soft skin."

Holly didn't know why he was turning on the charm but there had to be a devious reason. His sensuous touch was making her knees feel weak, but she forced herself to remember that it was all an act. "When you have so many women in your life it must be hard to remember little things like that," she said lightly.

He sighed and pulled her closer. "Could you manage to be quiet for a few minutes? I want to hold you close and pretend. . . ." He didn't finish the sentence.

Pretend what? That she was Marsha? That couldn't be it, he had only to go look for her in the other room. But Holly gave up the puzzle as the arm circling her narrow waist tightened and she surrendered to the magic this man could weave so easily around her.

The arm tightened and he held her so close against his lean body that she could feel his hard chest crushing her breasts. His muscular thighs brushed against hers and a quiver ran through her as she realized that they were almost as close as they could possibly get.

Holly's defenses were completely bridged as they moved to the slow music, their bodies locked in mutual pleasure. Her head was pillowed on his shoulder and his mouth rested on her scented hair.

"You've monopolized this beautiful girl long enough, Slade. It's time you gave the rest of us a chance."

The intrusion into their private world was jarring and Holly looked in bewilderment at the young man who was trying to cut in. Slade seemed to feel the same way. "Why aren't you in your usual place, Freddie—at the bar?" he scowled.

"Because I finally found a reason to leave it." The blond man with the bushy mustache took her hand and deftly swept Holly into his arms and away from Slade. "Since our mutual friend won't do the honors, allow me. I am Freddie Chatsworth and I would like to know you a great deal better."

In spite of his brash introduction, he was amusing and a very good dancer. When he had first cut in, Holly had been so drugged by Slade's aura that she had bitterly resented the intrusion, but now she realized that it had been for the best that the spell be broken. Slade could captivate her with a look and reduce her to a seething mass of desire with a touch. Of course, it was his vast experience against her total innocence but why was he doing it?

There couldn't be any doubt that he had brought her here to divert her attention from Alan. Freddie was the first man to make a move in her direction, but after he had broken the ice they crowded around her vying for dances. Slade didn't come near her again.

Even while she was talking and laughing, Holly couldn't help wondering about him. He had held her so intimately and seemed to be caught up in the same magic. And when Freddie had cut in, Slade had acted extremely annoyed. Surely she hadn't imagined it? And then the answer came to her and she felt a complete fool!

Slade was a famous man with a notorious reputation with the ladies. If he seemed interested in a woman all the men would flock around, assuming that she must be something special. He didn't even trust her to attract them on her own! Holly was so furious she wanted to do permanent damage to him but she controlled herself and smiled sweetly at her current partner. Let Slade think he had won—he would find out that she would go on seeing Alan as much as she darn well pleased! At least her popularity tonight was soothing to her wounded pride if nothing else.

Her sleek dark head continued to peep over the shoulder of one man after another as she was whirled around the dance floor. They were all jostling for her attention and Holly's laughing face seemed responsive, but actually her eyes searched the crowded room for the one man who wasn't interested in her.

Slade danced often with Marsha who fitted her body to his with an assurance that spoke for itself. She was a tall woman and his lips rested below her temple instead of on top of her head as they had with Holly. She was murmuring something in his ear and he smiled at her in that slow, senuous way that left no doubt about their relationship. Something curled up and died inside Holly but she was powerless to look away.

At that moment, Slade glanced in her direction and their eyes met. His immediately became contemptuous and Holly flushed. This was what he wanted wasn't it, so why was he looking at her that way?

Suddenly Holly was tired of the whole farce. Excusing herself from her current partner on a pretext of going to comb her hair, she slipped unobtrusively out of one of the tall French windows that led to the terrace. The crisp, starry night was beautiful though cold and she was soon shivering, but she didn't want to return for a wrap and risk acquiring unwanted company. She felt unaccountably sad and mixed up and she wanted to be alone.

Her teeth were chattering as she rested against a tree in a secluded part of the garden and leaned her head against the trunk. A warm coat was unexpectedly draped over her shoulders and as she looked up in surprise, Slade said, "What are you trying to do, catch pneumonia?"

"It was warm in there. I . . . I just came out for a little air."

"Alone? Where are all your eager conquests?"

"Waiting for me no doubt," she answered wearily.

"No doubt," he concurred ironically. "When I couldn't find you, I was afraid you had selected one lucky partner and slipped away with him."

"Afraid or relieved?" she asked shortly.

"Why would I be relieved?"

"With me off your hands, you and what's-her . . ." she stopped at the warning look on his face, "Lady Dillingham would have the whole night to yourselves."

"I don't need you to arrange my sex life," he told her mockingly.

"And I don't need you to arrange mine!"

"No, you've been doing that rather busily tonight. Have you settled on anyone special? I suppose they're all equally virile so one will serve the purpose as well as another."

Holly was close to tears but she bit her lip to stop it from quivering and threw back her head defiantly. "I might have to try all of them if there's time while we're here. After I do I'll give you a rating, if that's what you want."

Slade swore savagely and his fingers bit into the soft skin of her upper arms as the jacket he had draped around her fell to the ground. "Do you know what I'd like to do to you?"

"Yes, I believe I do," she answered coolly, "but you can forget about it. You aren't even in the running."

His eyes narrowed dangerously and his fingers tightened until she winced with pain. "Oh, no? Those aren't the signals you've been sending out. Ever since we met you've been throwing suggestive little statements my way."

"You're out of your mind!" She struggled to get away but he held her easily. "I wouldn't sleep with you if you got down on your knees and begged."

"Are you sure?" His lips curled cruelly. "Let's go back to the hotel and find out. Shall we use your bedroom or mine—or would you prefer that we frolic naked through the suite and make love on the floor of the living room? Would that appeal to your jaded palate?"

The graphic suggestion was meant to be insulting and Holly had to force herself not to show how much it hurt. The tears she had been trying to hold back welled up in her gem-colored eyes and she pounded desperately on his chest. "Let me go, I hate you, I hate you!"

"Show me how much, you little pagan." He jerked her against his hard body and his mouth crushed hers brutally, bruising her soft lips and forcing them apart with a savagery that was frightening.

She fought desperately but he anchored his fingers in the cloud of her hair, pulling her head back until her creamy throat was exposed to his questing mouth. His lips burned a trail down its length to the soft cleft between her breasts. Her heart started to pound wildly and Holly shuddered and tried to push him away, uttering tiny cries of protest which went unheeded.

Very deliberately, he slipped the wide-necked gown from her shoulders and knowing she was helpless to stop him, deftly unfastened the front closing of her wispy bra.

Her breasts gleamed whitely in the moonlight, the rosy tips quickly hardening under his ardent gaze. She gasped as his hands cupped the firm mounds, his thumbs lightly brushing the coral nipples, and when his tongue flicked each one lightly, an unwilling moan escaped her and she arched her slender body.

Slade's avid mouth fastened on her breast and then slid to her bare shoulder, raining burning kisses that seared her skin. Holly's resistance was disappearing under his sensual touch and her fingers fluttered up to thread through his dark hair without her even being aware of it.

His touch was gentler now as he muttered, "You're so beautiful . . . so incredibly lovely."

His hands slid voluptuously down her body, molding her hips and pressing them close to his demanding ones. His desire lit a matching need in Holly that engulfed her and swept everything before it.

"I want you," Slade murmured against her throat.

Her body sprang to life against his and she yearned for the fulfillment that only this man could give. Holly tried to remember the brutal way he had started to make love to her but it was no use. It didn't matter that he felt only lust for her. Alan was right, no woman could resist him when he used all of his expertise.

"I want you too," she whispered. But even in surrender, while her body was clamoring for him, she was bitter. Bitter enough to tell him what Alan had said so Slade would know she was an unwilling victim. "Alan—"

The hands that were caressing her neck suddenly tightened painfully, cutting off the rest of her words and she looked at him in shocked disbelief.

"The name is *Slade!*" he ground out viciously. "That can be fatal—mixing up the names of your lovers."

His eyes blazed into hers and the pressure of his fingers frightened her. It was difficult to speak but she forced out the words. "Slade, please . . . I only—"

"Save the explanations, they aren't necessary." His contemptuous gaze raked her half naked body. "You can cover up now. I've seen the merchandise and it's used."

He turned on his heel, leaving Holly utterly shattered. The enormity of what had happened left her shaking so badly that her trembling fingers had trouble fastening the lacy bra. Pulling up her dress hastily, she leaned her forehead against the rough trunk of the tree and closed her eyes while wave after wave of pain and humiliation flowed over her. She was too numb to feel the cold and too desolate to leave the protective darkness. Would her body ever stop trembling in the aftermath of the fire storm of emotion that he had put her through?

Time passed unnoticed and when a coat dropped roughly around her shoulders, Holly looked up in a daze.

Slade's face was as cold as the night and there was a white line around his mouth. "We're leaving. I've made your excuses to our hostess," he said grimly, surveying her tumbled hair and ravaged face. Holly stared at him wordlessly, crystal tears welling up in her tormented eyes. After a harsh intake of breath, he said angrily, "You're determined to use every trick in the book aren't you?"

She turned around, bowing her head. "Go back inside, Slade. You needn't bother with me, I can find my way alone."

He grabbed her arm, covering the distance to the house with great strides and hauling her roughly after him. "I advise you to keep quiet if you know what's good for you," he grated. "At this moment, the urge to break that beautiful body of yours in two is almost irresistible but I'm trying to restrain myself."

Those were the last words he spoke to her all the way home and sensing the inexplicable fury in him, Holly sat huddled in a corner of the limousine. Slade thrust her through the door of the suite, still without speaking but as she started toward her room he said tautly, "You're in for the night whether you like it or not so don't try sneaking out again."

She turned to look at him in bewilderment but saw only his retreating back as Slade vanished into his bedroom and slammed the door so hard that it reverberated throughout the suite.

Holly collapsed on the bed in her own room in a huddled little ball. Quivering with shame, she remembered her abject surrender to Slade's practiced lovemaking. Lovemaking? That was a laugh! It was a callous assault calculated to bring every one of her senses into play until she was so aroused that she was helpless in his arms. Holly folded her own arms over her breasts, trying to forget the feel of his long fingers expertly caressing her in the places that would make her completely vulnerable.

But why had he done it? Why had he set out to humiliate her in that way? He was the one who had taken her there to meet other men, yet when everything went according to plan, he was angry. It didn't make sense. And then Holly realized that even though his plan had worked, Slade was disgusted at seeing how easily she seemed diverted from Alan. He made love to her deliberately in order to prove that *any* man could arouse her. When she had been about to tell him that Alan was right and he could charm any woman into submission, Slade thought she was confusing him with Alan.

Holly's cheeks burned at the horrible implication. He didn't know that no other man had ever touched her like that—that no other man had ever aroused such feelings in her. It was only because she loved him that. . . . Her eyes opened wide at this soul-spinning thought. She must be crazy, it couldn't be true! But even as she was denying it wildly, Holly knew it *was* true.

She had fallen in love with Slade the first moment she laid eyes on him and, although she had fought against it desperately, every passing day brought her deeper under his spell. Nothing could ever come of it because Slade had women much more beautiful than herself but if she told him the truth about her innocence, at least he wouldn't hold her in such contempt.

He thought she was completely indiscriminate and that was her own fault. If only she had set him straight in the very beginning! But it wasn't too late. Her love for him would have to remain a secret, but she could confess that she had never been intimate with a man.

Slade might be angry at her for the willful deception but that kind of anger she could take. And after he got over it, maybe they could be friends. Maybe he might even begin to like her a little bit. Holly was willing to settle for that if it meant being able to be with him and see those gray eyes smile approvingly instead of freezing her with a wintery blast.

She got up and ran a comb through her tousled hair and then smoothed away the traces of tears that marked her pale cheeks. Once she had made up her mind, there didn't seem any reason to wait until morning. She had to settle this thing between them once and for all.

Holly's heart was beating fast when she knocked on Slade's door and when there was no answer, it speeded up even more. She called his name softly but that too was greeted with silence. If he was asleep should she wake him? She stood there irresolutely for a minute but the need to talk to him was too great to be postponed.

Turning the knob gingerly, she entered the room. The drapes were drawn, making it difficult to see anything except the bulk of the large bed against the far wall and she made her way toward it silently. But when she got there, Holly found that her caution had been unnecessary. The bed was empty.

Desolation followed her back to her own room plus a sense of loss that caused an actual pain in her breast. Slade had gone back to his mistress.

Chapter Five

Slade was gone by the time Holly got up the next day—if he had come back at all—and the shadows under her eyes attested to the sleepless night she had spent. It was almost morning before she fell asleep and if Slade returned, she didn't hear him. It was a temptation to peek in his room and see if the bed had been slept in but she resisted the urge. That smacked too much of masochism.

Holly dreaded the thought of seeing Slade because the office was scarcely the place for her confession yet without it, she didn't know if she could bear being with him. But her apprehension was groundless. He never appeared and in the late afternoon Holly discovered the reason.

"Slade went to Paris for a few days," Alan told her.

"Lucky him," she forced herself to say disinterestedly. Holly wondered if he had gone alone but she couldn't bring herself to ask.

"How was the party last night?"

She shrugged. "It was all right."

"Just all right? Those circles under your eyes indicate that it went on until all hours."

Holly changed the subject determinedly. "What did you do last night?"

"Moped around missing you," he grinned. "How about having dinner with me tonight?"

"Not tonight, Alan, I guess I am kind of tired. Maybe tomorrow night."

She really was exhausted and after an early dinner, Holly climbed into bed. She was trying to read when the phone rang.

"Holly? It's Slade."

Her breath caught in her throat. As though she wouldn't know that deep voice anywhere! But why was he calling? Was it to check up on her, to see if she was with Alan? "Slade, I thought you went to Paris."

"I did. I'm in Paris now."

"Oh, it's . . . that's nice." She had trouble talking to him even over the phone.

"I had to leave suddenly but I didn't want to wait until I got back to tell you that I know my behavior was inexcusable. I want to apologize."

"Ap . . . apologize?"

"Yes. Your life is your own and the way you choose to live it is up to you."

"But I don't . . . I mean I haven't . . ." she began desperately.

"You don't need to explain. I have no right to try and impose my values on you."

"But Slade, that's what I want to talk to you about."

"Yes?" His voice was impassive.

"Not . . . not over the telephone," she stammered nervously. "When you come back, can we have a talk?"

"Right," he said indifferently. "Well, that's all I wanted to say. I'll be returning in a few days."

Holly hung up the receiver slowly, chilled by his disinterested manner. But he *had* apologized, that was something wasn't it?"

Slade was pleasant when he returned and on the surface everything was the same as it had been before the party, but there was an undercurrent between them that had never been there before.

Holly had expected to set things straight as soon as he got back but there never seemed to be an opportunity. It was almost like Slade was consciously avoiding her, although there was no evidence she could put her finger on.

It was normal that he should be too busy for her to approach him in the office, but he always managed to come and go from the suite when she was out. And on the few occasions that they met there, Slade was always in a hurry to keep some appointment or other. Holly began to despair of ever cornering him but she couldn't fault his manner toward her. It was impersonal but courteous.

If it hadn't been for Alan, she would have been reduced to a state of despair. He took her out almost every evening and coaxed her to laugh and have as good a time as possible under the circumstances. He was such a dear that Holly regretted with all her heart that she couldn't fall in love with him, especially since he seemed to be patiently waiting for just that.

One night Alan took her to a private gambling club on a courtesy card of Slade's who was a member. Holly had been to Las Vegas and Reno but this was completely different. Instead of the raucous atmosphere that prevailed at the American casinos with their noisy crowds of jean-clad tourists, this club was quietly elegant.

There was ample room between the tables and

everyone was beautifully dressed, many in formal evening clothes. The long room was discreetly lit and the croupiers all wore tuxedos. Waiters hovered unobtrusively, ready to respond to the mere lift of a patron's finger.

Alan led her to a cashier's window and explained that they were Slade Rockwell's guests. When he took out some money to buy them each chips, the man smilingly shook his head.

"There is no need, sir, we will extend a line of credit and send you a statement tomorrow morning. You can send us your check at that time. Welcome to our club and we do hope you have a pleasant evening."

Holly's eyebrows rose. So that was how the rich people did it. If you had enough money, you didn't have to carry it around.

Alan gave her a stack of chips but she was hesitant about playing so she followed him to a blackjack table and sat beside him while he played. A waiter brought them each a drink and perhaps because she gulped hers rather quickly, her nervousness soon vanished.

When Alan lost consistently, Holly decided that she was bringing him bad luck which he denied. "You could never do that, honey. Besides, it's only chips."

"No, Alan, I have a feeling about it. I think we'll both be lucky if we play at different tables. Don't worry about me, I'll be just across the room."

She hadn't asked him what the chips were worth but his casual attitude indicated they probably didn't add up to much. Holly had played dice a few times and, although she didn't know much about the game, she headed for a dice table. Two men smilingly made room for her between them and she carefully placed one chip on the intricately marked green felt surface.

At first she stayed about even, winning a few times

and losing as often. Then luck seemed to go against her and in a remarkably short time, her whole stack was gone.

"You're not very lucky tonight, little lady," one of the men remarked commiseratingly.

Holly shrugged. "It's only chips," she answered since that appeared to be the thing to say.

At the cashier's window, she got another stack. "Please put these on my own account," she told the man, giving her name. As an afterthought she decided, "Perhaps you'd better give me two stacks. Good fortune isn't exactly smiling on me tonight."

He murmured polite regrets and deftly slid another stack toward her.

Holly selected a different table this time and she had just made her first bet when Alan came to check on her progress.

Eyeing the large pile of chips in front of her he said, "It looks like you're on a winning streak, love, maybe your hunch was right. I just won a bundle too."

"Oh, Alan, that's wonderful!" She didn't bother to disabuse him of the notion that she was winning. Why spoil his pleasure?

"I won't break your luck." He kissed her on the cheek. "Is there anything you want before I leave?" When she assured him that there wasn't, he signaled to a waiter to bring her another drink anyway.

Holly was indeed in Lady Luck's bad graces. Nothing that she did that night worked out. Switching to twenty-one didn't help and roulette was a disaster. But the drinks took the sting out of losing and she felt relaxed and very happy. This was great fun!

When she went back to the cashier for two more stacks, the man looked at her strangely. "Are you sure that's what you want, Miss Holbrooke? Perhaps it would be better if you called it an evening."

Holly was affronted and when she drew herself up to her diminutive height and insisted, the man reluctantly pushed a pile of chips toward her, handing her a slip of paper to sign.

The nerve of the man! After all, it was her own money she was losing. He reminded her of Uncle Ralph who couldn't stand to see anyone have a good time. As a matter of fact, that's who he looked like. The thought struck her funny and she started to giggle.

It was getting late when Alan came to get her and she was down to her last few chips. "Too bad," he comforted, "it looks like you didn't end up very well but don't worry, I won enough to make us both even. I think we'd better hit the road now, don't you?"

He cashed in his winnings and retrieved his marker and as they were walking out to get a cab, Holly asked idly, "How much were those chips worth? I never did know."

He named a sum that made her blood run cold. She sobered instantly and seeing her white face, Alan was concerned. "What is it, Holly, you're pale."

"I had no idea the stakes were that high!" she gasped.

"Is that all?" he chuckled. "You had me worried for a minute. I didn't tell you because you didn't ask but what difference does it make? They didn't lay a glove on us," he joked.

Holly was silent, making rapid calculations in her head. Four stacks at—good Lord, she had lost a whole month's salary! What on earth was she going to do? Alan must never know. He would blame himself and it was really her own stupidity.

"Holly?" He was looking at her worriedly.

"I'm all right." She managed a weak smile. "I guess I'm just not cut out to be a high roller."

After worrying about it all night, Holly knew she would have to tell Slade and ask him to pay her losses and give her an advance on next month's salary. It would be a bitter pill to swallow because he already thought she was hopelessly irresponsible and this would put a cap on it. But what else could she do? When the little bit of ready cash she had ran out, she wouldn't have enough for toothpaste or shampoo or even lunch for that matter. Alan would give her a loan of course, but if Slade ever found out she took money from Alan there was no telling what interpretation he might put on it!

Holly tracked Slade down in his office the next morning and his expression on seeing her wasn't exactly welcoming. Swallowing nervously, she said, "I'm sorry to disturb you but could . . . could I speak to you for a minute?"

He sighed irritably. "Ah, yes, that little talk you're so determined on having."

She shifted uncomfortably. "No, this is something else. I'm afraid I'm in a little . . . um . . . trouble."

Slade stiffened ominously, his eyes narrowing as they swept her slight body and Holly had the frightened feeling that his control might snap as easily as the pencil he now broke in two. "Since I'm obviously not the cause of it, don't you think you ought to go to the source?"

"What do you mean?" She looked at him uncomprehendingly.

"The father," he said bluntly. "The man who got you in this predicament, or don't you know his name?"

Holly felt as though he had slapped her and she went

pale, clutching the desk for support. Then fury engulfed her. "You unspeakable, disgusting man! I'm not pregnant I'll have you know, and if I were you would be the last person I'd come to. I must have been out of my mind to ever think I could even *discuss* a problem with you let alone ask you for help!" Angry tears welled up in her eyes and she turned blindly toward the door.

Before she could get there, Slade grabbed her by the shoulders and turned her to face him. "I'm sorry if I misjudged you, Holly, tell me what's wrong."

"No! Let go of me! I wouldn't tell you what day it is."

A little smile touched his mouth but it didn't reach the worry in his eyes. "Tell me what kind of trouble you're in." When she stubbornly refused to answer and renewed her efforts to get away, he shook her hard. "Tell me!" he commanded.

Impotent rage filled her. It wasn't bad enough that she might go to jail for not paying her gambling debts, she also had to submit to the indignity of having Slade shake her until she rattled. "I lost a whole month's salary at the casino last night and I don't have the money to pay it. Now are you satisfied?"

He looked at her incredulously. "*That's* the trouble you're in?"

"Would you rather I was pregnant?" she asked sulkily.

The hands that had been gripping her shoulders so painfully, moved up to frame her face and Slade looked at her wonderingly. "Holly, Holly, what am I going to do with you? I think you're taking years off my life." Before she could answer, he pushed her firmly into a chair and stood over her so she couldn't escape. "Tell me the whole story."

Since there was no getting out of it she explained the

circumstances, ending with, "I know it was stupid of me, but in Las Vegas I never played with more than dollar chips and it just didn't occur to me to ask."

Amusement warmed his gray eyes. "Another lesson learned I trust."

"Oh, yes! But the thing is now what am I going to do? Will you pay the casino and advance me some money on my next month's salary?" she asked anxiously.

"Yes and no."

"What does that mean?"

"It means yes, I will pay your debts and no, I won't advance you any money."

"But I don't have enough to live on! I'm not asking to buy anything, just the simple necessities."

"Such as?"

"Well, lunches and dinners for one thing. Or is starvation to be one of my punishments?" she asked bitterly.

"Scarcely," he laughed. "There isn't enough of you to begin with." She squirmed as his glance traveled over her slight body. "You can sign for your meals at the hotel—if you ever find yourself alone that is," he added sardonically.

"That might take care of dinner but how about lunches? Or are you suggesting that the hotel fix me a brown bag every day?"

"No, I don't want you getting crumbs all over the office," he teased. "If Alan or Victor aren't around, I'll make the supreme sacrifice and take you out to lunch myself."

"I don't want that any more than you do!" she flared. "Wouldn't it be easier to advance me a few paltry dollars?"

"Easier but not nearly as instructive."

"All right, keep your rotten money," she cried childishly, "I'll get it somewhere else."

"I wouldn't try it," he warned. "You will only make yourself look foolish since everyone in this office will be instructed not to lend you any." The firm set of his jaw told her he meant exactly what he said and Holly subsided into impotent fury. "Be ready at one o'clock and I'll take you to the Knightsbridge Club for lunch. Good food but no gambling," he told her mockingly.

"No, thank you, I'd rather go without," she told him stiffly.

"Suit yourself," he shrugged, "but you're going to be awfully hungry by the end of the week. I've seen you eat, remember?"

In the end she gave in as he had known she would, although Holly was rigid with resentment as she walked beside him into the dignified dining room. Slade was completely relaxed and seemed to be enjoying himself hugely. All the coldness that had been evident toward her before was gone and a casual observer would have thought that he had chosen to be by her side.

Holly sulkily refused to utter a word during lunch, although the food was delicious and ordinarily she would be bubbling over with comments. It didn't seem to bother Slade though and by the end of the meal she gave up trying to annoy him.

One of her favorite desserts was on the menu and since the waiter was nowhere in sight, she unwillingly asked Slade, "May I have some trifle?"

"Do you think you can afford it?" he asked casually.

"You mean I have to pay for this?" she gasped.

"Wasn't that what you proposed?"

"Their prices here are horrendous," she cried. "I can't afford to eat in places like this, especially with that terrible amount I have to pay off."

Her eyes were turquoise with dismay and Slade relented. "I was only teasing you, little one. Of course you don't have to pay for your own lunch. What kind of man do you think I am anyway?"

She sighed with relief. "Please don't do that to me again. My nerves are already on the ragged edge of nowhere."

"I'm sorry, honey." He tipped her chin up with a long forefinger. "I didn't think you would get so upset."

This was the old Slade and his touch was doing remembered things to her. She lowered her lashes under his smiling gaze. "You're really right and I can't keep coming to fancy restaurants like this with you. I'll just get deeper and deeper in your debt."

"And would that bother you?"

"Yes, of course." They were sitting on a banquette against the wall and Holly was suddenly aware of how close their bodies were and how very masculine his was. Seeking to change the subject she said, "Would you please lend me five dollars or whatever the equivalent is in pounds?"

"I thought we'd settled that. What do you need it for?"

"I have to buy some panty hose. You can see that those come under the heading of a necessity can't you?" she begged appealingly.

"Definitely," he smiled, "where do we find them?"

We? Surely he wasn't going shopping with her? "At any department store," she said uncertainly.

"Good. As soon as you finish we'll go to Harrod's."

"You don't have to go with me."

"I do unless you plan on shoplifting." His wide grin told her he was enjoying her discomfiture.

"But I also want to buy some lingerie," she told him

desperately, forgetting for the moment that he knew she didn't have any money. It was only an attempt to discourage him since men hated shopping in those departments. "I didn't have time to buy what I needed before we left."

"Capital idea," he said smoothly, "I enjoy picking out pretty nightgowns."

Holly blushed. "You have to be out of your mind to think I would let you. What would the saleslady think?"

"That I'm a very lucky man." He gave her a slow look. "And that you wouldn't have it on long if you belonged to me."

Holly's flushed cheeks were burning and she couldn't meet his gaze. "Please, Slade," she murmured.

There was no way to dissuade him and it was a very disturbed girl who accompanied him to the big department store. The young hosiery saleslady kept giving Slade admiring glances out of the corner of her eye as he took an active interest in her wares.

Holly was ready to die of embarrassment when he picked up a sheer pair of lace-topped panty hose and said, "These are the ones I'd like to see you in." His double-edged meaning was unmistakable but he met Holly's furious gaze blandly.

It was even worse in the lingerie department to which he insisted on taking her, although Holly declared she had changed her mind. The saleslady who waited on them there was elderly and Slade changed his tactics.

Holding a sheer peach-colored nightgown up to Holly, he said critically, "Yes, I think my wife will look beautiful in this don't you? We would also like to see something in satin. I love the feel of satin don't you, darling?" He put his arm around her lovingly while the saleslady beamed approvingly.

When the woman had gone in search of other gowns, Holly pulled away from him angrily. "Why did you let her think I'm your wife?" she hissed.

"Would you rather have her think we *aren't* married?" His eyes sparkled with amusement.

Slade insisted on buying several gowns and Holly had a chilling thought. She knew he was enjoying her embarrassment but was the real purpose of this shopping trip a present for Lady Dillingham? He had taken great care in picking each one and they would probably fit her, although the other woman was more voluptuous. When he held them up against Holly, was he actually picturing Marsha's well remembered curves lightly concealed under the filmy chiffon? The idea was so painful that she bit her lip.

Holly was very quiet in the limousine and Slade reached over and took her hand. "Are you angry with me?"

"No." It wasn't anger it was jealousy and the hopelessness of her love for this handsome unattainable man.

"Then why so quiet?"

"I was just thinking about things," she answered truthfully, trying to withdraw her hand. But his fingers tightened around hers.

"Care to tell me about them?"

She looked up into his strong face and the pulse in her wrist beat so wildly that she was afraid he would feel it. What would happen if she said yes, I want to tell you how much I love you and beg you to love me back. Her lashes dropped in panic at the insane idea, fearful lest even a hint of it should be reflected in her eyes. "It isn't anything you would be interested in," she said sadly, unable to see the inexplicable look on his face.

Something came up unexpectedly at the office and Holly had to work later than usual. When she returned to the hotel, Slade was already there. He was relaxing over a drink and he raised his glass and said, "Care to join me?"

It was the casually intimate way he asked that enchanted her, as though he really wanted her company. Could that be possible? Holly decided not to question her good fortune. "I'd love to. Just let me take off my jacket."

As she started toward her room, Slade called to her. "You forgot something." She turned to look inquiringly and he held up a long box. "Your nightgowns."

She caught her breath. They weren't for Marsha after all! Her cheeks were flushed and her eyes were shining as she accepted the package. "Thank you," she murmured shyly.

Holly put the parcel on a chair in her room and hurriedly shed her jacket. She paused only long enough to run a comb through the soft dark curtain of hair and dab on a little perfume before going to join Slade. It was quiet in the suite for once and they had just commented on it when the telephone and the buzzer rang simultaneously.

Slade raised a rueful eyebrow. "So much for tempting fate. I'll get the door, you get the phone."

Victor's spare figure appeared in the doorway as Holly reached for the receiver.

"Sorry to bother you, Slade, but I think we should go over those contracts before I leave for Zurich in the morning," Victor said.

"Good idea, Vic, I want to be sure everything is in order before we make an offer."

The voice in Holly's ear said, "Hello, lovely, this is Freddie."

For a moment she drew a blank, possibly because she wanted to forget everything about that dreadful party. Then it came to her—Freddie Chatsworth, the man who had cut in on Slade. Holly wasn't especially glad to hear from him but she said politely, "Hello, Freddie, how are you?"

"Simply ripping now that I've finally gotten to speak to you. Doesn't anyone ever give you messages at that hotel?"

Victor's voice was droning on in the background and as Holly turned to glance idly at the two men, she found Slade eyeing her enigmatically. She had repeated Freddie's name aloud, was Slade too being reminded of that terrible night?

"Holly? Are you still there, luv?"

"What? Oh . . . er . . . yes, I'm still here."

"I want to see you again. How about dinner tonight?"

"Tonight?" she said vaguely. "No, I'm sorry but I'm busy." She wasn't but Freddie, through no fault of his own, was mixed up in her mind with the most traumatic evening of her life.

When she declined the invitation, he suggested the next night and then a succession of different dates. Holly was painfully aware of Slade listening impassively in the background. It was difficult to think of enough tactful excuses with her attention thus distracted, but she finally managed to get rid of him, although Freddie declared that he wasn't defeated and was going to try again.

After carefully replacing the receiver, Holly avoided Slade's eyes and murmured, "I'll leave you two alone."

"Don't run off on my account, Holly, it's always nice

to have you around," Victor told her in his usual courtly manner.

Slade was silent though and she said hurriedly, "Thanks, Victor, but I . . . well, I have a few things to do."

As she went to her room, Holly was unaware of Slade's thoughtful eyes following her.

Chapter Six

Holly continued to spend more time with Slade but it was a mixed blessing. Since she now admitted that she was hopelessly in love with him, every moment in his company was welcome, especially with his renewed friendliness toward her. But being with him so much meant that she found out more about his personal life than she cared to.

Holly burned with helpless resentment when his many women called. Lady Dillingham was by no means Slade's only romantic interest, although she appeared to hold the favorite's spot. The beautiful blonde felt so sure of her welcome that she even came to the office to carry Slade off to luncheon or tea and he never seemed to mind, although if she came unannounced and he was busy she had to wait like everyone else.

But Marsha managed to turn even this into a triumph. She spent the time making sure that everyone in the office knew she was there to collect her personal property. Holly often wished that one of her rivals would show up at the same time but it never happened.

Sometimes Holly would return from a date with Alan and meet Slade coming home from one of his constant social engagements. He never asked her out in the evening again after the fiasco of Lady Dillingham's party, but they would often have a nightcap together.

His manner toward Holly was that of a big brother and he seemed interested in where she had been and what she had done. He always asked if she needed anything and was quick to sense if she was tired or upset but it was done in a filial way, that's what was hardest to take.

Slade listened courteously to all the little everyday things she had to recount. The gray eyes that studied her face were impassive, without a glint of the desire she had once seen there. Holly told herself that she ought to be grateful for just the opportunity of being with him, but there were times when she found herself aching with vague longings after they had said their casual good-nights and each gone to their own rooms.

One night Holly told Alan she had to stay in and do a lot of "girl" things. There were overdue letters to write and stockings to rinse out and after a prolonged soak in a scented bubble bath, she washed her hair. When it was dried to a long gleaming swathe that curled around her bare shoulders, Holly went barefoot into the bathroom for a clean nightgown. One mirrored panel of the closet concealed a chest of drawers and she opened one absently and then froze. Staring up at her was the peach-colored chiffon that Slade had selected.

She had never worn any of the lovely gowns that he had insisted on buying for her, feeling a curious reluctance to accept such an intimate gift. In the back of her mind was the intention to return them to him, but she had delayed doing it because she was sure it would precipitate an argument and she didn't want to disturb their fragile rapport.

The seductiveness of the exquisite garment weakened her resolve and Holly slipped it over her head. It settled around her slim body in a pale peach cloud, the diaphanous folds floating from a fragile lace yoke that skimmed her ivory shoulders. Holly whirled around, looking at her image from every angle and the soft fabric whispered around her bare ankles like a caress. The lovely pastel gave a glow to her flawless skin, making her feel utterly feminine and desirable.

Suddenly her shoulders slumped. What was the point in looking desirable when the one you desired didn't want you? But that line of thought was dangerous to her peace of mind and Holly determined not to pursue it. She would go to bed with a good book and have an early night.

Slade had given her a best seller, telling her it was frothy but good reading and that was just what she needed tonight. Now where had she put it? After searching the room with a glance, she remembered that she had left it on the coffee table in the living room.

The long room was softly lit by the glow of the one small lamp they left on when one or the other of them were out at night. The last one in turned it off. Holly was just reaching for the book when a key sounded in the lock.

She froze in sudden fear. It was much too early for Slade to be coming home. Who could it be? She was rigid with panic when the door opened and Slade's broad shouldered frame filled the entry.

"Oh, Slade, you startled me!" She let out her breath with a shaky sigh of relief. "I didn't think you would be back yet."

He closed the door and walked slowly into the room. "Who were you expecting?"

"No one, that's why I was so frightened."

He moved steadily toward her. "Were you alone all evening?"

His tone of voice disturbed her. "Yes, I . . . I washed my hair."

His eyes inspected the scented black tresses. "What a pity that all that loveliness went unseen," he remarked skeptically.

She hadn't imagined it. His manner was cold again, the way it had been that night. Surely he didn't think she had been entertaining a man here? His eyes were raking her body and Holly realized with a flush of embarrassment that she was practically naked.

She clutched the transparent folds of chiffon together in a vain effort at concealment and stammered, "I have to . . . I think I'd better go to my room."

"Don't go. Stay and have a nightcap with me."

"No, I . . . it's late."

"You just said it was early."

"I don't have my robe," she said desperately.

"Are you cold?" He was standing very close and Holly instinctively shrank away from the tall muscular body, every nerve shrieking a warning. "It's strange how much more seductive women are when they're lightly covered than when they're completely naked," he said, eyeing her deliberately.

His insolent manner provoked her ready anger. "I'm sure you're an expert on the subject, but if you don't mind I'd rather not hear about it," Holly said, turning away.

"Wait." His hand on her arm stopped her. "Does it bother you that I'm as much of an expert on women as you are on men?"

It was a golden opportunity to tell him what she had been wanting to for weeks, but Holly had no intention of having that discussion in her present state of undress.

Besides, his hand on her bare arm was lighting tiny flames in her blood.

"Nobody could equal your track record," she said shortly.

"Not even you, Holly?" he asked softly.

Her heart plunged like a stone and she tried to pull her arm away but his hand tightened. "Let me go, Slade," she said coldly. "I want to go to my room."

His fingers were combing through her hair, moving to massage her scalp. "Would you like me to come with you?" he murmured.

Her body quickened in response. That was what she did want but not like this. Not with this practiced seduction because he didn't have any other woman tonight. "Certainly not!"

His hands traced the shape of her slender neck and shoulders, sliding down to cup the fullness of her breasts. "Think what magnificent love two experienced people like us could make."

"That's disgusting!"

"Is it?" There was a curiously bitter twist to his mouth. "We both know that we want each other. Why don't we just bow to the inevitable?" He pulled her roughly to him, his hands hard on her soft body.

Holly struggled fiercely in his arms, her spirit wounded beyond repair. "The only way you'll ever get me is by rape and I don't think you would descend to that!"

He clamped her body to his and anchored his hand in her hair, pulling her head back so she had to look at him. His eyes were blazing as he said, "You're right but I don't think I'll have to resort to rape. Before I'm through with you, my little nympho, you'll be begging me to make love to you."

Anger was all that sustained Holly. "I'll see you in hell first!"

There were deep lines around his nose. "What makes you think I'm not already there?"

His mouth fastened brutally on hers, bruising her soft lips and forcing them apart for the invasion of his tongue. Her body was bent into an arc making it difficult to fight him effectively. In any case, she was no match for his superior strength.

Holly was making soft cries of protest which he ignored, grinding his mouth against hers until she felt his teeth on her lower lip. The pain registered in her frightened brain and she whimpered softly. That sound finally penetrated Slade's fury and his mouth eased its punishing pressure, but his lips still kept possession of hers. They moved seductively now though, his tongue outlining the shape of her mouth before thrusting in and out so sensuously that the room started to spin.

Holly's muscles were strained with the effort of trying to hold Slade off and they failed her abruptly, leaving her limp and defeated in his arms. As soon as she stopped struggling, he loosened his savage grip, holding her more gently. But that was infinitely worse in a way.

Slade's hands started stroking her body slowly and voluptuously. They wandered from her bare shoulders over her breasts and the flat plane of her stomach to the small rounded hips and Holly shivered uncontrollably.

"Slade, please don't," she begged, but he didn't even hear her.

"Your body is so perfect," he murmured, his eyes drugged.

He slipped the gown from her shoulder and down one arm until her breast was revealed, the rosy nipple betraying her arousal. When his lips brushed against it, Holly moaned and he lowered the other strap, stroking both breasts with feather-light fingertips that sent a cascade of emotions through her body.

His mouth sought hers once more but this time the kiss was gentle, exploring the soft inner recesses with an expert seduction that destroyed her defenses. Holly's arms stole hesitantly around his neck and when his warm lips slid along the line of her jaw to her earlobe, she buried her hands in his thick hair and clung to him.

His tongue traced the contour of her ear and then he kissed the soft skin in back of it. The gown had slipped off, leaving her body bare in his arms and Slade trailed a languorous path down her spine that left her gasping with pleasure. She unconsciously pressed her body closer to his, molding herself to him until she could feel his muscular thighs against her.

He tipped her chin up and looked at her with molten eyes. "I want you, Holly. Do you want me?"

"Yes, oh, yes!" she moaned, burying her face in his neck.

He lifted her effortlessly in his arms, carrying her into her bedroom and putting her gently on the bed. His eyes drank in her body and Holly felt no shame, although it was the first time a man had seen all of her. She loved this man and wanted to give anything he asked. Lifting both arms wide, she welcomed him to her.

Slade lowered himself onto her with a groan, burying his face in her neck and muttering, "I was going to leave you like this do you know that? But I can't do it—God help me, I can't do it!" He rained feverish kisses over her face, murmuring all the while, "You're like a slow flame in my blood, always there to torment me and now I have to have you. I didn't want this to happen. You're only a child, how can you be so completely amoral?"

"Slade, don't," she whispered in pain but he was driven by a devil inside of him.

"Why does it bother me that you've slept with at least a dozen different men?"

"But I haven't!" she cried. "You're the first."

His eyes were tortured. "Don't try to lie to me. It doesn't matter. I'm going to take you anyway."

"But not like this," she begged. "Yes, I want you, I'll admit it. But I've never wanted any other man. No man has ever held me like this."

"I wish it were true," he said wearily, his hands trailing over her soft skin as though he couldn't help himself.

She took his face in her hands, a shimmer of tears in the huge aquamarine eyes. "I can't stop you from doing anything you want to me, but after you do you will know I'm telling the truth."

He shifted his weight and lifted her to a sitting position, gripping her shoulders with steely fingers. "Are you telling me the truth?" Her unwavering gaze gave him the answer but he seemed unable to accept it. "I don't believe you," he said tautly. When she remained silent, innocence shining out of her eyes, he said wonderingly, "My God, I *do* believe it!"

He gathered her in an embrace that was so tight Holly could hardly breathe. Stroking her hair tenderly, he murmured little endearments that made her melt with love.

After a blissful time, Holly gently disentangled herself and kissed him on the chin. Winding her arms around his neck she pulled his head forward and whispered in his ear, "You said I would beg and I am, Slade. Won't you please make love to me?"

He stiffened in her arms and held her away from him. The urgent passion was gone and a wealth of emotions played over his strong face, none of which Holly could read.

"Slade, what's wrong?"

What happened next left her completely crushed and utterly bewildered. He stood up abruptly and pulled the covers around her, bending over to kiss her tenderly on the mouth.

Brushing back her tumbled hair with gentle fingers he said, "Go to sleep, Holly, I'll see you in the morning."

It was so unexpected that for a moment she couldn't comprehend what was happening and she stared after him numbly. Then realization set in and she scrambled to her knees. "Slade!" she cried out in agony, but he didn't turn around.

Holly sank slowly back against the pillows and watched the tall retreating figure with a sense of desolation that was chilling. Why had he left her when she had offered herself so completely?

Once more Slade had rejected her but this time was the worst of all. This time she had come so close to becoming a woman in the arms of the man she loved. Why had he turned away when he had seemed to want her as much as she wanted him? Was it possible that he still thought she was promiscuous? Yet he had seemed to believe her.

Holly's unfulfilled body throbbed with actual pain as she tried to remember every word he had spoken, looking in vain for an answer. It was hurtful to remember some of them, but when she had finally told him the truth everything had changed. Surely she hadn't imagined the fierce joy in his eyes or the broken words that told her of it? Then why? *Why?*

It was impossible to lie there on this bed that Slade

had shared so briefly and Holly sprang up and put on a robe. For most of the night she paced the floor but it didn't help. Nothing did.

The sound of distant church bells woke her the next morning and even before she opened her eyes, Holly had a sense of foreboding. Then it all came crashing down on her and she buried her face in the pillow with a moan.

She lay motionless for a long time, willing the oblivion of sleep to return. After recognizing the futility of that hope, Holly finally got up and went into the bathroom. Turning the shower spray to needle sharp refreshed her drooping body but nothing could repair her soul.

She dressed automatically, pulling on a soft rose-colored sweater and a matching wool skirt, and then wondered what to do next. It was Sunday and there wouldn't even be the solace of work. What would she do all day? For that matter, what would she do with the rest of her life?

Trailing a warm jacket in nerveless fingers, Holly picked up her purse. Maybe a walk in Hyde Park would clear away some of the cobwebs.

Slade was standing at one of the long windows looking out at the park, his eyes narrowed in thought. He was dressed casually in a black turtleneck pullover and jeans that sat low on his narrow hips. It was unusual attire for him and it made him look younger and very macho, like a race car driver or a champion skier. His hands were jammed in his pockets, tightening the denim so that it outlined his powerfully muscled thighs. After a brief hesitation, Holly started wordlessly for the door.

He turned and saw her and his eyes lit up. "Good

morning, Holly," he said softly. When she didn't even acknowledge his presence, Slade crossed the room in a few long strides and caught her arm.

She shuddered away from him and cried, "Don't touch me."

"Holly, don't be foolish, we have to talk."

He refused to release her and since she knew from experience how easily he could subdue her, Holly forced herself not to struggle. "What about? Are there some insults you forgot to deliver last night?" she asked coldly.

"I've ordered breakfast. You'll feel better after you have a cup of coffee." He led her firmly back from the door.

"I don't want any. I'm going out."

"Not until we've had a talk."

There was a hardness in his voice that warned her he didn't intend to be dissuaded. There was nothing she could do about it but abject misery made her try. "Haven't you humiliated me enough? What more do you have planned? I can't bear to look at myself in the mirror now."

"There isn't any reason for you to feel that way, little one." His fingers touched her cheek gently but she flinched away.

"Why the sudden turnaround? Ever since we met you've believed my morals were nonexistent. You never missed a chance to show how easily you could get me into bed. Well, you proved your point, isn't that enough for you?"

"Can you really blame me for having that opinion? You were the one who led me to believe you slept around." He watched her intently. "Why did you want me to think that, Holly?"

"It was what you wanted to believe."

"That isn't true but I won't argue the point now. The fact is that you could have set me straight so easily. Why didn't you?"

She shrugged. "It didn't seem to matter."

"I can't believe a girl would *want* a man to think that about her."

All the misery her lies had caused rose up and threatened to engulf Holly. "What difference does it make? We fought from the first minute we laid eyes on each other and you formed your impression of me then. Nothing I said would have changed it."

"Are you sure?" When long eyelashes veiled her troubled eyes, he continued softly, "I wouldn't say we fought all the time. I can think of some notable examples when we got along rather well."

Hot color rose along her creamy throat and she looked away. "I don't see why my morals are such a burning issue anyway. Are you equally concerned about Monique Duvall's or Lady Dillingham's? Or are you under the apprehension that you were the first with them?"

A chuckle broke his tension. "Far from it."

"And that doesn't bother you?" she demanded.

"My dear child, I'm a man not a boy. I'll admit I have enjoyed the . . . favors shall we call it . . . of beautiful women and their experience has added to the pleasure. I have never seduced a virgin."

Holly's feeling of rejection was choking. "I'm sorry I almost spoiled your evening!"

"Will you stop being such a little idiot? I'm trying to explain why I left you last night. It was the hardest thing I've ever done in my life, incidentally." Slade put a hand to his neck and massaged the tight muscles ruefully, walking up and down as if what he had to say was difficult. "I don't suppose there are many details of my private life that haven't been publicized, unfortunately. My views on marriage are especially well known. I never really saw the need."

Sudden comprehension swept over Holly. "And you thought I would expect you to marry me if we made love? That never entered my mind!"

"Well, it damn well should have," he said grimly. "For whatever reason, you have reached the ripe old age of twenty-three without experiencing a man. Do you know what a gift that is to your future husband?"

The injustice of it enraged Holly. "Talk about male chauvinism! It's all right for you to go around the world bed hopping, but just because I never met a man I wanted to sleep with, I'm doomed to celibacy until I find a man who wants to make it legal, is that it?"

In spite of her protests, he took her face between his palms and stroked her cheek with his thumb. His eyes fastened on her trembling mouth and he said softly, "But you did meet a man you wanted didn't you?"

She jerked away and faced him defiantly. "Yes, one who has a hang-up about virgins. I never knew it was such a crime but now that you have been kind enough to point it out, I'll be sure and do something about it."

Before he could stop her she ran to the door and flung it open, startling the waiter who was on the point of ringing the buzzer. Holly skirted the breakfast cart and ran down the hall straight into Alan's arms.

"Holly! What's the matter, you look upset." His concerned face surveyed her flushed cheeks.

"Oh, Alan, take me away from here *please!*"

"Of course, honey. Do you want to tell me about it?"

"Not now, let's just get out of here," she panicked.
The wheel of the rolling table stuck in the doorway and by the time Slade could skirt it, the elevator doors were closing. He had only a brief glimpse of Alan's arm around Holly and her tearful face upturned to his.

Chapter Seven

Holly's tears had subsided and she was staring wanly out of the window of the car Alan had rented. He had been wonderful, not asking any questions once she had begged him not to. After taking a look at her shattered state, he put his arm comfortingly around her and declared that he was going to take full responsibility for the day. And that was how they found themselves on their way to the small town of Bath.

"I think you will really enjoy seeing it," Alan said, tactfully keeping the conversation impersonal. "They've done a remarkable job of restoring the old Roman baths."

"Yes, I've heard about them and I'm looking forward to it," she said politely.

At least that was the way she had felt before the recent traumatic events, but now Holly wondered if she would ever enjoy anything again. But Alan was being so kind that she determined to make an effort.

He told her a bit about the history of Bath as the beautiful English countryside rolled by and gradually, a little color began to return to her pale cheeks.

"Are you feeling better?" he asked, squeezing her hand.

She managed a tiny smile. "Yes, thanks to you."

"Care to tell me about it?"

A shiver ran through her. "No!"

"Okay," he said cheerfully, "but if you change your mind, I have a broad shoulder you can cry on."

"You're so good to me, Alan, how can I ever thank you?" she said impulsively.

His hazel eyes were serious as they rested on her delicate face. "I'd like to do a lot more. You know that don't you, Holly?"

She bent her head in misery. Alan was in love with her and she would sell her soul if she could only love him back. But it didn't belong to her anymore. It belonged to Slade who didn't want it. Why had she fallen in love with him of all people? It wasn't as though she hadn't known what kind of man he was right from the beginning. But who ever said that love made sense?

"Hey, don't look so serious. We're out for a good time, remember?" Alan joked.

They took a slow tour through the town of Bath before Alan parked the car and he pointed out the restored council houses standing in an impressive crescent behind a stately iron picket fence. They got out and walked along the cobbled streets and Holly admired the beautifully tended lawns and rounded flower beds of massed blue and yellow and red and white flowers.

After that they strolled through the narrow streets of the town, stopping to browse in quaint little stores. By then it was lunchtime and Alan led her to a charming tea shop. It was during lunch that Holly began to throw off the paralyzing weight of depression that had been crushing her.

She looked around with real instead of feigned

interest and said, "Alan, I do love it here. This was an inspired choice."

"I hoped you would like it, it's always been one of my favorites. I've been coming here for years. That's one good thing about the countryside, restaurants don't open and close like clam shells."

"I suppose the job brings you to England regularly doesn't it?"

"Yes, but I discovered this place even before I went to work for Slade."

"You had been to Europe before you joined the Rockwell organization?" Holly couldn't bring herself to use Slade's name. When Alan merely nodded without elaboration, she looked at him appraisingly. "You never mentioned that. As a matter of fact, I'm just beginning to realize how little I truly I know about you. In all the time we've spent together, you never once talked about yourself. Are you concealing some deep dark secret?"

"Yes, actually my name is Bluebeard but if I told you that you wouldn't marry me."

She hurriedly changed the subject. "Be serious, Alan, what did you do before you got this job?"

"Not very much I'm afraid," he said ruefully. "I was a rich man's son, just drifting and getting into trouble."

She looked at his clean-cut rather boyish face and clear hazel eyes. "Not you, Alan, I can't believe that."

"Well, maybe not trouble exactly but I was a pretty mixed-up kid. I had graduated from college and couldn't decide what I wanted to do. Maybe because I didn't really have to work. Oh, my father was a little impatient with me, but he made sure I had plenty of money and my mother could always find excuses for me."

"That sounds normal," Holly smiled.

"It was a time when being rebellious was almost expected of you and I did the typical thing."

"You grew a beard," she teased.

"Of course, and a mustache too." It was hard to imagine him that way and she studied his face with interest. "I also bummed around Europe for a year, complete with backpack and knapsack."

Her eyes sparkled with laughter. "My, you *were* wealthy. Rich hippies went to Europe, poor ones stayed home and went to rock concerts."

"Strangely enough, that trip changed my whole life," he said seriously. "It's where I met Slade—in Amsterdam."

The mere mention of his name was enough to spoil the conversation for Holly. "And I suppose you were so impressed by his magnificent life-style that you wanted to emulate him and when he made you an offer you couldn't refuse, you jumped at the chance to don a three-piece suit," she said scornfully.

"Not exactly." He eyed her speculatively and hesitated for a moment.

Holly was contrite. He didn't deserve that acid-tongue treatment. "I'm sorry, Alan, please go on, I really do want to hear it. How did you and Slade meet?"

It was a story he obviously relished telling so Alan continued. "I had hitchhiked my way from Brussels to Amsterdam and I was just moseying around the streets doing some sight-seeing. Slade was coming out of the Amstel Hotel with a lady."

"Naturally," Holly murmured nastily but low enough so that Alan didn't hear her.

"A little boy came from behind them and snatched her purse and ran right toward me—right into my arms actually. He was just a little kid, not more than eleven or twelve. He was scared when I grabbed him but when Slade came up he was terrified. You know how imposing Slade can be when he's just displeased and this time he was really sore."

"What did he do?"

"He skewered the boy with those ice cold gray eyes and told him that he wasn't going to call the police because they would be too lenient on him. He said the only thing thieves understood was swift punishment so he was going to mete it out right there. I think I would have thought twice if that menace had been directed against me and I'm almost as big as he is. By this time the kid was crying his eyes out and I was beginning to be sorry I had intercepted him."

"I can imagine!" Holly exclaimed indignantly. "Of course the child had to be punished but it wasn't necessary to scare him to death."

"Wait, you haven't heard the whole story," Alan laughed. "Just as I was about to mix in, Slade winked at me and said, 'Since this man is the one who caught you, he's going to help decide what to do with you.' I realized then what he was doing. If the boy went to a detention home, or whatever they do with them over there, he would just get out and do it again. Slade was determined to put the fear of God into him and did he ever!"

"What did he threaten him with?" Holly asked curiously.

"Everything except drawing and quartering. And when we were sure he had gotten the message, we played the good cop, bad cop game. You know, where one man wants to use force and the other persuades his partner to go easy."

"Which cop were you?"

"The good one, naturally," he grinned. "Slade

makes a much more convincing heavy." Alan shook his head reminiscently. "I'm telling you when we finally let him go, that little fellow shot off like a rabbit into its warren. I would be very much surprised if he ever stole so much as a jelly bean again."

"But how did you and Slade get together after that?"

"I told him I admired his tactics—after I found out what they were—and he suggested we go have a drink together. We sort of got to know each other and Slade asked me to have dinner that evening."

"I'll bet that didn't delight his lady friend," Holly said dryly.

"I suppose not since she wasn't invited," Alan smiled. "Slade told me to meet him at his hotel which was very super deluxe and although I liked the guy, I was still full of all those juvenile rebellions. I had one fairly decent outfit with me, but I decided to show him I wasn't going to be patronized so I turned up in my scroungiest pair of jeans."

"I'll bet he didn't show how furious he was," she said, knowing Slade's ability to control his emotions. "Or did he?"

"Not at all. He was one step ahead of me as usual. When we met in the lobby, he was also in jeans but his were even mangier than mine. We were a really disreputable duo. If the manager hadn't known him, he might have called the cops. As it was, he probably thought we were both eccentric millionaires. That was one of the best nights of my life." He covered Holly's hand and smiled at her. "Outside of the ones I've spent with you of course."

"And did he offer you a job that night?"

"Yes, a very challenging one. As you so aptly put it, something I couldn't turn down."

"You millionaires do stick together," she said lightly.

"I didn't start at the top," he chided gently. "Surely you know Slade better than that. He put me at the bottom of the ladder, but with duties so interesting that I couldn't wait to climb the next rung."

"I'm sorry, Alan," she said sincerely. "I know you did it all on merit. It's what I like about you. I didn't even know until now that you were rich."

"It isn't important," he shrugged. "So is Slade—a lot richer of course, but it isn't the first thing you notice about him. He's equally at home in a drawing room in Mayfair or a Soho flat. His society pals wouldn't recognize the man who showed *me*, the smart hippie kid, the dives of Amsterdam."

Holly knew that everything he said about Slade was true but each word was breaking her heart. Slade could be both charming and ruthless and she had seen him both ways. Giving her that melting smile that made her a willing slave or dominating her with that taut male body that made a different kind of slave of her. She carried his image around like a portrait in her heart. He might almost be sitting at the table with them, his long frame stretched out and a sardonic smile on those rugged, handsome features as he listened to their conversation.

Holly drew in her breath. "I'm sure he's all you say he is but I don't want to talk about Slade," she said sharply. "We were supposed to be talking about you."

Alan reached across the table and took her hand. "Holly, I would be less than bright if I didn't know that whatever upset you today has to do with Slade. But I can tell you with complete assurance that whatever it was, he didn't mean it."

She withdrew her hand. "Your loyalty is commendable but I'm afraid you see him from a man's point of view and that's apt to differ sharply from a woman's."

"It's more often the women who don't have any complaints," Alan grinned.

"Those are the ones who thrive on his attention. I'm not one of them," she said shortly.

Alan looked his surprise. "Did he make a pass at you? I can't believe Slade would force himself on a woman," he said slowly.

Holly dropped her eyes to her clenched hands. If he only knew, it was the other way around! A vivid picture arose of herself curled up naked in Slade's lap, clinging to him and begging him to make love to her. "If you don't mind, I'd rather not discuss it."

Alan was very quiet and Holly's misery had returned, but fortunately the magnificence of the Roman baths which were the next stop drove it from both their minds.

There were a succession of them on different levels. The largest was a huge rectangular pool open to the sky, but surrounded on all sides by stately marble columns. Beautifully carved statues stood on top of the colonnade, looking down at the inviting water with the same serene expressions they wore when ancient Romans came to frolic.

The classic columns were reflected in the pale green water and just under the surface at one end, broad stone steps were visible leading into the bath.

After marveling at the engineering feat that must have been involved without the use of modern equipment, they walked down sloping ramps alongside roughhewn rock tunnels that led down to the hot springs that fueled the spa. Some of the baths on the lower levels were small, almost like oversized bathtubs and others were more elaborate. They were all different sizes—square, rectangular and free form and they varied in depth from shallow to fairly deep.

In ancient days this must have been a busy meeting place, alive with both patrons and attendants. Alan and Holly were fascinated by this glimpse into the past where Romans came to take their leisure much as modern man goes to his health club.

By the time they emerged after having explored, inspected and commented, all memory of the slight unpleasantness at lunch had vanished.

"What say we go back to London for dinner?" Alan asked. "Some of these little country inns are long on charm but short on food."

Holly was in agreement and they drove back to an elegant restaurant that Alan assured her had gourmet food. If the expensive decor was any criterion, they were in for a treat, she thought.

As they were following the headwaiter to a table, a voice rang out. "Alan Beale, upon my word!" A slender young man stood up and pumped Alan's hand enthusiastically.

"Kevin Forsythe, speak of the devil!" Alan seemed equally delighted. "I can't believe it! I was just thinking about you today." He turned to Holly, "Remember at lunch when I was telling you about that year in Europe? Well, Kevin was part of it. We knocked around together."

"That we did, mate, and a jolly good year it was too till you ran off and joined the establishment. Here, let me take a look at you." He went over Alan critically. "Yes, I can see it agrees with you—everything including the gold watch," he grinned.

Alan introduced Holly, adding a jocular warning, "And don't believe a word he says."

She gazed curiously at the young man standing before them. He was of medium height with a wiry frame and his dancing blue eyes were inspecting her with equal interest. Holly noticed that his suit was a trifle shabby and his hair a little long, but he projected an air of complete confidence.

"Are you two alone? Will you join us?" Kevin asked eagerly. "We have a lot of catching up to do."

Kevin's companion was a pretty young girl with a long mop of frizzy hair that was the height of fashion. Her outfit, however, looked like it had been assembled in bits and pieces from various thrift shops. They were seated at a table for four so Alan signaled the headwaiter that they would join the other couple. After the introductions they learned that the girl's name was Mavis Brown.

"But of course I'll have to change it if I ever become a star," she said. "I was thinking of something really posh like Regina Rothermere." She tipped her head to one side. "What do you think?" She was so completely ingenuous that Holly liked her immediately.

"I assume that you're an actress," Alan smiled.

"Oh, yes, Kevin and I are in a marvelous play. It has a message and everything." Her brown eyes were wide with wonder and Holly decided that she couldn't be more than nineteen.

Alan turned to Kevin. "So that's what you ended up doing. I always wondered."

"It's only little theater but it's a step in the right direction," Kevin said deprecatingly. He looked at his friend admiringly, taking in the superbly tailored suit. "I don't have to ask how things are going with you. But then you always were a rich bloke."

Alan waved that away and said, "You must be doing all right too."

Kevin grinned. "You mean this place? Don't let it fool you. Mavis and I won a dance contest and this was one of the prizes. The headwaiter almost came down with the pip when he saw us, but I put on my Sheridan Whiteside act—you know, *The Man Who Came to Dinner*. Sometimes it pays to be an actor after all."

The waiter took their order and when the food came, it was as delicious as Alan had promised. He ordered a fine French wine to accompany it and Mavis was suitably impressed.

After several glasses, she informed everyone within hearing distance, "This is ever so much better than beer."

"Don't you go getting tipsy on me, Mavis," Kevin scowled. "We have a class tonight and Dushensky will have your hide if you mess up."

"I didn't know professional actors still went to school," Holly remarked to divert him. The young girl was having such fun that she didn't want him to spoil it for her.

"It's an improvisation class and actors have to keep up on their trade like anyone else," he told her seriously.

"I've heard of it," Holly said, "isn't that where you make up the lines as you go along?"

"That and a lot more," he agreed. "We also study method acting."

"That's where you pretend you're an inanimate object," Mavis volunteered. She stumbled a bit over the word inanimate and Holly and Alan exchanged a smile.

"I have a wizard idea," Kevin exclaimed, "why don't you come with us? It will be a real giggle."

"Would you like to?" Alan asked Holly.

"I think it would be great fun if you won't get in trouble for bringing us."

"Piece of cake," Kevin assured her.

The waiter brought the check while they were all

laughing and talking animatedly and Alan paid the bill unobtrusively. When Kevin discovered it, he objected strenuously but Alan waved his protestations aside. "Save your freebie for another time. It's on the expense account anyway," he added untruthfully.

"What's a freebie?" Mavis asked.

While Kevin was explaining to her, Holly squeezed Alan's hand. "That was very nice of you."

He shrugged it off. "I was always a rich bloke."

When they got to the class which was held in a dilapidated warehouse, they found that Kevin had been less than truthful about their being welcome. In order to get them in, he had told the instructor they were prospective students who wanted to try out.

"But I couldn't possibly get up in front of everyone and perform," Holly gasped. "How could he do a thing like that?"

"Kevin is a very good fellow but he does have a way of bending the truth," Alan laughed. "Don't worry about it, honey, who knows, we may discover we have hidden talent."

The teacher who went by the single name of Dushensky, was a portly man in a disreputable green sweater. He had a thick mop of steel gray curls that contrasted strikingly with bushy dark eyebrows. He lumbered around the cavernous room shouting at everyone and his intimidating manner was made more so by the thick middle European accent in which he delivered his barbs.

"No, no, no," he shouted at a pretty girl who was wearing a red leotard. "You are in luf with the man. You are begging that he is not leaving you, not asking when is the time for the next train to Pinsk!"

No one seemed to take offense at his criticism. In fact, no one seemed to pay very much attention to him.

Holly was watching the lively proceedings with great interest when Dushensky marched up to her and pointed a stubby finger. "You. You are a tree."

She looked at him in amazement, sure that she had misunderstood because of his accent. "I beg your pardon?"

"A tree. Make like a tree," he said impatiently.

"It's method acting," Mavis, who had drifted over, explained helpfully. "You imagine you're a tree and after a while—well, you just are one."

Holly and Alan exchanged looks of merriment but when she turned to Dushensky, Holly tried her best to conceal it. "An oak tree or a maple?" she asked innocently.

"Oak, maple—what difference it makes?" he asked suspiciously.

"I want to know what shape to make my leaves," she told him seriously.

Alan could no longer control his laughter but the rotund teacher wreaked his revenge. Alan was instructed to be a doorknob.

They were still laughing over the evening as they walked down the hotel corridor. Alan had wanted to stop for a nightcap but Holly declined.

"Anything after Dushensky would be an anticlimax," she declared.

"I guess you're right," he agreed. "He's something else isn't he?"

"Do you think Kevin and the others take him seriously?"

He shrugged. "Who knows? Actors are crazy anyway."

Holly felt relaxed and happy. All of her troubles of the morning had been pushed to the background. They still existed, of course, but somehow at the moment they didn't loom quite as large. Maybe tomorrow she would be back in the depths but Holly resolved not to think about it now. It had been a fun evening and nothing was going to spoil it she vowed.

They had reached her door and Alan opened it with her key. The suite was in darkness and she turned to say good night. All of Holly's gratitude welled up and she suddenly felt a lump in her throat. What could she say that would convey her appreciation for his being there when she needed someone so desperately?

"Thank you for today, Alan. It . . . it was wonderful and I'll never forget it."

"You won't get a chance to," he told her confidently. "We're going to do it again—like tomorrow night."

Holly smiled gratefully at him, putting her arms around his neck and hugging him unself-consciously.

An arm went around her, pulling her close, and his hand tipped her face up to his. He kissed her tenderly and she didn't pull away but after a moment, Alan released her, saying ruefully, "Good night, honey, see you tomorrow."

Holly closed the door and flipped on the light, smiling happily. But when she turned around, a frightened cry escaped her. "Slade! What are you doing here?"

He was sitting on the couch with his arms folded and he had on the same clothes he had worn that morning. "I live here, remember?" he replied with heavy sarcasm.

His manner was ominous and a pulse in her temple began to throb. "I mean, what . . . why are you sitting in the dark?"

Ignoring that, he said, "Where have you been?"

"I went out with Alan."

"I figured that much out for myself but I repeat, where did you go?"

Although he didn't raise his voice, there was controlled fury in the glance he directed at her and Holly was suddenly terrified. What had she done that could have incensed him to this extent? He actually looked like he wanted to do bodily harm. She measured the distance to her bedroom but as though he could read her mind, he stated calmly, "I wouldn't try it." When she stood there mutely, he said, "I asked you a question."

"What? Oh . . . we went to Bath."

"And did you enjoy yourself?"

"Yes," she answered meekly.

"Tell me about it," he said pleasantly, still with that dangerous calm.

Holly shifted nervously. "You wouldn't care to hear about it."

"On the contrary. I can't think of anything that interests me more."

"Why are you cross-examining me?" she cried. "We went to Bath and we had lunch and we saw the council houses and the Roman baths. Now are you satisfied?"

"Not completely." He stood up with the lithe movement of a cat and came to stand very close to her, his taut body menacing her with its potential danger. "It's the part you left out that interests me."

"What did I leave out?" she asked, honestly puzzled.

"Suppose *you* tell *me?*" When she shook her head and looked at him questioningly, a muscle started to twitch in his jaw. "Did that take you until the present?"

"Oh, you mean this evening."

He nodded grimly. "Now you're catching on."

Holly felt a strange reluctance about telling him of

the acting class. It had been weird and crazy and fun. But if she tried to describe it to a sophisticated man like Slade, it would sound juvenile.

"Well, we . . . uh . . . we had dinner. At a really wonderful place. The food was delicious. You've probably been there, of course, because you've been everywhere but I was quite impressed." She was babbling on in an attempt to distract him but Slade merely waited until she ran down.

"It must have been a remarkably long dinner. I didn't realize that restaurants stayed open this late."

"Well, after dinner we did . . . some other things."

"And did you accomplish your purpose?" he asked harshly.

Anger was starting to replace some of the fear and Holly looked at him in exasperation. "I honestly don't know what's the matter with you tonight, but I do know that I don't have to stand here and take this third degree." She started to brush by him but he caught her arm in a grip that made her gasp with pain.

"Answer my question, you little———" He ground out an epithet that made Holly blanch. "Did you take care of that little condition you were so determined to rectify when you ran out of here this morning?"

At last Holly understood and she looked up at him in horror, the pain in her arm momentarily forgotten. "You think I slept with Alan?"

His eyes were demonic as he doubled her arm back and jerked her against his rigid body. "You're half right, my beautiful little witch, I don't think there was any sleeping involved."

Anger flooded her at this crude injustice. "I'll have you know that Alan is a wonderful, generous man, he—"

"Generous?" He gave a bark of humorless laughter

as he interrupted. "That's a curious word. I'm sure any man would be *generous,*" he gave it sneering emphasis, "if you made him the same offer. Does Alan know why he was so fortunate? That it was merely because he was lucky enough to be the first man you encountered?"

Tears of pain filled Holly's eyes. "You can't really believe that?"

"No, I suppose he had preferred status. If you can't call on a friend, who can you turn to?" he asked bitterly.

Holly was drowning in misery. Slade's soul-shattering words were destroying her and if she didn't get away from him soon, she would break down completely. The savage light in his eyes told her he was beyond reason and she twisted desperately, trying to break his steely grip. "Let go of me," she cried but it was like speaking to the wind.

"Don't you want to tell me about it?" he asked mockingly. "That's supposed to be a big event in a girl's life. I thought maybe you would like to talk about it."

"Please, Slade," she begged piteously.

"Was he gentle with you?" he continued inexorably. "Did he touch you like this?" His hand cupped her breast, the fingers moving sensuously until his expertise evoked a response. Bending his head, his lips found the hardened nipple and rolled it between his lips through the thin wool of her sweater. "Did he make you want him the way you wanted me?" Holly moaned involuntarily and he transferred his mouth to her neck, sliding up to nuzzle the vulnerable spot behind her ear. "Alan isn't as skillful as I thought. Would you like me to finish what he started?"

Tears were streaming down her pale cheeks and Holly bent her head defenselessly. He jerked her chin up violently and when she raised the protective lashes, her anguished eyes were like jewels shimmering under water.

Uttering a savage oath, he thrust her away as though the contact was unbearable. Without another word, he strode into his room and slammed the door.

Holly's knees threatened to buckle under her but she got to her room somehow. Lying face down on the bed, a storm of weeping racked her slender body and even when it was over, she didn't have the strength to move. The hideous scene had completely drained her and left her mind empty of everything except pain.

When conscious thought returned, it hurt even more. How could Slade think such horrible things about her? He had jumped to conclusions without even giving her a chance to explain. Why did he always think the worst of her? It had been that way from the beginning, no matter whose fault it was, and Holly realized that this was the end.

He was tearing her apart and she couldn't stand it anymore. Slade had once delcared that his purpose was not to break her spirit but he was slowly doing it. The self-reliant, happy-go-lucky Holly was almost gone and if she didn't get away from him soon, she would be destroyed.

It had been building up to this for a long time but she had refused to admit it, justifying everything in her aching need to be near him if nothing else. But no longer. Tomorrow she would tell Slade that she was leaving. Perhaps with an ocean between them, she would even begin to forget—in time. Maybe in a million years, she thought bitterly.

Chapter Eight

Slade was gone by the time Holly was up and dressed the next morning but she decided it was all for the best. Her resignation should really take place in the office. Everything between them from now on was going to be completely businesslike.

Before tendering it, she diligently typed up a detailed report on the progress of her work to date and made recommendations for her successor. With that in order, she went to Slade's office prepared for the confrontation. After keying herself up for the ordeal, she discovered with considerable dismay that he had flown to Antwerp and wouldn't be back until the next day.

The thought of existing in this vacuum for another twenty-four hours was intolerable and Holly knew she couldn't do it. She had to get away—today with any luck. Was it possible that fate had taken a hand? A letter of explanation to Slade would be infinitely less painful.

But it suddenly occurred to her that she didn't have the money for her ticket home. After a worried moment, Holly's brow cleared. Alan would loan it to her. But after scouring the *Metro* offices from top to bottom, she couldn't find a trace of him. He hadn't come in that morning and no one knew his whereabouts.

The day and night that followed were among the worst in her life but Holly survived them somehow. The next day she was at Slade's office promptly at noon. That was the time he was expected back. There was still no word from Alan which was perplexing and Holly was getting slightly worried.

"I'm sorry, Miss Holbrooke, but you can't go in," Slade's secretary told her as Holly made for Slade's private office. "Mr. Rockwell is busy."

Frustration threatened to consume her and she said impatiently, "I simply have to see him."

"But he has a visitor."

The words fell on empty air as Holly, after a perfunctory knock, disappeared into Slade's office. Her headlong rush took her almost to the desk before she realized that the visitor was Lady Dillingham. The Englishwoman was sitting on an edge of the desk, her long legs crossed provocatively and Slade was leaning back in his chair, smiling at something she had said.

The smile disappeared as he looked around at Holly. "I believe it's customary to be announced," he said coldly.

"I . . . I knocked," she stammered.

"But you didn't give us much time." Marsha smiled maliciously. "It might have proved . . . embarrassing," she purred. "Hello again, Miss Holbrooke."

Holly's misery deepened. Ignoring her, she said to Slade, "I have to speak to you."

"As you can see, I'm busy at the moment," he frowned.

"Well then, give me an appointment," Holly said desperately. "After lunch?" She had correctly assumed that he expected to spend that with Marsha.

"Oh no, not today," Lady Dillingham cut in before he could answer. "Slade has promised me the whole afternoon. We have marvelous plans don't we, darling?"

Slade took her hand and kissed it as Holly died a slow death. "Of course, my dear, you know I never go back on a promise."

It was a calculated act, designed to show Holly how he treated someone he really cared about and it hit home. Tears blinded her and she whirled around and headed for the door before either of them had the satisfaction of seeing them. Marsha's trilling laughter, however, provided the final humiliation.

It was late afternoon when one of the secretaries came into Holly's office with a letter.

"I don't know how this happened, Miss Holbrooke, but Mr. Beale left this note for you yesterday and somehow or other it got buried under a pile of papers. I'm so sorry. I do hope it hasn't caused you any inconvenience."

Holly smiled at the worried girl and reassured her, but it was a good thing that she had left before Holly read the contents. The hurried note told her that Alan had returned to New York! He expressed his regret and assured her the problem that took him there would be cleared up quickly but Holly knew better. This was Slade's punishment for both of them.

How *could* he, she raged? How could he be so vindictive? Poor Alan, he was the innocent victim in all of this. Well, as soon as she was out of the way he would be restored to favor. That much at least she could do for him. Not that any incentive was needed now to change her mind. Slade was an evil, ruthless man and the sooner she was quit of him the better. He couldn't avoid her forever. The showdown would come tonight.

Holly left her bedroom door open so she wouldn't miss Slade when he returned. The sickening thought crossed her mind that he might be spending the night with Marsha but she endeavored to put it out of her mind.

The hours ticked by and after a while she began to feel a little light-headed because she had been unable to eat anything all day and very little the day before. And when his key sounded in the lock, a surge of adrenalin made everything sway alarmingly.

She had left all the lights on in the living room and Slade looked rather tired in the bright illumination. His mouth tightened as she confronted him and he said, "Not now, Holly."

"I'm afraid it's now or never," she said hardily. "I'm going home tomorrow."

He stopped in the act of turning away, his attitude watchful. "That's very interesting. And just how do you propose to do that?" he asked sardonically.

Holly shook her head. "I don't want to play any more word games with you. I'm quitting, Slade."

"I see." His eyes were enigmatic. "Did you have any thoughts on what you're going to do after that?"

"I'm going back to San Francisco."

"Are you indeed?" he drawled. "That should be quite a trick."

"What do you mean?"

"Unless you were planning to stow away, I don't see how you're going to manage it." When she looked at him blankly, he said, "Money, my dear Miss Holbrooke, you don't have any."

"Do you mean . . . but you. . . ." Holly was stuttering with distress. "You said if it didn't work out you would give me a ticket home!"

"I have no complaints. I'm perfectly satisfied with your work."

Holly was trembling with nerves. "Don't play with me, Slade. You know what I'm talking about. I can't take any more."

He surveyed her coldly. "What I know is that you agreed to do a job and I expect you to stick to the agreement."

"Why? So that you can torment me some more?

His eyes were bleak. "I don't think I have a corner on that department."

Holly wasn't even listening. "I can't go on like this," she cried passionately. "You have to let me go!"

"Slavery has been abolished," he shrugged. "If you want to be a little coward and run away, I can't stop you."

She ignored his insult to pursue the more urgent matter. "How can I if you're not going to honor your word."

Deep grooves appeared in his face. "Do you really want to talk about honor?"

"You *owe* me the money. My salary is due in two weeks. Just pay me what I have coming so far."

"Have you forgotten the little matter of a month's wages that you lost in the casino? Actually, you don't have any money coming until the end of next month."

She looked at him in horror. "You can't mean to keep me here that long?" His implacable face gave her the answer. "But I'll pay you back, I swear it! I'll get another job and I'll pay you off so much a month."

If her distress affected him it didn't show. "That wouldn't be very good business. I have vested interest in you and as long as you're working for me, I know my investment is safe."

"You're a devil," she whispered. "The money means nothing to you. It's just a way to grind me under your heel."

"Don't you think you're over dramatizing just a little? I'm a businessman. When I lend money, I like to ensure that it will be paid back."

"Preferably in blood," she said bitterly. "You know that I would repay every penny. I'd scrub floors if I had to rather than be beholden to you!"

His glance roved negligently over her slight figure. "You're not exactly built for the job. No, I think my only guarantee is to keep you for collateral."

"And suppose I refuse to work for you?" she asked defiantly.

"In that case, when we move on you would be left here to fend for yourself which could prove to be rather disastrous." His mouth curved cruelly. "Americans are only welcome in a foreign country when they have money."

The hopelessness of her position overwhelmed Holly and she stared at him in anguish. "You wouldn't do that."

"Would you like to bet?" One look at his granite face convinced her and he added, "Whether you like it or not, you're completely dependent on me."

"Yes, you've seen to that haven't you?" she asked furiously. "You've made sure that the noose is tight around my neck and anyone who might help me has been warned off or gotten rid of. Poor Alan was sent into exile for daring to be kind to me."

His level gaze was noncommittal. "A problem arose in New York that needed Alan's handling," he said.

"How very convenient! Of course the fact that he cares about me has nothing to do with it."

A muscle twitched in Slade's jaw. "I don't believe I have to justify myself to you."

"You couldn't possibly! Alan might believe that fiction because he trusts you, poor soul, but you and I know better. No matter how you feel about me, how could you do this to *him?*"

"I don't think we're getting anywhere with this conversation and I suggest you turn in. Perhaps you'll be less emotional in the morning."

The hard purpose in his face warned Holly that he wasn't going to change his mind and there was nothing she could do about it. Without money, she was his helpless victim and he could turn the emotional screws until her spirit broke on the rack. She vowed fiercely not to give him that satisfaction but as she turned toward her room, Holly's shoulders were drooping.

The days that followed merged into a gray haze. She got up in the morning and went to work, remaining at the paper until late at night. Often she was the only one in the offices except for the cleaning crew, but keeping busy was her only salvation.

At night she returned to the suite and dropped into bed exhausted enough to fall into a dreamless sleep for a few hours and awake like a robot when the alarm clock went off. Sometimes she skipped meals entirely and when she did remember to eat, it was such an effort that she usually gave up after a few bites. Her eyes were enormous jewels in her pale face and her slender body looked slight enough to be blown away in a light wind.

One day she bought a sandwich in the commissary and took it to the park across from the *Metro* offices. It was a brisk day but the sky was blue and she welcomed the wintery sun on her chill bones.

The sandwich was tasteless and she was breaking off pieces and throwing them to the fat pigeons that swarmed around opportunistically when a shadow blotted out the sun.

"What the hell do you think you're doing?" Slade asked furiously, his face carved out of rock.

She looked up in surprise. Until this moment, Holly had seen Slade rarely and then only from a distance. Lady Dillingham had come to the office to pick him up once and another time, Holly had seen him leave with a tall, willowy redhead. If he slept in the suite, she wasn't aware of it. By the time Holly returned at night, sleep was the only thing that interested her.

His appearance in the park was the last thing she would have expected. "I'm feeding the pigeons," she said in answer to his question.

"I can see that," he ground out tautly, "but I think you need it more than they do. What are you trying to do, starve yourself?"

Why would he pretend to care, she wondered? He seemed to be spoiling for a fight for some reason but Holly knew there was no point in arguing with him. She always got the worst of it. Looking carefully at the half-eaten sandwich, she said, "It isn't very good."

"Then get something that is," he ordered. "You look like a disaster victim."

"I am," she said simply, looking at him with enormous eyes.

Grabbing her by the wrist, Slade jerked her to her feet, swearing viciously under his breath. He strode down the street at a furious pace and Holly was half running to keep up with him. "Where . . . where are you taking me?" she asked breathlessly.

He didn't answer. A half block up the street they came to a small pub and he dragged her inside and shoved her into a booth. "You're going to have something to eat," he said finally.

"But I'm not hungry."

"You'll eat or I'll hold your nose and force it down you," Slade said savagely.

Without consulting her, he ordered soup and steak and kidney pie with plum tart for dessert. Holly looked at the mountain of food with dismay, but after the first bite she found she was ravenous. Under Slade's watchful eye, she cleaned her plate.

"That's better," he said with satisfaction. "A few more days the way you were going and you wouldn't have needed a key to get into the hotel. You could have slipped under the door."

"That's an idea," she said lightly. "Maybe I could get in an envelope and mail myself back to the States."

Her head was bent over her plate and she didn't see the pain in Slade's eyes. "Where would you address it . . . San Francisco or New York?"

She looked up in surprise. "Why would I . . . ?" And then it came to her. "Oh, I see."

"Do you miss him that much?"

Slade was convinced that she was pining away for Alan and nothing she could say would change his mind. Just as nothing she could say would convince him that they hadn't slept together. There was no point in even trying and it only opened up old wounds.

It seemed best to change the subject. "How much longer will we be in London?" she asked.

He was silent for a long moment and then he said, "We're almost finished. Another week or so ought to do it."

"That's good." She nodded her head without interest. It had just been something to say.

His eyes softened as he looked at the small delicate face framed by shining dark waves that curled around her slender shoulders. "You haven't had a very good time here have you, little one?"

Sudden tears pricked her eyelids at the unexpected endearment. It brought back memories of happier times when he used to tease her and their relationship was one of easy camaraderie. At the time she had wanted more than that, never dreaming that the day would come when one kind word would make her choke up.

Pushing the last of her dessert around the plate, Holly said carefully, "London is a very interesting city and I enjoyed the things I saw."

"We'll try to do better in Rome," he said gravely.

She caught her breath. Was Slade beginning to soften toward her? He was certainly different than he had been in a long time and she had to take the chance, no matter how slim. Tentatively, she asked, "Do you really need me there, Slade?"

"You'll enjoy it, Holly, I promise."

Holly sighed. She had her answer. Although he had decided to be nicer to her for some devious purpose of his own, it didn't mean that he was relinquishing his grip. Like a small trapped animal that realizes the futility of struggling any longer, she bowed her head in acquiescence. If she had looked up, Holly would have surprised an expression of great tenderness on Slade's face.

He started to tell her about Rome, describing it so graphically that Holly's attention was caught in spite of herself. She asked interested questions that he took pains to answer fully and Holly felt a stirring excitement as the prospect of seeing the eternal city. Her face grew animated and a casual observer would have taken them for a handsome couple who didn't have a care in the world.

They continued their conversation on the short walk back to the newspaper and, as her head bobbed up and down near his broad shoulder, Holly felt the tension drain out of her. A feeling almost of euphoria enveloped her when Slade's gray eyes smiled down like they had in the old days.

Holly paused at the bend in the hall that would take her to her own office. "Thank you for lunch, it was very nice of you to take the time." He was very tall and masculine and she felt suddenly shy.

"It was a pleasure," he smiled. "I want—" His words were abruptly cut off by an angry female voice.

"Slade, you dreadful man! Do you know what time it is? I've been cooling my heels in your office for—"

Holly didn't wait to hear the rest of Lady Dillingham's irate words. It was midnight for Cinderella and the prince was going back to his lady. But at least she didn't have to listen to Slade's soothing words or endure any of Marsha's barbs. Holly ducked into her office and closed the door quietly.

She worked late again that night, skipping dinner entirely. The big lunch was more than she had eaten in days. It wasn't any fun to eat alone anyway. In fact, nothing was any fun. The excitement over Rome had died away and Holly stared at the papers on her desk, feeling only an aching emptiness.

Finally, she forced herself into activity before black depression could completely immobilize her. She started to screen some microfilmed articles and hours passed as her interest was gradually engaged by the varied nature of the subjects.

When she finally shrugged into her coat and left the *Metro* offices, Holly discovered that it was raining. The vagaries of the London climate had double-crossed her again. It had been sunny that morning so she hadn't brought an umbrella. As in many large cities, taxis are scarce at most times and almost nonexistent when it rains. By the time Holly got a cab after walking for endless blocks, she was soaked to the skin and shivering so much her teeth were chattering.

She was a sorry sight walking into the elegant hotel and when her numbed fingers managed to turn the key in the lock, Holly opened the door and sneezed simultaneously.

Slade appeared in his bedroom doorway. "Do you know what time it is?" he scowled. "Where the devil have you been?"

"Working." Holly sneezed again.

"Working? Till this hour?" he asked incredulously. Was it possible he hadn't known, she wondered? He advanced into the room and inspected her carefully, taking in the black hair plastered to her pinched face and the limp coat that gave off an odor of wet wool. "You're soaking wet," he exclaimed.

"Yes, I know," she said acidly. "It happens when you walk in the rain."

"Why didn't you take a cab?" he demanded.

Holly gave a high pitched laugh that turned into a sob. "Leave me alone, Slade. I don't think I could stand another of your inquisitions tonight."

He crossed the room in a few long strides and grasped her by the shoulders, turning her to face him. "Are you all right?" he asked, inspecting her closely.

"Yes, I'm fine now." The warm luxury of the room was soothing after her cold and slightly frightening walk in the darkened city streets and Holly felt almost light-headed with relief. "I'm going to take a hot bath and go to bed."

"I'll fix you a brandy."

"No thanks, I just want to get these wet things off."

He cupped her chin in his hand and tilted her face up to his concerned eyes. "You don't look well," he frowned.

She pulled away impatiently. "You wouldn't look so good yourself if your hair was dripping in your eyes and your clothes looked like you swam the Channel in them." She gave a massive sneeze. "Now will you please let me get undressed?"

He didn't detain her any longer but his eyes were troubled as he watched her disappear into her room.

Holly awoke in the night with a burning thirst. Her head ached and her throat was sore but most of all, she was thirsty. It was an effort to get out of bed because her body was stiff, although her legs felt like rubber, but Holly knew she could never go back to sleep without a drink of water.

Weaving her way to the bathroom, she gulped down a whole glassful and then part of another. As she was about to stagger back to bed, she remembered a glass carafe that was in the medicine chest. It would be a good idea to fill it and put it on her bedside table in case she awoke later on.

Standing on tiptoes to reach the top shelf where it was kept, a wave of dizziness swept over her. The heavy bottle slipped from her tentative grasp and fell to the tile floor, shattering with a crash that sounded like an explosion in the quiet night. Jagged shards of glass surrounded her bare feet and Holly looked down at the mess and burst into tears.

"What the—!" Slade's exclamation was broken off as

he took in Holly's woebegone face and the debris at her feet. "Don't move," he commanded.

Sweeping her into his arms with one lithe movement, he carried her into the bedroom while she turned her face into his bare chest and sobbed against his comforting shoulder. Slade's lips brushed her forehead and he made soothing noises as he moved toward the bed.

"Don't cry, sweetheart, it's all right. You didn't cut yourself did you?"

Her sobs were lessening. "No, but there's glass all over the bathroom."

"Don't worry, the maid will clean it up." He brushed the hair out of her eyes and then looked at her narrowly, putting the back of his hand on her cheek. "You're burning up!" he exclaimed.

She gazed up at him piteously. "My throat hurts."

Placing her gently under the covers, he strode to the telephone. She looked at him through a languorous fog. Who on earth could he be calling at this hour? But when she heard him demanding a doctor be sent up immediately, Holly sat up in bed.

"I don't need a doctor! I'm just catching a little cold, that's all."

"Be quiet. You have a raging temperature and we're going to do something about it." He opened one of the mirrored closet doors and was rummaging through the chest of drawers.

"What are you looking for?" she asked.

"Never mind, I found it."

Slade had a fresh nightgown over his arm and as he approached the bed, Holly stared at him wide eyed. Before she had an inkling of what he intended, he lifted her easily and stripped off the gown she had on.

Holly was too surprised to resist but as he cradled her bare body in his arms, a blush started that began at her toes and swept upward. "Wha . . . what do you think you're doing?"

He was slipping the fresh gown over her head, expertly guiding her arms into the sleeves. "Don't be embarrassed. You aren't the first naked female I've ever seen."

Was that supposed to be comforting? "How . . . how dare you?" she spluttered.

"Very easily," he teased and then the smile disappeared. "Your gown was soaking wet. You have a fever."

"I could have changed it myself. You didn't have to—" Her tirade was cut short as the buzzer rang in the living room and Slade went to admit the doctor.

If her temperature was soaring it was his fault, Holly thought crossly. It had happened so quickly and been over so soon, but she still tingled from the indescribable feeling of his arms around her nude body and the feel of those sure fingers on her heated skin.

The doctor was a rotund older man with a pleasant manner in spite of the fact that he had been roused in the middle of the night. "So this is our patient. Let's take a look at you," he said cheerfully.

Holly looked pointedly at Slade, expecting him to leave the room but to her indignation, he lounged nearby watching the proceedings.

Dr. Welbourne put a thermometer in her mouth and took her pulse, doing all the other things that doctors do. When he read her temperature, his eyebrows rose a fraction but his manner remained calm.

"You have a touch of the flu, young lady. You're going to be fine but I think I'll give you a shot to hurry things along."

Realizing that it wouldn't do any good to make a

fuss, Holly obediently turned over on her stomach. But her face was very red, knowing that Slade was once more viewing a part of her anatomy usually kept hidden.

"She seems awfully warm, doctor. Is her temperature very high?" Slade's concern was evident.

"It's a little high but nothing to worry about. These things look a lot worse than they are. She should sleep through the night and I'll be back tomorrow to check on her. Don't worry," he said soothingly. "A few days in bed and your wife will be just fine."

Holly opened her mouth to set him straight and then closed it again. The truth would only be misunderstood. After writing out a prescription, the doctor left a few instructions and then Slade ushered him out.

Holly was rubbing her bottom gingerly when Slade returned. "Now don't you feel silly?" she challenged. "All that fuss over nothing."

"I wouldn't exactly call the flu nothing."

"Well, it isn't anything serious."

He smiled. "That's good. I'm relieved to know that you're going to be all right, my dear wife."

"That's another thing," she said crossly. "If you had had the decency to go out of the room, he wouldn't have jumped to the ridiculous conclusion that we're married."

"Is that so ridiculous?" he murmured huskily.

Holly thought she knew what he meant. With her in bed and Slade in his pajamas, no wonder the doctor assumed what he did. It didn't bear thinking about and she said distantly, "You'd better start being more discreet or one day you're going to get yourself into a situation you can't get out of. Or should I make that one *night,*" she amended acidly.

"You mean I might have to make an honest woman of you?"

Amusement mixed with an emotion she couldn't define, flickered in his gray eyes and Holly felt herself getting even warmer. "Don't be silly, I wasn't referring to myself," she said shortly. "You're safe with me but I wouldn't be so sure about those girl friends of yours. It would serve you right if you woke up to find yourself married to that Marsha woman."

"I take it you don't approve of her as my prospective mate?"

The idea caused an actual pain in her breast and Holly couldn't meet his eyes but she tried to keep her tone casual. "Why should it bother *me?* You're the one who would have to live with her."

He sat down on the edge of the bed and picked up her hand, playing with the fingers. "Do you have any more appropriate candidates?"

His nearness was sending a ripple of excitement through her feverish body, causing the funniest floating sensation. The doctor had given Holly some pills in addition to the shot and the combination of fever and medication was making her unbearably drowsy. There was something peculiar about the tone of Slade's voice, something that puzzled her. She felt that it was important to figure out what it was, but the contours of his face were getting fuzzy and her drooping eyelashes kept fluttering with the effort to keep them open.

Slade stood up abruptly, tucking the covers around her with incredible gentleness. "Never mind. Go to sleep, little one, you'll feel better in the morning."

Holly curled up and sighed contentedly. "You're

being very good to me. No one ever took care of me like this before."

As she drifted off to sleep, Slade's answer seemed to come from a long distance and it didn't make sense. It almost sounded like he said, "From now on, I'm going to take care of you all the time."

Chapter Nine

A small lamp was still lit when Holly awoke, although the room was filled with daylight. For a moment she wondered if it was time to get up and then the events of the night returned. Holly sat up and uttered a startled cry. Slade was asleep in a chair next to the bed.

He looked defenseless somehow with his long legs sprawled out and a shock of dark hair falling across his wide, intelligent forehead. He still had on the black silk pajama bottoms and matching robe and there was a dark stubble of beard which shocked Holly. She had never seen him less than immaculately groomed and in command of every situation and her heart gave a funny little thump to see him looking so vulnerable now.

Slade's eyes flew open at her faint exclamation and he awakened like a jungle animal, every sense instantly alert. "How do you feel this morning?" His gray eyes assessed her gravely.

"Much better, thank you." Her temperature had broken during the night and the headache was all gone. "But what are you doing here? Why didn't you get into bed?"

"I didn't like to without asking first," he teased.

The ready color rose in Holly's face. "Don't be

ridiculous, you know what I meant. Have you been here all night?"

"Yes, I didn't think you should be alone."

"You . . . that was very kind of you," she faltered.

"Not at all. Your fever was pretty high last night." He stood up and stretched and Holly's fascinated gaze followed the lithe movement. The muscles rippling under the smooth black silk gave him the look of a supple panther. "I'll order breakfast and then see about getting a nurse for you," he said.

"I don't need a nurse!" she gasped. "I was just about to get up and dress."

"You will do no such thing," he said crisply.

Holly had swung her legs to the floor and a momentary wave of dizziness assailed her. "Well, maybe I will stay in bed," she conceded. "But only for today."

"You will remain there until the doctor says differently."

"And that's another thing—he doesn't need to see me again. Do you have any idea of what it must cost in a hotel like this?"

"Why don't you let me worry about that?"

"Because you're being ridiculous. I absolutely refuse to see the doctor and a nurse is out of the question."

Slade had pressed her resisting shoulders back against the pillows and he kept her pinned there while his gaze fastened on her mouth. "One more word and I'll use the only method I know of that will silence you."

He was very close and her pulses were behaving erratically, but she had to try and talk some sense into him. "At least listen to me about—"

His lips touched hers in a kiss that was sweet and gentle. It lasted only a moment, but afterward Holly could barely whisper, "Slade, you'll catch my flu."

He straightened up and smiled at her. "That will be entirely on your head. I warned you. Now if you're through giving orders, I'll get on the phone."

In the end they compromised with Holly agreeing to see the doctor if Slade would dispense with the nurse.

They had breakfast together in the bedroom and when they were finished, Slade put his napkin down regretfully. "I hate to leave you alone but I have an important meeting this morning. I would cancel it but Mueller and Schilling are flying in from Frankfurt and there is no way of heading them off."

Holly assured him several times that she would be perfectly fine and that yes, she would call if she needed anything, anything at all. When he finally left, she sank back against the pillows exhausted. Being with Slade was always a nerve tingling experience and his present solicitude left her limp—but happy. How long would his present attitude last? It was only because she was sick in a foreign country where she didn't know anyone and Slade felt sorry for her. She realized that. But after seeing the gentleness of which he was capable, she didn't think she could bear it if he returned to his former coldness.

The maid rapped on the bedroom door, interrupting that troubling train of thought. She was carrying a huge basket of deep red roses and when Holly's luncheon tray appeared later, it held an exquisite spray of pale green orchids in a slender vase that was just the right size for her bedside table.

Holly was overwhelmed by Slade's thoughtfulness and she loved the flowers, but it was the phone calls that she appreciated the most. He called three times during the afternoon, assuring her he would be back as soon as possible and asking what he could bring her.

"I feel like I'm accepting all this attention under false

pretenses," she told him. Slade had come home early with a huge box of chocolates and an armful of books and magazines. They had finished dinner and Holly was propped up against the pillows. Her hair was brushed to a blue-black sheen and she looked rested after a day in bed. "My temperature is almost normal and I expect to be up by tomorrow."

"No, you won't," he said promptly. "You're going to stay right there and get a complete rest. I had no idea you were working so hard," he frowned.

"I didn't mind."

"Well, you should have had more sense. Look at you—you're so delicate I could pick you up with one hand." There was a deeper undertone to the irritable words and Holly's heart leapt into her throat at the glow that lit his eyes as they traveled over her from head to toe.

Something intangible trembled between them and Holly was almost afraid to breathe for fear of breaking the fragile intimacy. The telephone did it for her.

The pealing instrument startled her at first and then she looked at it with dread. Who would be calling her? "It must be for you," she said woodenly.

Slade reached for the receiver impatiently but his look of annoyance was replaced by a lack of expression. "How are you? How's everything going? . . . Yes, I gathered as much. . . . Hold on a minute, she's right here."

Holly had been pretending not to listen to his conversation, but naturally she couldn't help it and the part she could hear puzzled her. It certainly wasn't Lady Dillingham as she had feared but who could it be?

"Alan!" was her delighted response to his greeting. "Where are you?"

"Still in New York, honey, but I had to talk to you. I

never got a chance to tell you how much I enjoyed that day with you."

"I . . . I did too," she murmured, terribly conscious of Slade sitting like a statue beside her.

"I hated having to leave without saying good-bye but something came up unexpectedly. You do understand don't you?"

"Yes, I do," she said softly. Slade got up abruptly and strode to the window, looking out at the darkened park with his back to her.

"We still have a lot of sight-seeing to do so don't start without me," Alan teased. "Will you hold off and let me take you around?"

"Yes." Her tone was absent as she watched Slade's rigid back.

"That sounds rather tentative," Alan complained. "I need reassurance, woman. Repeat after me, I'll wait for you, Alan."

With a sense of fatality, Holly said, "I'll wait for you, Alan."

Slade crossed the room with long strides. Pausing at the door, he broke into her conversation. "I have to go out, is there anything you need?" he asked levelly.

"No, but I—"

"Then I'll see you in the morning."

After Holly hung up, tears filled her eyes. Why had Alan picked that moment to call? She was delighted to hear from him, he was a good friend, but Slade would never believe that's all they were. Alan's call had awakened all his suspicions. Would he revert to his former savagery? There was nothing Holly could do about it because he wouldn't listen to any explanations much less believe them, but she couldn't bear to have Slade turn into an icy stranger again.

Holly needn't have worried on that score. Slade was pleasant when he came back to say good-bye the next morning. He didn't join her for breakfast but he very politely asked if she needed anything before he went to work. When she said no, he left her alone and desolate. The only phone call that day came from Slade's secretary who asked how Holly was getting along.

Although Holly felt a great deal better, Slade was adamant about her staying in and the long day stretched interminably. Also the next few days. He returned from the office every evening but after a few polite words exchanged in the doorway, Slade went out again.

By the end of the week, Holly was feeling rebellious. Her temperature had long disappeared and her health was much better than her temper. She had gotten dressed and wandered through the suite forlornly when toward evening, the phone rang.

"Don't tell me I've finally gotten ahold of you, luv!" a slightly irate voice demanded.

"Kevin?" she asked incredulously. "How wonderful to hear from you."

"Yes, well it would have been a lot sooner if anyone down at that bloomin' newspaper knew his ankle from his elbow," he complained. "I've been trying to reach Alan for days and I got switched everywhere but to obituaries."

"It's the reorganization," Holly giggled. "I guess everything is a little bit chaotic."

"I'm glad to hear it isn't a case of congenital idiocy," he said dryly. "What's all this nonsense about Alan going back to New York so soon?"

"He . . . uh, something came up rather suddenly."

"Too bad. I don't suppose he'll be back by tomorrow

night?" he asked hopefully. "No, I was afraid not. Well, you'll just have to come by yourself."

"Come where?"

"I'm having a party and you're the American contingent. Nine o'clock at my flat."

Slade had come in, unnoticed by Holly who was engrossed in her conversation, and he stood in the doorway listening with an impassive expression on his face.

"A party, oh, Kevin how super!" It was as if someone had opened her cage door. "Wait till I get a pencil and I'll take down your address." She turned and jumped as she registered Slade's silent presence. "Oh . . . Slade, you startled me. I . . . I'm on the phone."

"So I see."

She expected him to follow his usual pattern and leave but he remained, lounging against the door frame. Holly was a little flustered under Slade's watchful eye as she wrote down Kevin's address, but when she hung up the receiver and turned to face him she was prepared to do battle.

"Who is Kevin?" he asked without preamble.

"A friend of Alan's. I met him the night we came back from Bath." She looked him squarely in the eye. "Kevin is having a party tomorrow night and I'm going."

His firm mouth curved in a slight smile as he took in her uptilted little chin. "Why the defiance?"

"Because I expect you to say no and I'm going anyway."

A peaked eyebrow rose sardonically. "Never let it be said that I don't recognize defeat. All right, I'll take you."

"You'll do nothing of the sort," she said indignantly.

"I don't have to be taken and called for like a little girl at a birthday party."

"Who said anything about calling for you? I said I'm *taking* you. That means staying with you."

"But you can't," she gasped. "You . . . you don't even know Kevin."

"Is it so unusual for a single girl to bring an escort?"

"No, but. . . ." Her voice trailed off. The thought of Slade with Kevin and his crazy crowd was mind boggling. Slade was so elegant and these kids were so casual. What would he think of them and vice versa?

"I promise not to disgrace you if that's what you're worried about," he smiled.

"It isn't that," she protested. "I just don't think you would have a very good time. These people are . . . well . . . different from the ones you run around with," she explained carefully.

He looked at her for a long moment. "Holly, your perception about other people and your lack of it where I'm concerned never ceases to amaze me. But understand this, you're going with me or you're not going at all."

There was firm purpose in his gray eyes and Holly gave up the uneven battle.

She was afraid among other things, that Slade would stick out like a sore thumb in his handsome business suit and tie, but his appearance when he came to her door laid those fears to rest. The dark brown cords and toast-colored sweater over a silk shirt open at the neck were exactly right for the bohemian-type party Holly expected this one to be. The casual attire made him look younger and unbearably masculine and she stared at him wordlessly.

"Do I pass muster?" he asked gravely, although from

the twinkle in his eyes she knew Slade had been aware of her doubts.

"Yes, of course. I was ju . . . just thinking that we harmonize," she faltered, indicating her own beige skirt and yellow sweater.

"We must try to do it more often," he said dryly, taking her arm.

Holly's next worry was the big black limousine that ferried Slade all over London. Kevin had given his address as a loft in Soho and, although Holly wasn't familiar with the city she knew it wouldn't be a high rent district. That huge car parked in a working-class neighborhood might be taken as patronizing. When Slade hailed a cab in front of the hotel, she looked at him in surprise.

"Give me credit for a little sensitivity, Holly," he murmured.

Would she ever stop underestimating this complex man, Holly wondered.

The taxi pulled up in front of a dilapidated three-story building and judging by the volume of music drifting out to the street, the party was in full swing. They climbed the rickety stairs to the top floor, guided by the din, and entered a long high-ceilinged room that was packed with humanity. A small stereo in a far corner was responsible for part of the music and a number of couples were dancing. In a different section of the room, a young bearded man was playing guitar for an enthralled group. The rest of the guests were moving around restlessly, shouting to be heard over the noise.

Holly's heart sank. What had she let Slade in for?

Kevin appeared out of the crowd. "Good to see you again, luv."

Holly introduced Slade and the two men shook hands and looked at each other appraisingly.

"I hope you don't mind my standing in for Alan," Slade said easily. "I didn't want Holly to come alone."

"Glad to have you. Any friend of Alan's and all that. You aren't what I expected though." Slade raised his eyebrows and Kevin grinned. "From the way he spoke about you, I expected a cross between the Lord High Mayor and Francis of Assisi." Someone called to him and Kevin waved at a card table set up in a corner. "Get yourselves some wine, it's self help here, matey."

After he left, Slade asked, "Would you like a glass of wine or would you rather dance?"

Holly looked doubtfully at the wildly gyrating couples, unable to picture Slade dancing to that kind of music.

"Trust me," he said with a faint smile, leading her onto the improvised floor.

Once more he managed to surprise her. Looking completely natural and without getting in the least bit winded, Slade performed the uninhibited steps. But when the music changed to a slow number, he drew her close, folding both arms around her.

"I can't pretend that's my favorite kind of dancing," he said, his lips brushing her forehead. "This is much nicer."

"But you do it so well." Holly couldn't keep the amazement out of her voice.

"You act positively astonished." His expression was wry. "I do get out of my rocking chair every now and then."

"I didn't mean that you were too old," she protested. "It's just that. . . . I mean you seem so. . . ." Her voice trailed off.

He tipped her chin up. "What do I seem to you?"

"Intimidating." The word slipped out before she could stop it.

Slade groaned and held her close. "Don't be afraid of me, little one. I won't ever hurt you again, I promise."

Her body was molded to his from shoulder to thigh and Holly gave herself up to the ecstasy of being close to him and breathing in the male scent that was peculiarly his own. They barely moved to the slow tempo and the slight swaying motion was unbearably sensuous. She was completely enveloped by him, melting into his body until they were like one person. Her head was pillowed on his shoulder and Slade's long fingers massaged the nape of her neck, threading through the long silky hair and sending shivers down her spine.

The music stopped but she stayed in his arms and when his warm mouth touched her closed eyelids, Holly realized that it was a good thing they weren't alone. She would probably have acted like a fool and thrown herself at him again. Luckily, they were in the midst of a crowd. That thought brought her to her senses and she moved away, carefully avoiding his eyes.

"I think I'd better comb my hair," she murmured, leaving him abruptly.

Mavis Brown was in the small curtained alcove that served as a bedroom and she fell on Holly eagerly. "Who is that dishy man you're with? He acts like he really fancies you."

"Don't be silly," Holly said shortly. "That's Slade Rockwell, my boss. He brought me tonight because Alan is in New York."

"Alan is awfully cute but this one is gorgeous." Mavis eyes Holly speculatively. "You mean you really wouldn't mind if I had a go at him?"

"Be my guest, but I'd better warn you—the line forms on the left," Holly said dryly.

"I know. All the girls here tonight are crackers over him."

They would be, Holly thought. Slade would always be the main attraction no matter where he was or what he was doing. That blatant masculinity drew women like a magnet and the cool amusement in those thick-lashed gray eyes provided a challenge they couldn't resist. No wonder he wasn't willing to settle for one woman. Why should he when he could have his pick?

When Holly emerged from the bedroom, she noticed that Slade was the center of a small cluster of people. Several women were looking at him with open admiration, but he was listening interestedly to two young men who were explaining something earnestly. Each of the group were vying for his attention and he was trying to divide it courteously.

"Your Slade Rockwell is quite a chap," Kevin's voice said at her elbow.

"Yes, he seems to be making quite a hit doesn't he?" Holly said lightly.

Kevin looked at her soberly. "Poor Alan, he doesn't stand a chance does he?"

Dear Lord, was it that obvious? "I don't know what you're talking about. Alan and I both work for the man so naturally we admire him."

"Kevin, we're running out of wine and I don't know where you put the rest of the bottles," Mavis informed him.

Holly was grateful for the interruption but Kevin's perception troubled her. It was bad enough for other people to notice but the real danger was that Slade might guess.

She looked at the group across the room as he

glanced up. Their eyes met and he beckoned her. Holly moved to Slade's side and when he put an arm around her waist and drew her close to his hard body, she could have purred with happiness. He wasn't hers and never could be but for tonight, at least, he was on loan and she was going to treasure every moment.

"All right everyone, it's show time!" Kevin was standing in the middle of the floor waving his arms. "Everyone prepare to sing for his supper."

This was evidently an accustomed practice among the guests who were all in show business or on the fringes of it and everyone formed a circle, leaving an empty space in the middle. Folding chairs were dragged up but many people simply sat cross-legged on the floor.

There was a lot of talent in the group and Holly clapped enthusiastically, enjoying even the performers who were less than adequate. The entertainment went on for a long time and when it was almost over, Kevin pulled Holly to her feet and dragged her into the cleared area.

"And now at great expense to the management, we bring you direct from the States, Miss Holly Holbrooke!"

Holly's face was stricken. "Are you out of your mind? I don't know how to do anything!"

Unperturbed, Kevin announced, "Miss Holbrooke will give us her world famed imitation of a tree."

Perhaps it was the wine or the wild applause that greeted his introduction but Holly was swept up in the fun. Assuming the stance that she had affected at the drama class, she posed gracefully with outstretched arms and lifted head, her long shining hair rippling down her back.

Cheers and whistles rewarded her performance but when she laughingly glanced over at Slade, the smoldering look in his eyes as they devoured her body made the breath catch in her throat. Abruptly dropping her arms, she stumbled back to her seat.

"And now for the pièce de résistance," Kevin shouted when the noise had died down, "the one and only, the inimitable, Slade Rockwell!"

"Oh, no," Holly whispered. It was all right for her to make a fool of herself but Kevin couldn't do this to Slade!

She jumped to her feet but Slade pushed her gently back into the chair. Striding into the center of the circle, he took the guitar from the young bearded man. Someone pushed a stool forward and Slade sat down and started to play.

The first haunting notes of the malaguena brought complete silence. His long fingers were sure on the strings and as his dark head bent in concentration, every woman's eyes were riveted on his handsome profile. When the last note died away there were cheers and foot stomping and encores weren't merely requested, they were demanded.

Slade played for half an hour and each selection was accorded rapt attention. They were unwilling to let him go but at the end of that time he stood up and smilingly shook his head.

"I don't know what plans the rest of you have for tomorrow, but I have a very early morning appointment."

Holly looked at her watch and promptly went into shock. It couldn't be that late!

In the taxi going home her eyes were big with wonder. "Where did you ever learn to play the guitar like that?"

Putting his arm around her casually, he said, "I'm a man of many parts, didn't you know?"

Holly was beginning to believe she didn't really know anything about him. This whole evening had been an eye opener. Slade was at least ten years older than anyone at the party and yet he had fit in easily. Not only fit in, they had jostled for his attention. Anything they could do, he could do better. How was it possible for one man to be so talented?

While she was considering all this, Holly leaned against his shoulder and closed her eyes for a moment. The combination of wine, the late hour and her recent illness combined to take their toll and her body gradually relaxed against Slade's. The next thing she knew, he was shaking her gently.

The hotel doorman had his hand extended and Holly looked at Slade in confusion. "Did I fall asleep? How dreadful!"

Slade smiled and shook his head. "It's my fault, I should have brought you home sooner."

When they were in the suite, he took her chin between his thumb and forefinger and inspected her tired face carefully. "You're to stay in bed all day tomorrow."

"Oh no, Slade, I'm coming into the office."

"You'll do no such thing," he said firmly. "Now off to bed with you and no more arguments. It's late and I have to get up early."

He put his hands on her shoulders and for a moment Holly thought he was going to kiss her good night. Her drowsiness vanished as something flickered in his eyes and his hands tightened, but as her heart began to race Slade turned her around and gave her a gentle nudge toward her bedroom.

"Sleep well, little one," he said quietly.

Chapter Ten

The plane for Italy soared upward after takeoff and Holly craned her neck for a last look at London. It had been pleasure mixed with pain, but she had fallen in love with the city. Her only regret was that she hadn't seen enough of it.

As though reading her thoughts, Slade said, "We'll come back and it will be better next time."

"I enjoyed it very much," she said like a polite child.

In truth, Holly was feeling very shy with Slade. They were traveling alone this time and she missed the refuge that Alan and Victor had provided. She knew that she couldn't keep a man like this interested for long, although his manner didn't indicate that he was bored.

Since her illness, Slade had been uncommonly kind to her. When he finally allowed her to go back to the *Metro* offices, he had checked often to be sure she wasn't over tiring herself. And he had taken her out to dinner every night to see that she ate, carefully bringing her home at an early hour.

Lady Dillingham hadn't shown up at the offices in those last days they spent in London and Holly finally decided that she must be out of town. That would account for Slade's having so much free time to spend with her. But being with him was an unexpected delight and Holly had gloried in his company, refusing to care about the reason for it.

"Will Victor be joining us?" she asked, more for something to say than because it really mattered, although she liked the older man.

"He will be in and out." A curtain dropped behind Slade's gray eyes erasing all expression. "Was that who you were really inquiring about?"

The specter of Alan was between them again and Holly looked down at her hands. Should she ignore it? He wouldn't believe her true relationship with Alan and Holly didn't want to bring up the painful subject, but ignoring it didn't make it go away.

Choosing her words carefully, she said, "I wasn't referring to Alan if that's what you're implying but since you mentioned it, yes, I wish he could be with us. There's so much to see in Rome and Alan is good about taking me sight-seeing."

Slade's large hand covered her clenched fingers. "Will I do as a surrogate?"

It was so unexpected that she looked at him breathlessly. "I . . . I couldn't ask you to do that. I know how busy you are."

His smile encompassed the wide aquamarine eyes. "Haven't we decided that you don't know anything about me?"

"Yes, but you've been all those places before. You would be . . . incredibly bored."

"Why don't you let me be the judge of that. We have the whole weekend before we have to report to work, do you want to give me a list of your choices or will you trust to my judgment?"

Was he really proposing to spend two whole days

with her? Holly's eyes were shining as she cried, "I'm completely in your hands."

"That's another subject entirely," Slade said dryly.

The Hassler Hotel was world famous and Holly was suitably impressed as Slade was greeted with the decorous familiarity that spoke of a long association. She knew that its location atop the famed Spanish Steps was one of the best in Rome and it was accorded a deluxe rating in all the tour guides.

Her room was enchanting, a large spacious chamber with a terrace that overlooked the city. Holly exclaimed with delight at the massive antique armoire and graceful tables and chairs, at which Slade commented wryly, "You finally got your wish—a private room. I believe we do share the terrace though."

Holly blushed, remembering the fuss she had put up in London. She had been right though. That terrible evening would never have occurred when they had almost—Closing her mind resolutely, she said brightly, "It's perfectly lovely."

He quirked a sardonic eyebrow at her. "Yes, well, get unpacked and I'll see you in half an hour."

Holly was ready and waiting expectantly when Slade knocked on her door. The ever present black limousine was waiting at the hotel entrance. Either he owned a fleet of them in every city of the world or they were rented, but it was certainly a luxurious extra.

"Where are we going?" she asked excitedly.

"I thought we would start with the Forum and the Colosseum, they're on the must see list for any first time visitor. Does that meet with your approval?"

"Oh, yes!"

The long limousine pulled away from the curb and Holly sat on the edge of her seat. She didn't want to miss anything but the traffic in Rome was so horrendous that she closed her eyes more than once as small cars darted in and out, seemingly bent on murder and suicide.

Slade finally chuckled and put his arm around her, drawing her close to his comforting body. "Don't worry, Angel Eyes, strange as it seems they all know what they're doing."

Such was her confidence in him that if Slade said it, it had to be true. She felt safe in the circle of his arms looking out avidly at the sights.

Their destination was the Colosseum but as they drove past the magnificent Arch of Constantine that stood opposite it, Holly drank in the beauty of its carved bas-reliefs and marveled at the fact that this very arch was erected seventeen centuries ago and was still standing, almost completely intact.

The Colosseum itself was mind boggling. It was a huge arena with a seating capacity of fifty thousand which sounded tremendous except that ancient Rome, incredible as it seems, had a population of about a million. The stadium was impressive but the knowledge that this was where the early Christians had met to do uneven battle with the lions sent a shiver down her spine.

The Roman Forum was more to her liking. Slade explained that this was the source of our entire legal system, not to mention the root of our language and much of our culture. As Holly stood among the ruins, she squinted her eyes and could almost imagine she saw chariots driving up to disgorge toga clad statesmen with laurel wreaths on their heads. The whole atmosphere was ageless and she felt as though she had stepped into a time machine and was transported back into history.

They toured the Casa de Livia and Holly marveled at the mosaic floors and the beautiful frescoes that decorated the walls. The fact that this had once been a luxurious home was evidenced by the many salons, the library and the private passageway which the servants used to bring food. It was difficult to realize, but many centuries ago, other human beings had stood on this very floor.

Viewing Holly's dazzled eyes, Slade smiled. "I think lunch is in order. There is a limit to how much you can absorb at one time."

Reluctantly, she had to agree with him. "I feel disoriented. As though I don't know which century I'm in."

They went to a charming restaurant where the menu was, of course, in Italian and Holly looked helplessly at Slade. "Would you order for me?" He did in fluent Italian and she commented admiringly, "Is there anything you can't do?"

His eyes swept her heart-shaped face, lingering on the soft mouth and he said softly, "Yes, I'm afraid so."

She didn't understand his meaning but Holly's breathing quickened at the intimate look he gave her and she sought frantically for something to say. Business was always a neutral ground. "Tell me about the *Novita Roma.*" It was the weekly magazine here in Rome that was their next project.

Her ploy didn't escape Slade and a faint smile tilted the corners of his firm lips. "What would you like to know?"

"I've never worked on a magazine and I think you'd better brief me. The deadlines are a lot more relaxed aren't they?"

"Yes, but for that very reason, the libel laws are stricter. In a newspaper there is more tolerance because of the immediacy of getting the news to the people. A magazine has time to double check every fact."

A frown creased his forehead and Holly said, "Do you disagree with that premise?"

"What? Oh, no, of course not, I was just thinking. . . . We have one employee that I'm afraid is a bad apple." His face cleared. "But that can wait until Monday. This is your weekend."

Slade refused to talk business, although there were many things Holly felt she should know about. But he didn't become personal either for which she was grateful, choosing instead to regale her with interesting stories about Rome.

After a long lunch he said, "I think a change of pace is in order now, how are your feet?"

"Fine, why?" she asked with surprise.

"Because we're going shopping. It occurred to me that since tomorrow is Sunday and the shops will be closed, we'd better take care of that today."

"Maybe it would be wiser to wait until tomorrow. Window shopping is all I can afford anyway."

Slade reached in his breast pocket and took out a long white envelope. "This is for you. I meant to give it to you at the hotel but I forgot."

"What is it?" she asked questioningly. When he didn't answer immediately, she opened the envelope and found a thick packet of bills.

"It's your salary for the month," he said finally.

"But I owe that to you. You said—"

"I said a lot of things," he interrupted, "most of them I'd like to forget." She bent her head remembering and there was an unreadable expression in his eyes. "Now you're independent again. You can do anything you want," he said softly.

Holly had a premonition about the money. The envelope seemed to burn her fingers and she looked at it with mixed feelings. If he had given it to her when she asked, she wouldn't be sitting here with him now.

She raised her eyes and looked at him shyly. "I'm glad you didn't give it to me before."

The watchful quality left his face and he reached across the table and covered her hand with his, the fingers squeezing tightly. "I was hoping you would say that."

Slade dismissed the car and they walked down the broad Via del Corso, stopping to look in the windows at such an array of elegant merchandise that Holly was dazzled. There were fine leather jackets, intricately wrought silver cups and bowls, colorful ceramic dishes, Venetian glass vases and figurines and much, much more.

Although Slade wanted to lead her inside, Holly contented herself with window shopping. Then they turned the corner into the narrow winding Via Condotti where there were more shops and she was enchanted by the cobbled streets, but confused by the plethora of merchandise.

"Surely you can find *something* you want to buy. You're destroying the myth about women shoppers," Slade teased.

"I don't know where to start, everything is so gorgeous." They were passing a leather shop and she stopped to look at the display. "I could use a new black purse," she mused.

They went inside and Holly looked at the handbag that had attracted her, but she couldn't make up her mind. The saleslady brought out others and Slade leaned against a showcase, watching the proceedings with amusement. Soon the counter was littered with bags while Holly considered and rejected. But when she finally settled on one and asked the price, her eyes widened with dismay. Where were all the bargains one was supposed to get in Europe?

The saleslady was very high pressure and Holly looked around for Slade to rescue her but he wasn't there. Like all men, he had probably gotten bored with the proceedings and was wandering around outside, she decided. After telling the woman she would have to think about it, Holly made her escape and met Slade on the sidewalk.

"You deserted me," she accused. "I didn't know how to get out of there."

"What's the matter, didn't you like their things? I thought they were very nice."

"They should be at those prices!"

"You have plenty of money now."

"Yes, but I don't intend to spend it all in one place," she said tartly.

His eyes brimmed with laughter. "Too bad you didn't feel that way at the casino. I do believe there's hope for you yet."

She knew he was only teasing her and when he held out a small box she asked, "What's this?"

"A little something to remember Rome by. Something you probably have a collection of but this is one to add to it," he told her obliquely.

She opened the little square box and inside, nestled on a bed of white velvet was a lovely gold heart suspended from a fragile gold chain. "It . . . it's lovely, Slade."

He fastened it with fingers that felt very warm on the back of her neck. The delicate heart slipped inside the open neck of her blouse and nestled between her breasts. Holly touched it softly and his eyes followed her hand to the shadowed valley. "Thank you," she said simply.

"Don't I get a kiss?"

They were standing in the middle of the crowded sidewalk where streams of people divided and re-grouped around them. "Do you mean here?" she asked incredulously.

"Sure, why not?" he chuckled.

"But all these people. . . ."

"They'll think we're in love. That's something Italians understand and approve of," he assured her with a twinkle in his eyes.

Putting his hands on her shoulders, he kissed her gently on the lips. Holly closed her eyes and when she opened them, Slade was looking at her, all the amusement gone from his face.

Their next stop was the famed Fontana di Trevi, presided over by the gloriously baroque chariot-drawn statue of the god Neptune. The dancing jets of water leapt high in the air, returning to the fountain in the form of diamond droplets and Holly exclaimed over its beauty.

"You know the legend don't you?" Slade asked. "If you toss a coin in the fountain, you will return to Rome."

"Oh, quick, give me a coin," she begged eagerly.

But when she prepared to throw it, he stopped her. "You have to turn your back and throw it over your shoulder."

She did as she was told and was rewarded with a satisfying plop. Turning excitedly to Slade she said, "You throw one too, I want us to come back together." Something kindled in his eyes and Holly realized how revealing her impulsive words had been. "I . . . it's a form of job insurance," she said brightly, trying to turn it into a joke. "That way I know you won't fire me."

Slade lifted a quizzical eyebrow but didn't comment as he obligingly tossed a coin over his shoulder.

"And now it's back to the hotel for you," he said. "I don't want you to get overly tired and risk a recurrence of the flu."

"But I'm not tired, honestly and there's so much more to see."

"Tomorrow," he said firmly. "We'll walk up the Spanish Steps but that's your last sight-seeing for the day. I want you to rest before dinner."

Holly knew better than to try to change Slade's mind when he got that look on his face so she went along reluctantly. It was the fastest way to get back to the hotel which was the only reason he had included them in their itinerary but Holly was grateful anyway. She had looked down from her room at them, of course, but it wasn't the same as climbing the broad stone steps.

Her delighted gaze took in the dark green orange trees that grew along the slope perfuming the air, and then rested on the house in which the famed poet Keats had died. Raising her eyes to the summit dominated by the magnificent Church of Trinità dei Monti, she looked wistfully at Slade but he shook his head.

"Tomorrow," he reiterated with a smile.

Holly hadn't realized how tired she was until she took off her clothes and climbed into bed. Her mind was filled with all the visions of delight she had seen that day and she wanted to take them out and examine them but her body betrayed her. After just a few moments, her eyelashes drooped and she was asleep.

It was dark when she awoke, the lights of the city sparkling like multicolored stars outside the window.

She took a worried look at her watch and then relaxed. Dinner was late in Rome as it was on much of the Continent and she had plenty of time to bathe and dress.

When Slade rapped at her door, she was just fastening the golden heart around her neck. It showed off to advantage with the dress she had chosen, a lavender silk print with a low vee neckline, long sleeves and a full skirt that fell from unpressed pleats.

"Very nice," he said warmly, helping her into her coat.

"Thank you." Holly glowed under his praise. "Where are we going?"

"A dress like that deserves to go dancing," he said, lifting her long hair out of the collar of her coat. The sensuous touch of his fingers on her skin sent a shiver through her body and she moved away, hoping he hadn't noticed.

The nightclub he took her to was discreetly lit and intimate. There was dancing but the floor was so small that the couples on it were pressed close together. Everyone was dressed beautifully and it was obvious that this was a very elegant spot not yet discovered by tourists.

Slade had ordered for both of them and the food was delicious. "I'm afraid if I lived here I would get very fat," Holly sighed appreciatively.

"I don't imagine that's anything you've ever had to worry about. You eat like a—well, let's just say you eat heartily," he grinned, "and you never gain an ounce."

"I know, it drives everybody crazy," she giggled. "It's a good thing I didn't live in the days of the old South when a girl was supposed to have an appetite like a bird."

Slade agreed. "Somehow I can't imagine you just sitting around under a parasol all day, batting your eyes at love-sick swains."

"That part I could manage," she teased, fluttering her eyelashes intriguingly.

"Are you flirting with me, young lady?" he demanded severely.

"Why should I be any different?" she shrugged, thinking of his long list of conquests.

"You're a fine one to talk," he commented dryly. "Have you noticed all the admiring glances directed your way this evening?"

"No, really?" Holly was delighted. "I've been absolutely crushed because I always heard that Italian men pinch pretty girls but no one has laid a finger on me. Maybe it's your fault." Looking at his broad shouldered powerful frame she said sadly, "You probably scare them all away."

"You little imp! Would you like me to leave you alone to see how well you can do?" When she laughingly declined, Slade said, "All right, then come and dance with me. Perhaps on that crowded floor you'll get your wish."

Moving into his arms was like going to heaven. Her body remembered the hard contours and as she relaxed against him, they were like two parts of an interlocking puzzle. She breathed in his warm clean male scent and when Slade's lips touched her forehead and his hands moved slowly over her back, Holly's happiness was complete. If only it could always be like this.

But the music ended and they went back to their table.

A glow remained on her face and Slade regarded her gravely. "Are you happy, Holly?"

"Oh, yes! I can't thank you enough for . . . for everything."

"I didn't mean just tonight."

"Oh . . . my job? Yes, of course, I love it."

"I think you're willfully misunderstanding me. What I mean is, are you satisfied with your life?"

Holly looked down at the tablecloth. Loving Slade as she did and knowing that he would never return that love, how could she be truly happy? These last days alone with him had been heaven, but she knew they would be followed by hell. In California it had been Monique Duvall, in London, Lady Dillingham. Who was the woman—or women—here in Rome who had the inside track? And could she bear watching him with them? The memory of Slade kissing Marsha's hand made her feel faintly ill. But he had been angry at her then, maybe he would be more discreet in the future. The thought brought little consolation.

"Is it such a hard question to answer?" Slade's voice broke in on her introspection.

"What?" For a minute she had forgotten what he asked and then it came to her. "Why shouldn't I be satisfied? I have everything any girl could wish for." Holly was glad the pain between her breasts wasn't visible.

"How about a husband?" he asked dryly. "Or doesn't that figure in your overall plan?"

"Oh, sure, I guess I'll get married some day when I'm old and gray," she said lightly.

"Then I take it that you don't intend to have children."

The casual statement struck a nerve. Children—Slade's children. Suddenly the dimly lit nightclub dissolved and Holly was in a sunlit park. A sturdy little black-haired boy was clinging to one hand while her other was pushing a stroller that held a rosy gurgling little girl with black curls and blue eyes. Any children of theirs would have to have dark hair and light eyes.

"Does the thought of tiny tots strike you numb with terror?" Slade asked sardonically. "I should think as an only child yourself, you would want to have youngsters but evidently I'm wrong."

"You don't have to sound so judgmental," Holly said defensively. "You're an only child and you don't seem in any rush to have any."

He raised his eyebrows. "What makes you think I'm an only child?"

"You mean you aren't?" she asked incredulously.

"No, I have a sister."

"You are without a doubt the most closemouthed man I've ever met," Holly said indignantly. "Everything I know about you I've had to drag out."

He shrugged. "I didn't think you would be interested. What would you like to know?"

"Tell me about your sister. Is she older, younger?"

"She's two years younger than I, her name is Felice Brent and she's married to a lawyer named Phillip Brent. They have three children and he specializes in international law. There, is that detailed enough for you?" he smiled. "As a matter of fact, you'll meet her yourself. Phil has to be in Paris on Monday and they're stopping off in Rome tomorrow."

"How wonderful for you! But I wouldn't think of intruding, especially since you have only the one day together."

"Don't be a little goose, of course you're coming. Felice will be delighted. Be prepared for the third degree though, I must warn you that my sister is incurably nosy. But after that's over we can all settle down and enjoy each other's company," he laughed. "I think you'll like both of them."

Holly did her best to dissuade him, really feeling that she would be in the way, but Slade refused to listen to her and she was much too happy to argue with him.

Chapter Eleven

Holly was unbearably nervous the next morning over the prospect of meeting Slade's sister. She had changed clothes three times and still wasn't satisfied with the result. Regarding herself in the mirror now, she was still doubtful. The unstructured blue silk dress was simple enough, but her small tilted breasts were outlined against the thin fabric and did it cling too sensuously when she walked? What difference did it really make, Holly asked herself? She meant nothing in Slade's life but the fact remained that she wanted to make a good impression on his sister.

They were meeting for lunch in the dining room of their hotel and as Holly walked in next to Slade, her hands were icy.

"Relax, what's the worst she can do to you?" Slade teased, taking her cold hand in his warm one. "After surviving Marsha, you're a veteran."

So he did know how unpleasant Lady Dillingham had been! Holly looked at him in amazement. Was there anything that escaped him?

Felice and her husband were already seated and they jumped up to greet Slade. They were both tall people and Holly's heart sank. She felt at an immediate disadvantage. Why couldn't she have been born tall and willowy like Monique and Marsha? Those were the kind of women Slade admired.

While the reunion was going on she had a chance to observe his relatives. Felice was dark like Slade with a stunning figure that did justice to her couturier clothes, but her husband had curly red hair and looked like an ex-football player.

"And now it's time you met Holly." Slade put his arm around her waist, drawing her into the group.

"She's a tiny little thing isn't she?" Felice's gaze was all-encompassing but her voice was thoughtful rather than disparaging.

"Haven't you heard that good things come in small packages?" her husband asked cheerfully, taking Holly's hand and engulfing it in his huge one.

"You must forgive Phillip, my dear," Felice told her. "He's terribly bright but he does tend to talk in clichés." The smile she gave her husband was fondly teasing and there was no sting in the words.

Over lunch, Holly got to know them and found that Felice was forthright and completely unaffected. She was obviously very wealthy but as totally unimpressed with the fact as Slade was. She did ask Holly a lot of questions and Holly could only conclude that it was because his sister had the mistaken impression that she was one of Slade's girl friends.

Holly evidently passed the test because Felice said, "There is one thing I must warn you about, when you meet Dad don't talk politics! He's a darling man but his mind is zippered shut on that subject."

"Thanks for the warning but I don't think I'll have occasion to meet your father," Holly said carefully.

Felice glanced over to where Slade was deep in conversation with Phillip. "I have a feeling you will," she murmured.

The rapport that had existed between the four of them through the long lunch was abruptly shattered when Felice announced that they were all going to a cocktail party that afternoon at the home of someone named Comtessa Ascaldi. Slade and Phillip groaned in unison while Holly looked bewildered.

"Not Holly and I," Slade said firmly. "I promised to take her sight-seeing today."

"I'll go with you," Phillip offered eagerly.

"You'll do no such thing," Felice stated. "I know Diane is a drag but we were at school together," she said as if that explained everything.

"The worst thing that ever happened to you was going to that school in Switzerland," Slade told her severely. "Your old school chum is a pain in the posterior."

"It won't be so bad," Felice answered defensively. "Diane does give marvelous parties and the trick is just not to let her corner you. I wonder if she's still into that Far Eastern religion," she mused reflectively. "Oh, well, it will be fun to see who she's gathered together this time."

In the end, Felice got her way as Holly felt she did most of the time, although the men were still grumbling when they drove up to the palazzo, a magnificent pink edifice that looked something like the public library at home.

The high-ceilinged rooms were full of people and Holly was enjoying herself even though she didn't know a soul except her own group. It was exciting enough just to be in Europe, but to actually go to a private party in a genuine palace made her cup run over. Until a throaty female voice trilled Slade's name.

"Slade, lover, I didn't know you were going to be here!"

An exquisite blonde in a flaming red dress that left little to the imagination, launched herself into his arms, giving him a long passionate kiss. Holly's heart plunged as she recognized Monique Duvall, the sex symbol of several continents.

For the first time since she had known him, Holly saw Slade's poise slip for a fraction of a second but he recovered so soon that it was almost imperceptible. "Monique, my dear, what are you doing in Rome?"

"I *told* you I was making a movie in Italy but you never listen to me," she pouted. Hugging his arm close to her body, she relented. "Never mind, we've found each other and that's all that matters."

Gently disengaging himself, Slade took Holly's hand. "I'd like you to meet Holly Holbrooke."

The glamorous movie star's eyes narrowed as she looked Holly over and then dismissed her negligently. After the briefest of greetings, she took Slade's arm and propelled him to the other side of the room, her voice floating back tantalizingly. "Darling, I've missed you terribly."

"How obvious can you get?" Felice snorted. "That woman is salivating like a head hunter contemplating a missionary."

"An apt analogy, my dear," Phillip said dryly, "but I don't think it's his head she's after."

"They're old friends," Holly offered, thinking she ought to make some comment but the slight quaver in her voice betrayed her.

Felice exchanged a look with her husband. "Two can

play that game," she murmured cryptically. Taking Holly by the hand she said, "Come with me, there are some people you should meet."

The "people" turned out to be several young men who were in delighted agreement with her. The only problem was that their English was minimal and since Holly spoke no Italian, their attempts at communication were hilarious. Holly would have enjoyed it very much if her eyes and ears hadn't been extended like antennae searching for Slade and his glamourous companion.

They had disappeared from the room and her imagination was supplying all kinds of unpalatable reasons when she felt a familiar arm around her waist. Slade greeted her admirers and engaged them in a rapid exchange of Italian, after which the young men smiled ruefully, kissed her hand and left.

"What on earth did you say to them?" she exclaimed.

"I told them you were mine and to buzz off. Only in politer terms of course," he laughed.

"You didn't! How could you do a terrible thing like that?" Her cheeks were bright pink with indignation.

"Those fellows don't play by your rules, honey, and I'm afraid you're not cut out for *la dolce vita,*" he teased.

"I can look out for myself," she stormed. "I don't need you to take care of me! Why don't you just go back to your movie star?"

His hand moved caressingly to her neck and he gently blew a lock of hair off her forehead. "Jealous?" he asked softly.

His touch was making her knees feel weak but Holly forced herself to say scornfully, "Don't flatter yourself."

"You're right, I would be flattered," he murmured.

Putting his arm around her rigid shoulders, he led her

over to Felice and Phillip. "I've performed above and beyond my filial duty," he informed his sister. "Holly and I are leaving."

"That's the first intelligent thing you've done today," she said approvingly.

Hoping to make his escape too, Phillip Brent turned a hopeful eye on his wife but after reading the implacable answer in her eyes, he sighed. "Why don't we meet you at the Bella Fontana," he suggested to Slade, naming a popular restaurant. "We'll be along as soon as Felice has immersed herself in the latest gossip."

By the time Holly and Slade were seated in the cocktail lounge, she had forgotten her resentment and was chattering away happily about the party. It took a while to realize that Slade wasn't listening.

"Is something wrong?" she asked tentatively.

"No, of course not." His attention returned and he smiled, covering her hand with his. "Have you forgiven me for chasing away your boyfriends?"

Had he been thinking about Monique? "They weren't even potential boyfriends," she said lightly, "just nice young men who were trying to be friendly." His lifted eyebrow was derisive and, although Holly didn't want to argue with Slade, she couldn't help saying, "You suspect every man I meet of having ulterior motives."

"They would have to be crazy if they didn't."

She sighed. "Okay, then let's agree that nobody's perfect. Now will you please stop screening my men friends? Your standards are impossibly high."

"They used to be." His mouth twisted cynically. "Just lately I find I'm willing to compromise them."

"Surely not you, Slade!"

Ignoring her sarcasm, he stared at Holly without really seeing her. "When you find something you can't do without, no matter how much it hurts to think—" he stopped abruptly.

There was a somber look on his face that frightened Holly. What was he trying to say? Was it connected with Monique turning up so unexpectedly? Or was it something else? He looked so tormented that her heart went out to him.

Touching his sleeve timidly she said, "Wouldn't it be better to forget it?"

Slade took her hands and held them so tightly that her fingers were numb. "That's not the answer! That's the fool's way out. I've wrestled with it, Holly, and I think I've come to terms with myself. I've finally decided—"

"Well, we made it," Phillip's relieved voice broke in on them. "It was a struggle but I managed to tear Felice away."

"It was the other way around," his wife declared. "That blonde bombshell of Slade's decided to extend her sphere of influence and *I* was the one who decided it was time to leave."

Slade stood up to pull out a chair for his sister and all the tumultuous emotion was erased from his face.

Holly had a feeling that a very important moment had slipped by but there was nothing she could do about it.

Monday morning was utterly chaotic at Slade's news magazine, *Novita Roma.* Holly was unfamiliar with the format, the operation, the language and the people and she realized for the first time how much Alan had done to smooth the way. Slade tried to help as much as he could, but he had more important matters to attend to and she was left to pick her way carefully.

She was walking down the corridor to her office with a stack of magazines under one arm when a handsome man approached. Holly smiled pleasantly and he returned the smile but, instead of going by, he stepped in front of her, barring the way. A rapid stream of Italian followed and she shook her head helplessly.

"I'm sorry but I don't speak Italian," she told him.

His dark brows lifted in surprise and he switched to English. "Ah, an American." He glanced at the pile of magazines. "You work here?"

"Yes, temporarily. This is my first morning and—"

A savoring light ignited in his eyes as he interrupted. "Perhaps I can do something to make it more permanent. I am Mario Donitelli."

He said it as though it should mean something to her but Holly hadn't the faintest idea who he was. Could he be a movie star? She didn't go to foreign films much but this man was definitely handsome enough. He was a few inches shorter than Slade but well built with muscular shoulders, unless they owed their width to the padding in that elegant suit. The medium brown hair spoke of his northern origins but the dark brown, almost black, eyes were pure Latin.

Holly gave up trying to place him and introduced herself politely. "I'm Holly Holbrooke."

"And who do you work for, *amorosa?*" His voice had a caressing sound.

"Well, actually, I—" She broke off as his hand cupped her cheek and slid down to fondle her neck. "Stop that! What do you think you're doing?"

His avid gaze travled over her body and both hands moved to span her narrow waist. "So delicate . . . mmm, *delizioso*. We must do something to make your stay here a long one."

"You can do something all right. You can take your hands off me," Holly said angrily.

The full mouth was suddenly petulant. "Be careful what you say. I can make your job here pleasant . . . or otherwise."

Holly put both hands against his chest and shoved him away but before she could deliver the irate words that threatened to choke her, Slade rounded the corner. His narrowed gaze took in the scene and his eyes grew flinty. "What's going on?"

Mario's smile returned with added candle power. "Mr. Rockwell! *Buon giorno.* I have been looking forward to your visit."

Slade's voice was frigid as he said, "I see you've met my assistant, Miss Holbrooke."

The emotions that played across Mario's face were so ludicrous that Holly could almost feel sorry for him. He was clearly horrified at having made a pass at the boss's aide and Slade's manner wasn't calculated to reassure him. His fury was all too obvious.

Holly sighed. She ought to be flattered that he had appointed himself her guardian but she could have taken care of this office Romeo herself. Slade was convinced that she knew nothing about men and needed protection, which was funny considering that he couldn't safeguard her against the one man who was the real danger.

"I want to talk to you, Holly," Slade said sternly. "Unfortunately, it will have to wait because I'm late to a meeting but I'll see you back at the hotel."

He strode off down the hall and she almost giggled. The temptation to say, "Yes, Father," had been strong but she had wisely resisted.

As soon as Slade was safely out of sight, Mario broke

into voluble apologies but with a cool look, she left him standing in the hall.

"Do you know a Mario . . . um . . . Mario something or other?" Holly asked her secretary a few moments later.

Rosa Vitale was an older woman who must once have been very attractive but was now rather faded looking. "Mario Donitelli? Yes, I know him." Her tone was completely neutral but Holly got the impression that she didn't like the man.

"Who is he? What does he do?" she asked curiously.

"He is a reporter on the magazine," Rosa answered without volunteering any more information.

Holly took the hint and went into the inner office, still not much wiser than she had been. But when she started to read through her stack of magazines, she discovered that Mario appeared to have star billing at *Novita Roma*. Maybe that's why he had been so confident that his advances would be welcome. That cornball routine of his went out with button hooks though, Holly grinned.

He seemed to be a competent enough writer, although his style was a little more florid than she cared for, but Holly decided not to prejudge the man because of an initial unpleasantness until she knew more about him.

That night she found out a lot more. Over dinner, Slade brought up the subject without any prompting.

"Mario was the bad apple I was referring to," he said grimly.

Holly was surprised. "I was reading over some of his stuff today and I thought it was rather colorful."

Slade snorted. "Colorful is a good word for it—imaginative might be a better one."

"I don't understand. What's wrong with that?"

"I don't know if you're aware of it but *Novita Roma* is being sued for a bundle because of an article Mario wrote. He was doing an exposé on the connection between organized crime and a certain high official. Mario uncovered evidence of bribery but that wasn't enough for him. He had to drag in some sex to make it more dramatic."

"Well, if the man was being offered sexual favors, that's a form of bribery isn't it?" Holly asked.

"It had nothing to do with it," Slade said disgustedly. "Mario discovered that this politician paid the rent on his secretary's apartment and immediately jumped to the conclusion that they were playing house. It turned out that the girl is his niece, a little bit of nepotism Mario ignored, and the guy only paid the rent *once*. He didn't even pay it technically. He only advanced it. His sister, the girl's mother, reimbursed him. So now we're being sued and the whole case against a really corrupt man has been weakened, perhaps irreparably."

"That's terrible! Have you talked to Mario?"

"Oh, sure. He claims he was an innocent victim." Slade's mouth twisted cynically. "Nothing is ever Mario's fault."

"Is it possible that he might be telling the truth?"

He looked at her sharply. "Don't tell me you fell for that Latin lover's line?"

"Of course not," she said impatiently. "I thought he was pitiful but I was trying to keep an open mind."

"You don't have to bother in his case. I can tell you that he's lazy and he's sloppy, two of the worst sins a journalist can be guilty of. And the hell of it is that I can't even fire him. At least not now."

"Why ever not?" she exclaimed.

"Because it would prejudice the case. It hasn't come to trial yet and firing Mario now would be like an admission of guilt."

He looked so tired that Holly's heart went out to him. All those tabloids that called Slade an irresponsible playboy should only know, she reflected angrily. Leaning forward, she said impulsively. "I wish I could do something to help."

His eyes softened as he looked at her. "You are helping just by being here." He squeezed her hand. "Do you mind if we make it an early evening? I have a lot of work to do tomorrow."

There was a beautiful long stemmed white rose on Holly's desk the next morning with a note propped up against the vase. She picked it up curiously and read: "*Scusami* a million times! May this rose express the purity of my intentions. Mario."

Her eyebrows rose cynically and she tossed the note in the wastebasket but the rose was lovely and she sniffed it appreciatively. Flipping the intercom key, Holly said, "Would you please ask Sophia Francesca to come to my office when she has a moment."

The dark haired young woman who arrived a short time later was beautiful, the sleek black hair pulled back from her face emphasizing the big dark eyes and classic Roman nose. Her clothes were the height of fashion, molding to a supple body and Holly looked at her in admiration.

"Won't you sit down, Miss Francesca," she invited pleasantly. "I'd like to discuss your work."

To Holly's surprise, the girl put her palms on the desk and leaned over it. "What has he been telling you about me?" she asked furiously.

Holly looked at her blankly. "Who?"

"Mario Donitelli!" she almost spat out the name. "It is true that I uncovered the rent receipt but that is *all*. I was never given an opportunity to discover more."

"I assure you, Miss—"

"We were supposed to work together on this story," Sophia swept on. "I was to share the byline but when it appeared that it would be a big story, Mario cut me out. And now he wishes to shift the blame to me. Well, I will not have it!"

"Mario never told me—"

Sophia pushed her thick hair back and directed a rapid stream of Italian at the ceiling. Then she eyed Holly contemptuously. "Why am I wasting my breath? You are like all the other stupid females! You are taken in by that phony charm and you believe the lies that come out of his mouth. I will not waste my time on you!"

Before Holly's astonished eyes, she whirled around and ran from the room. When Holly finally pulled herself together, she depressed the intercom switch once more. "Would you ask Mario Donitelli to step in here?" she asked thoughtfully.

Mario's manner was deferential in the extreme when he entered her office. His eyes went to the white rose and his face lit up. "I am glad to see that you did not throw away my peace offering," he said.

"It would be acting as childishly as you did to destroy something beautiful," she told him evenly.

"You are right of course," he said contritely. "But you are very lovely and I am Latin." He shrugged and spread his hands palm up and Holly had to smother a smile.

"Suppose we stick to business," she suggested. "I have just had a very interesting conversation with

Sophia Francesca." Holly paused, expecting him to explode into similar recriminations but he surprised her.

"Ah yes, Sophia," was all he said, shaking his head sadly.

"I'm sure you are aware of what she told me?"

"That we were to work together on that unfortunate article? That she was to share my byline?"

"That's correct." When he was silent, Holly asked, "What's your version of it?"

"You cannot ask me to be ungallant," he murmured.

"I don't think gallantry enters into it," Holly said crisply. "I think we need to get to the truth of the matter. Tell me your side of it."

"If you insist," he said reluctantly. "The truth is that Sophia Francesca is an ambitious woman. There is nothing wrong with that except that she is willing to do anything to achieve her goals. When I began this article, she came to me and asked to assist me. I told her that I have always worked alone but she said that she wanted no credit, only the experience that she would receive." He hunched his shoulders expressively. "Call me softhearted—and I will freely admit that I am where women are concerned." His boyish glance at Holly begged understanding.

"I will concede that point," she said dryly.

"Sophia came to me in great excitement," he continued, "claiming that she had further evidence of this man's duplicity. I asked her if she was absolutely sure, if she had double checked, explaining that we must not jeopardize our case with frivolities. She assured me that she had so I took her word for it. *That* is all I am guilty of—faith in my colleague."

Holly looked at him in perplexity. He looked totally

sincere and he hadn't rushed in with accusations the way Sophia had but she had seemed passionately sure of her facts too. Where did the truth lie?

Mario looked at her compassionately. "I know it is very difficult for you. You do not know any of us so you are swimming in a sea of doubt. Perhaps it would be best for you to put it out of your mind for a time. Come to lunch with me and we will talk of other things."

"Oh no, I couldn't. Thank you but I have work to do."

"But you must eat," he coaxed. "We will go to a *trattoria,* a fast food restaurant, is not that what you call it?"

Holly finally agreed to go, although she was unsure of the wisdom of it. But in the back of her mind was the idea that she might somehow find out the truth of the matter.

The restaurant that he took her to was by no means a fast food place. It had linen tablecloths and subdued lighting but it couldn't be called intimate either. A buzz of talk and laughter filled the long room which was packed to the rafters. This was evidently a popular restaurant.

True to his word, Mario didn't refer to the troubling matter of the contested article. Instead, he told her funny stories that made her laugh and although he was attentive, he never overstepped the bounds of propriety.

They were having coffee when two men stopped at their table and greeted Mario with a rapid spate of Italian. He introduced Holly, explaining that she spoke only English. They politely switched to her language, the younger of the two saying appreciatively, "Trust Mario to have the prettiest girl in the room."

"Do not dig my grave deeper, Carlo, Holly already has a bad opinion of me."

"Of Mario?" his friend asked incredulously. "No, no, he is a, how you call it, a pussycat."

"I think you have the wrong animal," Holly grinned. "In my country we call it a wolf."

At Mario's urging, the two men joined them for coffee and Amaretto and he explained Holly's connection with the magazine.

"You are fortunate to have the services of Mario," the older man who was named Nuncio, advised her. "He is the top journalist in all of Roma."

Mario appeared embarrassed. "What can you do with good friends?" he shrugged.

"But it is the truth," they both chimed in.

"No, no, it is too much! Holly will think that I have arranged this," he protested deprecatingly.

When it was time to go back to the office, Holly was actually reluctant. It had been a most enjoyable lunch. She hadn't found out anything about the disputed article but she had gained an insight into Mario's character. He was the kind of man who could inspire fierce loyalty in his friends and that wasn't consistent with the picture she had received at work.

That night at dinner, she sounded Slade out tentatively. He was so busy during the day that she almost never saw him except for brief glimpses in the hallway. Holly looked forward to the evenings when he took her to dinner because it was the only time she got to spend with him and she felt a brief pang, wishing they shared a suite as they had in London. But this was safer.

As she looked at his long lean body in the elegant suit, Holly knew that if there were no barriers between them, it would only be a matter of time until she threw herself in his arms. It was increasingly difficult to sit opposite him and make polite conversation when her eyes kept returning to his mouth, remembering the passionate way it had possessed hers.

Pushing those fruitless thoughts to the back of her mind, Holly said, "I had lunch with Mario today."

Slade's expression immediately darkened. "I thought I told you to stay away from him."

"No, you didn't. You only told me what you thought of him."

"And that wasn't enough for you?" he asked angrily.

"Slade, I don't think you're being objective. I know this lawsuit is very worrying but it's possible that Mario is really innocent."

"You've decided that after just one lunch?" he asked sardonically. "Mario is even better than I gave him credit for—or you're more naive."

"That's a rotten thing to say! Why do you have to bring everything down to a personal level?"

"Because I've seen men like Mario operate and I've seen silly little girls like you fall like ripe fruit."

"That's the most insulting thing I've ever heard!" she exclaimed passionately. "Just because I ask you to keep an open mind, you think I'm falling in love with the man."

A great stillness descended over him. "Are you?"

"Of course not," she said impatiently, "but I've seen facets of his personality that you haven't."

"No doubt," he said savagely. "Mario saves his charm for gullible women."

"What you're saying is that I'm so stupid I don't recognize a snow job when I see one isn't that it?" she asked furiously.

"You said it, I didn't."

"Well, if I'm so ignorant about people, why did you hire me?" she challenged.

There were deep lines running from Slade's nose to his mouth. "I didn't realize you had blind spots."

"That's your interpretation," she flared. "I told you in San Francisco that I was going to voice my opinion no matter what you thought."

"All right, you've voiced it, now let's drop the subject."

"No, I won't! Why are you being so dogmatic?"

"And why are you getting so involved?"

"I thought that was what I was hired for."

Slade's expression was enigmatic as he looked at her flushed face. "I don't want to pull rank on you but I must remind you that I'm the boss."

"If you're so omniscient then what do you need me for?" she cried.

"Are you going to quit your job again? I'm getting a little tired of that broken record," he said ominously.

"Don't worry, I wouldn't give you the satisfaction. I'm going to stick around like a thorn in your side until I prove to you that Mario is innocent!"

They finished their meal in silence. Slade called for the check and not a word was spoken on the short ride back to the hotel, where he had bid her a curt good-night at her door.

Now as Holly was lying in bed and staring at the ceiling, she wondered what had possessed her. Mario's guilt or innocence meant nothing to her except as it affected Slade. He was the one whose approval she coveted. She had only wanted to help, but Slade's derogatory inference that she was dumb enough to fall for any experienced man's blandishments had made her want to strike back. And now they were at sword's points again. Was this the end of the tentative relationship that had been developing between them? Holly had accepted the fact that she could never have his love, but could she live without his friendship?

Turning her face into the pillow, she wept like a lost child.

Chapter Twelve

Holly awoke the next morning determined to make up with Slade. She would apologize and admit that she had acted childishly. Nothing was worth the misery of being out of favor with him.

Dressing quickly in a dressmaker suit of soft gray with a pale yellow blouse, she hurried, hoping to catch him at breakfast but he wasn't in the dining room. Never mind, she would go to his office and maybe after she had made her confession he would take her in his arms and smooth her hair in that gentle way and tell her that he was sorry about the disagreement too.

But when Holly got to the office his secretary told her, "Mr. Rockwell telephoned and said he wouldn't be in today."

"He hasn't gone out of town has he?" Holly asked fearfully.

"No, he left a number where he could be reached if anything important came up." The woman reached for a slip of paper on her desk. "Here it is, would you like to have it?"

"Oh, yes, please!"

Back in her own office, Holly reached eagerly for the

phone and then paused. Suppose he was with somebody and couldn't talk? Well, that might be all for the best. He would have to listen to her without interruption and they couldn't argue, although Holly promised herself that was something they would never do again if she could help it. Smiling happily, she dialed the number and listened to the telephone ring.

"Bianca Film Studios," a voice announced in her ear.

Holly slowly replaced the receiver. It had never occurred to her that he would be with Monique Duvall but it should have. They had met her at the party on Sunday and this was Tuesday. Actually, his restraint was commendable, she thought wryly. Their first day at the magazine had been hectic and this was probably the first time he could break away.

Holly sat down at her desk and began to work on a personality profile she was developing. All of her movements were carefully deliberate as though she were made of glass and might shatter at the slightest impact.

A shadow fell across the desk and she looked up into Mario's smiling face. "Such industry on so beautiful a day," he teased. "Come out with me and we will have coffee at a sidewalk cafe and enjoy the sunshine."

Holly looked dispassionately at the man who had caused her such heartbreak. No, that wasn't fair. It was true that Mario was the cause of her quarrel with Slade but in any event, he would be with Monique now.

"I'm sorry, I have work to do," she told him.

"I know Americans take their work very seriously but even in your country you have, what do you call it—the coffee break?"

She looked at her watch and shook her head. "Not this early."

There was laughter in the dark eyes. "Everything must be on schedule? So much time to work, so much time to eat, so much time to make love? I do not think I would like that."

Holly smiled unwillingly. "No, you would have trouble with your priorities."

"Ah, you see, I have made you smile. When I came in here you looked oh so sad. I am good for you," he stated positively.

"I wish I could bottle your self-confidence, Mario. I could make a fortune selling it."

He was undaunted. "I only tell the truth—always," he added.

Holly was reminded of her rash promise to prove Mario innocent. She looked into his guileless, open face. *Was* he innocent? If he wasn't, she had made the world's biggest donkey of herself and that didn't bear thinking about.

"I really do have a lot of work," she said pointedly.

"*Scusami,* I will get out of your tresses. Is that the way you say it?"

"That's close enough," she smiled.

"But only for today," he warned. "Tonight I hope you will do me the honor of having dinner with me."

Holly shook her head. "I'm afraid that's impossible," she said firmly.

Going out with Mario would be like waving a red flag in front of Slade. He had made his feelings abundantly clear and she wasn't going to jeopardize their reconciliation by doing anything so foolish.

Mario was difficult to convince but she eventually got rid of him and settled down to a day that seemed endless.

After work, Holly rushed back to the hotel and made

straight for Slade's room but her knock went unanswered. She checked with the switchboard but there were no messages from him. As if there would be. Why would he bother to think of her when he had the luscious Monique in his arms, Holly thought mockingly, but the logic did nothing for the sharp pain in her chest.

After a solitary dinner, Holly came back to her room just in time to hear the phone ringing and she ran to it joyously.

"Holly, you sound breathless. Did I get you away from something?"

The elation died. "Alan, how are you?"

"Missing you like the devil," he said ruefully. "How are things going in Rome?"

"Pretty good but I need you terribly, Alan."

"That's good to hear," he said huskily.

Too late, Holly realized he had misinterpreted her impulsive statement. "I could sure use your help at the magazine," she said quickly.

"I knew it was too good to be true," he said dryly. "Is there anybody special who is giving you a hard time? Just name the villain and I'll flatten him when I get there," he joked.

"No, it isn't that exactly. I . . . Alan, do you know a man named Mario Donitelli?"

"Oh, that one." The humor vanished from his voice. "Stay away from him, Holly, he's no good."

She felt a stirring of irritation. Mario wasn't all *that* bad. The way everyone was down on him you'd think he was public enemy number one. "You're as bad as Slade! The two of you must think I'm a little country girl."

"Oh, oh," Alan groaned.

"What's that supposed to mean?" she demanded.

"Look, honey, I know he's a very handsome guy and he's very hot stuff with the ladies but—"

"I couldn't be less interested in him personally," she interrupted. "I only want to evaluate him in a business sense."

"That should be easy," Alan said succinctly. "Do you know about the lawsuit he's embroiled us in?"

"Yes, I do but Mario has an explanation for that. He says—"

"Listen, Holly, I don't want to argue with you," he broke in. "I don't even want to talk about him. Tell me what you've been doing. I miss you, honey."

Holly allowed him to change the subject because what was the use in pursuing it? He had a closed mind just like Slade.

They talked for awhile and after she hung up, Holly felt even more restless. Wandering out onto the terrace, she looked over the beautiful city. Slade's windows were dark and a stab of anger jabbed her. It was London all over again, only the cast of mistresses had changed.

Well, this time it was going to be different! She wasn't going to pine away like some rejected little waif. Slade might not find her attractive but Mario did. Tomorrow she would ask him if his invitation still stood.

Mario was ecstatic that she had changed her mind and the next evening, Holly dressed very carefully. She selected a black full-skirted organza dress with a deep U-neckline made more dramatic by the white ruffles that outlined it. White ruffles also cuffed the long narrow sleeves and a pair of spike-heeled black sandals complimented her slim legs.

Mario's glowing eyes made the effort worthwhile. "You look like a *principessa, mi amore,*" he breathed and his admiration was such a balm to her wounded spirit that she didn't discourage him.

After dinner, Mario took her dancing and as he held her close, Holly waited hopefully for an emotion that didn't come. Why could Slade make her tremble just by catching her eye across a room, yet she felt absolutely nothing with her entire body pressed against Mario's? He was handsome, he was charming, he was good company—what on earth was the matter with her?

"I am so happy that you have changed your mind and I hope you realize that this is only the opening gun in my campaign," he murmured in her ear.

"My, that sounds ominous. What campaign is that?"

"The one to make you fall in love with my city."

"Only your city?" she inquired dryly.

"If you would choose to extend the privilege to one of its citizens, I would not mind," he said throatily.

Holly laughed. "Mario, you don't have to trot out the whole seduction bit for me. I'm sure Italian girls expect it but I don't so save your energy."

He seemed hurt. "You think I was giving you a . . . what do you say, a line?"

"I *know* you were giving me a line but it isn't necessary. Let's just be friends and enjoy each other's company."

He ran a finger gently down the curve of her cheek. "Whatever you say, *mi amorosa,* but know this, I could feel very differently."

Mario's admiration was apparent but not intrusive and Holly had a very good time. They laughed together and he never mentioned the magazine which she appreciated. Slade and Alan were really hung up on that lawsuit, but Mario's very insouciance seemed to point to his innocence.

It was late when she returned to the hotel but Slade's

windows were still in darkness. He ought to get a rebate on his bill, she decided bitterly.

The next day, Slade appeared in her office. "Where were you last night?" he asked without preamble.

She looked at his beloved long rangy body and her heart began to race but she remembered where he had been for two days. Banishing the hateful picture of those long legs twined around the voluptuous Monique, she said coldly, "Out."

"I know that," he scowled, "I'm asking you where?"

"I don't think that's any of your concern."

Slade rounded the desk and pulled her out of her chair, his fingers digging savagely into her soft skin. "I asked you a question and you damn well better answer it."

Holly was shaken by his violence. "I was out to dinner with Mario if you must know."

He released her and looked down contemptuously. "Is that the best you can do?"

"We can't all go out with movie stars," she said defiantly, although inside Holly felt sick. Where was all the tenderness she knew he was capable of? All expended on Monique? Those cold gray eyes were ripping her to shreds.

"What makes you think I . . ." Slade broke off and turned away. "I have neither the time nor the inclination to discuss it with you. I just stopped by to say that I'll be tied up for a couple of days but I'll expect your reports on my desk."

He was gone before she could say anything and Holly looked bitterly at his retreating back. Monique was evidently even more alluring than Lady Dillingham. At least in London, Slade had made a little time for business, fitting Marsha in rather than giving her all his time. But when Monique whistled, he answered. That must be what he wanted though, because no woman could lead him around by the nose.

Mario was in and out of her office, although Holly thanked her lucky stars that he hadn't been there when Slade appeared. He showed up regularly with a bunch of violets or a delicious chunky chocolate bar, not elaborate gifts, but thoughtful little tokens and Holly was increasingly grateful. She realized it was a concerted effort to get in her good graces, but after Slade's abrasiveness any attention was welcome.

Mario had once more elicited her promise to go out with him and he stood in the doorway blowing her a kiss. "Till tonight, *mi amore.* I will find it difficult to get through the day."

Holly was shaking her head over his Latin dramatics when her secretary entered. "Yes, Rosa, did you want to talk to me?"

The woman spread her hands helplessly. "I have something . . ." she paused and then said jerkily, "I do not know quite how to say this."

"Why don't you sit down?" Holly said pleasantly. "Please don't be nervous. I'm interested in anything you have to tell me."

Rosa perched uncertainly on the edge of a chair. "It is about Mario."

Mario again! "Yes, go on, what about him?"

"I think I should warn you that he—" Rosa stopped and then continued with difficulty. "You are very young and he is very experienced."

Holly sighed. Everyone seemed bent on protecting her. "I'm grateful for your concern, Rosa, but I'm well aware that Mario is what we call in my country a wolf."

Rosa looked at her obliquely. "It is not your virtue I am concerned about, *signorina.*"

Holly's surprise was mirrored in her voice. "What is it you're trying to tell me then?"

Rosa's face was a study in conflicting emotions. She was a very private person, but it was evident that she felt strongly enough about whatever was on her mind to overcome her usual reticence.

"Mario is a corrupt man!" The words fairly erupted. "He has no scruples and once caught, he will fight viciously, not caring who he destroys in order to protect himself."

Holly was shaken by the vindictiveness in the woman's face. "You are entitled to your opinion, of course, but I fail to see how this affects me."

In spite of her attempt to hide it, Holly's repugnance came through and Rosa shrugged. "I thought you should be warned," she said tonelessly. Without another word, she turned and left the room.

Holly was more disturbed by her secretary's indictment than by all of Alan or Slade's rantings and ravings. What could make this quiet woman such a bitter enemy of Mario's? Was it possible that they were right? But not everyone in the office felt that way. Many of the female employees adored him and Holly had seen the loyalty of his friends, Carlo and Nuncio. If only everything were completely black or totally white!

She was very troubled at dinner that night and, although she tried to hide it, Mario wasn't fooled. "Something is bothering you, *amorosa,*" he said softly. "Would you like to tell me about it?"

She gave him a bright smile. "You're imagining things. I'm having a marvelous time."

"Do not try to fool me," he said gently. "Tell me what is making you sad."

"Something *is* bothering me, Mario," she sighed.

"Can you tell me why Rosa Vitale . . . well . . . why you're not her favorite person?" she finished delicately.

Something flickered in his eyes and was gone before she could identify it. "She has been telling you bad things about me?"

"Well, let's just say she's not exactly one of your fans and I want to know why."

He shrugged. "I cannot defend myself against a woman."

"You *must,* Mario," Holly said sharply. "What is all this about?"

"I am a Latin and it goes against my every instinct to speak badly of a woman but if you insist." He sighed. "I wish there were some way to say this kindly. Rosa was once a very beautiful woman and there is no greater tragedy than for a lady to lose that beauty. Sometimes she will refuse to accept the evidence that her mirror gives." He looked down at his hands. "Rosa sought to renew her confidence in my arms but . . ." he spread his hands. "I felt great compassion for her but I could not."

Holly felt a wave of pity sweep over her. Poor Rosa! How terrible it must be to clutch so desperately after youth that you offered yourself to a younger man who rejected you.

Mario looked at her downcast face and put his hand over hers. "Let us talk of happier things," he said gently.

It was a relief to lose herself in work the following day and a further blessing that Slade wasn't around, Holly told herself. Let him steep himself in Monique's charms, maybe it would put him in a better mood, she thought viciously.

She was walking through the lobby of the hotel after another grueling day when she heard her name called.

"Victor, how nice to see you! When did you get into town?"

"A couple of days ago but Slade and I have been holed up for two days working on this lawsuit and I've barely seen the light of day. How's it going, Holly?"

"Fine," she answered absently. If Slade had been with Victor then he couldn't have been with Monique. Maybe that accounted for his foul temper.

"How about having dinner with me here in the hotel?" Victor asked. "I've been subsisting on sandwiches and rotten coffee and I feel the need of some decent food, not to mention charming company," he added gallantly.

"I'd love it, Victor," Holly said sincerely.

They were having a drink and some friendly conversation when Slade joined them. Pulling out a chair, he scowled at Holly. "What are you doing here? Did your Latin lothario have to make the rounds of his harem?"

She scowled back. "You can be sure that I wouldn't be here if I'd known you were going to be."

"Don't fight, children," Victor sighed. "I've had a hard day and I was looking forward to a peaceful dinner."

"Perhaps I'd better leave then," Holly said distantly.

But as she prepared to slide her chair back, Slade caught her wrist. "Stay where you are," he commanded.

His fingers were bruising her soft skin and one look at the steely glint in his eyes convinced her that he meant what he said. She subsided sulkily and was relieved when he removed his hand. Even in anger, Slade's touch had the power to move her.

Menus were presented and after they had ordered, Victor turned to Slade, evidently continuing a discussion. "I still think we ought to put up a fight."

Slade shot an oblique look at Holly and said, "Let's drop it for now shall we?"

Victor shrugged. "You're the boss." Turning to Holly, he said, "Have you had a chance to see anything of Rome?"

Holly busied herself with her soup. "Yes, we got here on Saturday morning and we . . . I saw quite a bit."

"Two days in Rome can only scratch the surface but it's a start," Victor said. "Did you enjoy it?"

Holly looked up to find Slade staring at her expressionlessly. All of his kindness in taking her to see places he'd been to a million times came back to swamp her and a lump rose in her throat. "Yes, it was wonderful," she said, unable to tear her eyes away from Slade's.

"When you've had enough of antiquity, you ought to get Slade to take you to the Bianca Film Studios," Victor said. "I was out there with him and it's a real experience. Of course, it can't measure up to the Colosseum but it has some of the same flavor of the Christians being fed to the lions." He shook his head ruefully. "Those movie people are something else. Slade, I really think you ought to reconsider—"

"Where is the waiter?" Slade cut in smoothly. "Holly's wine glass is empty."

He didn't want to talk about the studio and it was understandable, she thought miserably. Slade's private life was very much his own. For that matter, she didn't want to talk about it either. Visions of the sensuous Monique were conducive to indigestion.

Slade's attitude softened markedly toward her and the rest of the dinner was very amicable. Of course just being with him was an event and, although Holly tried to steel herself against his potent attraction, it was a lost cause.

They all went up in the elevator together. Victor said good night and went to his room down the hall but Slade paused at Holly's door. He hesitated and she had the feeling that he wanted to say something. She glanced up tremulously, every nerve ending aware of this handsome, masculine man looming over her. If he made the slightest move toward her, Holly knew she would launch herself into his arms, pressing her softness against his hard length. A delicious warmth spread through her and her lips parted involuntarily at the thought.

Slade stiffened and drew a sharp breath. "Good night, Holly," he said firmly.

He quickly walked the few steps to his room and disappeared before her eyes. Holly slowly closed her own door and leaned against it desolately.

After preparing for bed, she climbed in and pulled the covers up with a sigh. But sleep refused to come and after trying several different positions and twisting the sheets into an impossible tangle, Holly gave up. With her arms crossed behind her head, she stared at the ceiling for a while and then got up and put on a dressing gown.

Crossing to the French windows, she stepped out onto the terrace. Maybe some fresh air would clear her head of all the hurtful thoughts.

A voice spoke out of the darkness and Holly started violently. "Is anything the matter?" Slade asked.

The tip of a cigarette glowed in the blackness and she could just make out his dark bulk. "No, I . . . I couldn't sleep."

He walked toward her and she could see the gleam of white pajama bottoms and the contrast of his bare chest against the black silk robe. His face was in shadow though and she couldn't see his expression. "You should be tired, you worked hard today."

"So did you," she pointed out.

"Maybe it's being in Rome that's unsettling." There was a smile in his voice. "They say Paris is the city of lovers, but I would say this one has a lot going for it."

Holly looked out over the blinking lights. "I suppose you can fall in love anywhere."

Slade became very still. "Is that what you did?" he asked softly.

No, she wanted to answer, I fell in love in San Francisco—the first time I saw you. Holly turned so the moonlight didn't fall quite so clearly on her expressive face. "Falling in and out of love is for teenagers," she said carefully.

"That's merely sexual attraction. I was talking about a deeper emotion."

He was standing so close that she could feel the warmth of his body and his powerful magnetism was weaving its usual spell. It was all she could do to keep from reaching out to touch the crisp hair on that broad chest. She longed to put her arms around him inside his robe and spread her hands over his smooth muscled back. Drawing a shuddering breath, Holly averted her head.

"He's no good, you know," Slade said tautly.

"What?" Her bewildered eyes flew to his face and then she realized that he was talking about Mario. Sudden blinding anger filled her. She was melting with love for this dynamic, virile man, actually trembling with her need for him and all he had on his mind was that stupid Mario! "You never quit do you?" she asked bitterly, turning away so he wouldn't see the tears that threatened.

But Slade grabbed her by the shoulders, whirling her back to him. "And you never listen do you?"

"I've heard all I want to hear! When you get on someone's case you never let go." Holly's hurt was prompting her to lash out at him and Mario was just a good excuse.

Slade's fingers bit deeper. "I'd like to shake some sense into that stupid little head of yours," he grated.

"And if you weren't so darn big, I'd like to shake some sense into yours!"

They stared furiously at each other, but suddenly the angry emotion that crackled between them subtly changed. His head was so close that she could see the dilated pupils in his gray eyes and her heart skipped erratically as Slade's hands loosened and began to move tentatively over her shoulders.

It was a temptation to sway toward him but Holly wanted him so badly that she sensed danger. The danger that she might blurt out her love for this unattainable man. Offer him one more time the love he didn't want.

At her imperceptible backward movement, Slade's face hardened and he thrust her away. "I'm going to bed," he flung out savagely and strode away, slamming the French door.

Chapter Thirteen

Holly had a blistering headache the next morning and it was an effort to concentrate on the papers that littered her desk. Massaging her aching temples, she reflected that lack of sleep didn't help. It seemed she had just managed to doze off when the alarm clock summoned her to another nerve-racking day.

She was making little headway when Gina, one of the younger secretaries, popped into her office. "Oh, Miss Holbrooke, I was hoping Mr. Rockwell was in here," she said breathlessly.

"No, I'm afraid not. Is there something I could do for you?"

The girl shook her head. "I have to locate him right away, Miss Monique Duvall is on the telephone." She rolled her eyes expressively. "I would recognize that voice anywhere—such sex appeal!"

She was gone in a flash and Holly looked after the excited girl, thinking bitter thoughts. Slade would be unavailable again today no doubt. His lady love was sounding the mating call.

Mario arrived soon after, right on the schedule he had established for himself, and Holly greeted him with exasperation. "I don't know how you ever get any work done when you're always in my office."

"If I saw more of you outside of business, I would not have to pursue you here," he said unrepentently.

Holly laughed in spite of herself. "Mario, you are nothing but a grown-up child."

He gave her a provocative look. "Do not believe it for a moment, *amore.*"

She saw a great deal of him over the next week. Mario was persistent and Holly allowed herself to be persuaded without too much objection. Before she knew it, he was monopolizing all her time, but it was better than sitting alone in her room agonizing over Slade. Mario was good company and at least she was getting to see a great deal of Rome's night life.

Besides dinner and dancing, he took her to movies and one memorable night to hear *Otello* at the beautiful late-nineteenth-century Teatro dell'Opera with its effective red and white decor. It was performed with typical Italian gusto and the elaborate multitiered interior of the elegant opera house was the proper setting for such a colorful production.

Another night they crossed the Tiber River to the Trastevere section and went to a picturesque old tavern with ancient Roman wine cellars and centuries old brick walls. The attraction here was surprisingly enough, modern jazz.

Mario was anxious to show her the city he loved, taking her to places off the beaten track, and Holly knew she was experiencing a Rome that not many tourists were fortunate enough to see. When she tried to express her thanks, he kissed her hand and looked smolderingly into her eyes, telling her in florid phrases how much more he would like to do for her. Holly tried to discourage what she considered a phony romantic response, but she gradually began to wonder if he could possibly be sincere.

Outside of some passionate kisses, he had never tried to make determined love to her, but something happened one evening after they had been seeing each other steadily for over a week that indicated Mario might really be serious. They were on their way home when he stopped the car in a darkened spot a block from the hotel.

The moonlight was streaming in, giving his face a cruel, hawklike look and for a moment, Holly was disconcerted. There was something different about him that bothered her. It was more than just a feeling that he was going to kiss her. She didn't really mind Mario's kisses, finding them pleasant enough, although they didn't set her on fire the way Slade's did, but the imperceptible change that had come over him made her uncomfortable.

Before she could tell him that she would like to go home, Mario grabbed her and began to force her lips apart with such ardor that Holly became truly alarmed. Then his hands moved over her body in a practiced assault and she squirmed with disgust, pushing hard against his chest.

To her relief, he released her immediately, capturing her hands and covering them with kisses. "Forgive me, my darling, but you are so beautiful I could no longer control myself."

"It's no big deal, just part of the grand tour," Holly said, trying to make light of it. "You probably thought it was expected, but if it's all right with you I'll stick to something less torrid."

"You think I only want to satisfy my body?" he demanded.

"I'd rather not talk about it," she said uncomfortably.

"Yes, we *must* talk about it!" he exclaimed. "I cannot bear to have you think this of me."

She gave him a level look. "Mario, you are a very . . . um . . . virile man. Your reputation with women is well known so please don't try to insult my intelligence."

He gave an expressive shrug. "I am a man, I admit it. I have had my share of adventures, but never have I met a woman like you." He caressed her neck, his fingers roaming to the sensitive spot behind her ear. "You are very special to me, *amorosa.*"

His words left her unmoved. Did he think she was going to fall for that stale old line? "That's very nice, Mario and I'm flattered. Now will you take me home?"

He watched her intently. "You do not believe me. You think I want only to get you into my bed." Holly's cheeks were pink with embarrassment and she looked away but he cupped her chin in his palm. "Yes, I desire you, what red-blooded man would not? But I want more than that from you. I wish to possess not only your body but also your heart and soul—your *life!*" He gave a mournful little laugh. "I have never said that to any woman before and my poor mamma would be *infuriato* if she knew I saying this to an American girl."

Holly couldn't believe her ears. It almost sounded like he was saying he wanted to marry her. "Are you proposing to me?" she asked wonderingly.

He put his arms around her, drawing her head gently against his shoulder. She couldn't see his face but his voice was soft. "I do not have that privilege right now, *mi amore.* If you were my wife I would want to give you the moon for a wedding present but I must be practical. How could I do that if I am unemployed?"

She raised her head and gave him a startled look. "What are you talking about?"

He stroked her hair and smiled ruefully. "No, no, now is not the time to speak of it."

"I want to know what you mean, Mario." He shook his head but she said, "Yes, I insist."

"I should not have mentioned it." When she started to speak, he put his finger on her lips. "All right, my darling, you will find out tomorrow anyway. Mr. Rockwell has fired me."

"I don't believe it!"

"I could not either but it is true. It is the lawsuit of course. I am completely innocent but my enemies have brought me down," he said sadly.

"That's the most unfair thing I ever heard of," Holly stormed. "Magazines have been sued before but they always stand in back of their reporters."

"It is so and that is why I have wondered. . . ." His eyes were thoughtful. "Almost it seems as though Mr. Rockwell has something personal against me."

He sounded puzzled but Holly, knowing the truth of the matter, was furious. As one macho man to another, Slade couldn't bear the knowledge that Mario was equally successful with women. And the mistaken idea that Holly was attracted to Mario was insupportable to him. But the thought that Slade could use his power for such shameful ends was disgraceful.

"He won't get away with this!" Holly cried passionately. "I'll talk to him tomorrow."

"No, no, my love, I do not want to involve you in this."

"I *am* involved and I'm going to do something about it."

"I do not want you to jeopardize your own job."

"Don't worry about it," Holly said shortly. "When I first signed on I told Slade I was going to speak my mind and he agreed."

"In that case . . ." Mario hesitated.

"It's time Mr. Rockwell faced up to a few plain facts," she said grimly. "I'm going to talk to him first thing in the morning."

Mario pressed her hand to his cheek. "I would be most grateful. All I desire is justice, but since he will not believe me, I am forced to let you be my representative." He gave her a melting look. "We will both benefit from his decision, *mi amore.*"

Holly stormed into the office the next morning prepared to do battle. Not waiting for Slade's secretary to announce her, she gave a perfunctory knock and flung open the door.

He was dictating into a recorder and he looked up with a raised eyebrow, but before he could say anything sarcastic she attacked. "I found out that you fired Mario."

"Good news travels fast," he said ironically.

Any hope for a peaceful discussion vanished which was what she expected but it only strengthened her resolve. "How could you do such an unconscionable thing?" she demanded.

"I'm afraid you have your priorities mixed. That's a question you should have asked your boyfriend."

His derisive attitude inflamed her. "That's what it's really about isn't it—the fact that Mario is attractive to women. What's the matter, do you feel threatened?" she challenged.

Slade sprang out of his chair and gripped the edge of the desk. "If you were a man, I'd knock you down for that!"

"A typically male reaction but it doesn't solve anything. How can you justify getting rid of him?"

There was a white line around his set mouth. "I wasn't aware that I had to justify myself to you."

"The great Slade Rockwell isn't accountable to anyone except God, is that it?"

He looked at her contemptuously. "Certainly not to an hysterical female who can't see anything wrong in a man sending a woman to do his begging for him."

"I'm not *begging,*" she denied hotly. "I'm asking for an explanation—one that is due *Mario,* but since you're too prejudiced to give it to him, I'm asking the question. How can you justify firing him?"

"How about a three-million-dollar lawsuit for starters?" Slade asked grimly.

"In our country a man is innocent until he's proven guilty. Why don't you at least wait for the outcome of the trial?"

"There isn't going to be a trial. We settled out of court."

Holly was taken aback. "But . . . but why?"

"Because we didn't have a hoot in hell of winning and we decided to cut our losses." Contempt etched deep lines in his face. "Your boyfriend isn't even a clever libeler—he didn't make any attempt to cover his tracks, depending no doubt on the power of the press to back up his lazy, sloppy investigative work—if you can call it that. But we don't operate that way."

"It wasn't his fault! You're putting the blame on the wrong person. Talk to Sophia Francesca, she's the one responsible. She was so ambitious to get ahead that she offered to help Mario on the story, supposedly without any reward. She's the one who is guilty of slipshod work. I'll admit he was gullible but he trusted her."

Slade looked at her almost with pity. "Sophia Francesca was assigned to this story along with Mario, but when it looked like it might turn into a headline grabber he cut her out. She happens to be a dedicated reporter with a lot of awards to her credit, not merely sexual scalps hanging from her belt."

"You always have to bring it back to a personal level don't you?" Holly cried. "Isn't it strange that you'll believe anything a woman tells you but not a man."

A wintery smile flickered over his granite face, not reaching the cold eyes. "Our present disagreement proves that I'm not necessarily prejudiced in that direction."

"That doesn't count. You never believe anything *I* say! But you go out of your way to look for women who have it in for Mario."

"Like Rosa Vitale?" he asked with an unpleasant smile.

"Yes, I suppose she's given you an earful too."

"Why don't you give me your version of what she has against Mario?"

"I wouldn't descend to your level," she said disdainfully.

"That's a cop-out, Holly. Tell me Mario's version of it since you have appointed yourself his champion."

Holly was loath to repeat the sordid little story but once challenged, she had to go through with it. When she had finished, Slade shook his head.

"I have to give him credit, he does concoct a good story—too bad he's not a fiction writer. Would you like to hear the real story? Rosa's husband was the assistant manager of a big hotel. There was a fire and several people were killed. Mario covered the story. There were irregularities in the safety measures and Antonio told Mario about them, asking for anonymity of course. He trusted Mario because he thought they were all friends; the three of them had shared many a drink together. Everyone had been speculating about the safety abuses, but Mario scored a scoop because he was the only one with quotes from an unimpeachable source. Antonio not only lost his job, he can't get another one in that industry."

"I don't believe you," Holly whispered.

He smiled mirthlessly. "Why don't you go talk to Antonio? He's doing janitorial work while he tries to figure out what to do with the rest of his life."

Holly's head was reeling and she felt tossed on a sea of uncertainty. Mario and Slade were pulling her in opposite directions. Which one could she trust? "You've always disliked Mario, isn't it possible that you've been misled?" she asked hesitantly.

"Oh, for God's sake, Holly, can you possibly be that naive? Or is he that great a lover?" Slade's face was tortured. "After Alan introduced you to sex did you go on to more ambitious things?"

Holly flushed a deep rose and she confronted him furiously. "You have a rotten, evil mind! I don't have to tell you this but I will—I haven't slept with Mario and for your information, he isn't the kind of man you think he is. He wants to *marry* me!"

Slade's face registered his incredulity. "You've got to be kidding!"

"Is it so unbelievable that a man should want to marry me? They aren't all like you. But you managed to toss a monkey wrench into the works didn't you?" she commented bitterly.

He seemed to be in shock. "What are you talking about?" he asked almost absently.

"If Mario is out of work we can scarcely get married can we?"

"Is that his observation or yours?" He watched her intently.

"What difference does it make, it's true."

"It makes a lot of difference. Tell me exactly what he said that sent you here to plead his case so eloquently." All of Slade's attention was focused on her answer.

"He didn't send me here," she said impatiently. "He . . . we just . . . he merely explained that he couldn't ask me to marry him if he didn't have a job."

Slade closed his eyes for a moment in an effort to control himself. "I realize you're young and inexperienced, but how can you be such a little idiot? Don't you see that he's using you?"

Desolation seeped into her bones. "You can't imagine any man wanting me can you?" she asked in a voice thick with tears.

He put his hands on her shoulders and said gently, "I think any man would be fortunate to have your love, but Mario isn't a man he's a slimy gutter rat."

Holly thought she detected pity in his eyes and it dried her incipient tears. "You're talking about my fiancé," she said coldly.

"You mean you're going to marry him?" he asked ominously.

Hearing it put into words made her feel almost faint. The man she loved was standing a few inches away but he could never be hers. Even so, how could she marry anyone else? But she was committed. If she confessed now that Mario meant nothing to her, she would look like a fool. Slade must never know of her hopeless love for him.

"Yes, I'm going to marry him," she said, although she felt as though she were suffocating.

"Then I hope you're prepared to support him,"

Slade said savagely, "because I'm going to see to it that he's blacklisted in every publication in Rome, and not only that—in all of Italy if I can manage it!"

They faced each other furiously. "I'm not surprised, it's just what I would have expected, but we'll get by in spite of you. And by the way, don't bother to fire me because I quit!" She whirled around and ran out of the room, the tears finally coming, but thankfully too late for Slade to see.

Holly's momentum carried her down the stairs and out the door, but as she walked along the sidewalk she rejected what she had to do next. Her defiant intention to marry Mario was ludicrous. How could she marry a man she didn't love? But how could she face Slade's cynical derision if she didn't? Would it be such a terrible alternative after all?

Holly knew that she would never love anyone except Slade, but going through life alone was a terrible prospect. Mario was kind and generous and if she tried hard, she could be a good wife to him. Still, her footsteps faltered and she had to force herself to hail a taxi.

The piece of paper Mario had given her with his address written on it was clutched tightly in her hand. Holly held onto it like a talisman, but it didn't help. She still felt as though the cab were a tumbrel and she was on her way to the guillotine. Was she insane to be doing this? But even as she leaned forward to tell the driver she had changed her mind, a vision of Slade's mocking face rose up before her and she settled back in her seat.

Mario answered the doorbell on the first ring, drawing her eagerly into the apartment. "I did not dare hope you would come so soon, my love. Have you seen Mr. Rockwell?"

"Yes, I saw him."

He inspected her grim face and the light died out of his eyes but he managed a tentative smile. "It went well?"

"I'm afraid not, Mario."

"What exactly did he say?" he asked carefully.

Her failed mission weighed heavily on Holly and she exploded into frustrated speech. "Slade Rockwell is the most bigoted man I've ever run across! He is a close minded, pigheaded—"

"Tell me what happened," he cut in impatiently.

"I went into his office this morning—very calmly," she emphasized. "He had no right to call me hysterical, no right at all."

"Never mind that, what did he *say?*"

Holly knew she had to edit Slade's words severely. "He was very angry because evidently his attorneys told him they didn't have a chance of winning the lawsuit and it had better be settled out of court. Slade is a fighter," she conceded grudgingly, "and I guess it went against his grain."

Mario shrugged carelessly. "He has so much money that he will not miss it."

It struck a jarring note but Holly attempted to dismiss it. "That's true but it wasn't calculated to put him in a good mood."

"Did you not tell him that it was not my fault?" he demanded. "Did you not put the blame on Sophia?"

"Yes, but he didn't believe me. Slade claims that Sophia is a very competent journalist. He said she was assigned to the story with you." Mario loosed a rapid stream of Italian that sounded very much like a string of oaths. "It isn't true is it, Mario?"

Ignoring her hesitant question, he said tautly, "Could you not convince him otherwise? I thought you had influence with him."

"Nobody has influence with Slade," she said dismally. "But it wasn't just Sophia's word against yours, there was Rosa Vitale too."

Mario became suddenly alert, like an animal sensing danger. "What does she have to do with this?"

"Rosa told Slade about something you had supposedly done to her husband." Holly looked at him in startled appraisal. "You didn't tell me she was married."

"What difference does it make?" He dismissed the fact carelessly. "What matters is that——" he said an Italian word that sounded vile, "dug my grave. She has been waiting for her revenge and now she has gotten it—in spades as you Americans say."

"But it isn't true is it?" Holly begged. "You didn't do what Slade said you did to her husband?"

"Women!" The way he said it sounded like a curse. "You can never count on them. Like you." He looked at Holly scornfully. "I invested much time in you. You led me to believe that you had influence with Rockwell but you misled me."

His face was ugly with anger and it was like seeing Humpty Dumpty crack into a thousand pieces. Once the mask was gone, Holly saw him for what he was, a treacherous man with minimal talents who traded on his sex appeal to achieve dubious ends.

"You used me," she whispered, unconsciously echoing Slade's words. "You gave me that big whirl just to ensure that I would be your friend at court."

His smile was sharklike. "Why should you complain? You got more out of it than I did. All that time I lavished on you was wasted—all wasted!" The smile vanished and he slammed his fist into his palm.

Holly stared at him in horror. "And if I had succeeded? How far were you prepared to go? Last night you intimated that you wanted to marry me. What would have happened if I had secured your job for you?"

His eyes swept contemptuously over her. "Once I had what I wanted, you would have been expendable and I would have dealt with you easily. You were an easy mark. A few love words and you were putty in my hands. Could you really believe that I would *marry* you?"

She looked at him with loathing. "The only thing that makes me feel a little better is that Slade saw through you even if I didn't and you'll probably never work in the media again. Of course, you can always live off of women can't you, Mario?" As a confident smile took possession of his face, she paused and then said tauntingly, "But have you ever thought about what's going to happen when you get too old?"

The uncertainty that clouded his eyes as her barb hit home was the only satisfaction Holly had as she fled from the apartment. His hateful words followed her like a swarm of insects and she was stung painfully by them. How could she have been such a fool?

Holly knew deep in her heart that she could never have gone through with marrying Mario, but the depth of his perfidy was shattering. She hadn't pretended even to herself that she loved him, but how could she have misjudged him so completely? Slade must be right, she was hopelessly naive and inexperienced. When it came to men she was indeed the village idiot.

In the taxi going back to the hotel, Holly huddled in a corner and tried to pull herself together. Her life was in ruins and she had to decide what to do next. One thing she was sure of, she wouldn't go crawling back to Slade. That was what he expected, but she couldn't bear to let him know what a fool she had been. Not that she could keep it from him, but at least she didn't have to face him and see the derision in his eyes.

There was only one choice open to her and that was to go home. Now that she was no longer working for Slade, there was no reason to stay. She certainly couldn't expect him to go on paying for her room, and it was best to leave before she was asked to. Not that she thought he would actually do that but, then again, she was certainly no authority on the male animal!

When she arrived at the hotel, Holly's first stop was at the front desk. "I'm checking out. Will you please send a bellman up in fifteen minutes and I'll need a taxi."

The desk clerk raised his eyebrows. "Certainly, Miss Holbrooke." He hesitated and then said, "This is very sudden. I hope nothing is wrong?"

"Oh, no, everything has been just . . . dandy." But her lopsided smile didn't quite make it.

In her room, she dragged her suitcase out of the far recesses of the closet and threw things in helter-skelter with no attempt at neatness. Speed was the only consideration because it had suddenly occurred to her that Slade might come looking for her. Not because he cared one way or another. Holly was well aware that he considered her a nuisance—or worse after today. But he had this crazy notion that she wasn't able to take care of herself and he might even insist on taking her to the airport. Probably to be sure he was rid of her, she told herself bitterly, and a long lecture was something she just couldn't handle right now.

Her fears were groundless, although when she got to the airport another problem presented itself. In her hurry to get away, it hadn't occurred to her that airplanes didn't run like city buses. The next flight for San Francisco didn't leave for eight hours.

"Eight hours!" she echoed. "That's terrible! I simply have to get out of Rome."

The reservation clerk obligingly looked through thick books of schedules but the result was the same. No other airline left any sooner. "You could take a flight to Paris or London," he finally offered helpfully. "Perhaps they can give you better connections."

"Oh, yes, that's a wonderful idea! Just get me out of here."

For once, Holly was in luck. A plane for London was on the point of departure and after the clerk had made a hurried phone call, she ran down the ramp as though a thousand devils were pursuing her.

In a way, her precipitous departure was a blessing. There was no time for either regrets or postmortems. Almost as soon as she had buckled her seat belt, the plane taxied into position and thundered down the runway. As it soared steeply into the sky, Holly looked down at the beautiful ancient city.

Slade was down there somewhere. Was he breathing a sigh of relief—or was he laughing at the silly girl who had made such a mess of things? Holly closed her eyes as a sharp pain stabbed through her.

Chapter Fourteen

The plane swooped in low for a landing at San Francisco International Airport and Holly watched listlessly as it seemed to barely clear the water before touching lightly down on the long runway. Her eyes felt dry after hours of staring out of the window at the endless ocean and her whole body felt stiff.

It had been a long trip. She had tried to sleep, as much to rest her troubled mind as her weary body, but the seats in tourist class were cramped and she couldn't get comfortable. Inevitably, that raised memories of the trip over—was it just a matter of weeks ago? The contrast could scarcely have been greater. That flight had started with champagne and high hopes and this one was ending in despair.

She had taken the small pillow the airline provided and tucked it under her head, trying to forget how Slade had held her on his lap and the way her body relaxed and snuggled into his arms with a feeling of belonging. The mere thought of it banished any hope of sleep.

After deplaning, everyone filed through customs and Holly dutifully stood in line, although she had nothing to declare. Passengers all around her were displaying the treasures they had bought in Europe, an incredible amount of merchandise ranging from genuine antiques to downright junk.

When Holly's turn came, the customs inspector looked at her disbelievingly. "You mean you didn't buy *anything* in Europe?"

It was ridiculous but he actually made her feel guilty. "I wasn't on vacation," she tried to explain. "I was working."

"No souvenirs at all?" the man persisted.

Suddenly Holly remembered that she did have one souvenir, a remembrance of happier times. The gold heart that Slade had given her was nestled inside her blouse and she slowly brought it out to show him. In a voice choked with tears she said, "This is all I have."

He waved her through, shaking his head incredulously. "Lady, I wish my wife was like you."

Holly hailed a cab outside the airport and gave directions to a downtown hotel. It felt strange to be going to a hotel in her own city but she didn't know where else to go. She had given up her apartment and, although there were friends she could have called, Holly didn't feel up to seeing anyone yet and having to face the inevitable curious questions that would arise.

She purposely chose a busy commercial hotel where she wasn't apt to run across anyone she knew. However, once she was settled in the characterless little room, Holly eyed it with dismay. What next? It was terrifying somehow to realize that no one knew her whereabouts. Or cared. No, that wasn't true, she mustn't over dramatize. She had a lot of friends and besides them, there *was* someone special who cared—Alan.

The thought of him was comforting and Holly had an

impulse to call him in New York, just to hear his voice. But even as she reached for the phone, something held her back. It wasn't fair to him. She didn't love Alan but he loved her. Holly knew that feeling the way she did now she might weaken and accept the proposal that would inevitably come after she had poured out her tale of woe. Alan deserved better than that.

Holly wandered over to the window and looked out at Union Square. The tiny scrap of park was surrounded by buildings and people were going about their business as though this were just an ordinary day. They all had a destination and a sense of purpose. She was the only one who seemed to be suspended in time like a butterfly caught in amber.

This nonsense has to stop, Holly told herself. She had to make some plans and the sooner the better. What were her priorities? First of all, she needed a job and a place to live. Then, of course, she would have to think about buying another car since she had sold her old one. The mere thought of all the decisions those things entailed drained her energy and Holly's slender body drooped like a wilting flower.

Then the solution presented itself. For weeks she had been surrounded by people, all pressuring her in one way or another and forcing her into impulsive actions that had proved disastrous. Before she made another mistake, it was time to find a quiet place and think things through for a change.

When she checked out just a few minutes later, the desk clerk clearly thought she was crazy but Holly was past caring. The hotel had a car rental agency in the lobby and in just a short time, she was driving over the Bay Bridge to Lake Tahoe, a mountain resort north of San Francisco. It was between seasons—after the winter skiing crowd had departed and before the summer people arrived—so there should be no trouble finding a place to rent. The wind blew through the open car window, whipping Holly's long hair around her shoulders and she inhaled deeply, feeling at peace for the first time in weeks.

The cabin she located was made to order for her purposes. It was set in the middle of a dense stand of tall pine trees with no neighbors in sight. The cabin itself was rustic but comfortable with a huge fireplace in the living room and an abundant supply of logs. In addition, there was a kitchen and bath and two bedrooms.

The light was fading by the time Holly unpacked and put away the store of groceries she had stopped to buy. She lit a roaring fire and made some coffee, taking it into the living room where she curled up on the couch to watch the dancing flames. Soon she would have to make some dinner. When was the last time she had eaten? Holly yawned and closed her eyes for a minute. The next time she opened them it was morning.

At first the unfamiliar bird sounds puzzled her and then memory returned and she sprang up and went to the window. It was a beautiful crisp day with sunshine slanting through the trees, their dark green providing a vivid contrast to the deep blue sky.

The next thing that registered was that she was famished. After bathing hurriedly and dressing in wool pants and a heavy sweater, Holly cooked herself a big breakfast of bacon and eggs. Carrying the last bite of toast with her to the sink, she cleared away the dishes and then went outside.

The woods were alive with bird songs and little rustlings in the underbush as Holly trudged through the pine needles. The lake was a huge shining blue platter in the distance and she stopped to admire it, inhaling deep breaths of the clean mountain air. Just being in this beautiful solitary spot was having a calming effect on her nerves and Holly was sure that she would find a solution to her problems. But not now. It was difficult to focus on anything unpleasant. Every time she started to think about the future, Slade's face rose up to haunt her and she resolutely made her mind a blank.

The following days blended together in a kind of blur. Holly walked for miles, exhausting herself physically. One day she walked all the way down to the lake, deliberately picking a deserted spot where she wouldn't have to talk to anyone. At night she tuned her little transistor radio to music and sat in front of the fire reading, or at least turning the pages automatically even though little of what she read registered. And very often she slept on the couch instead of bothering to go to bed.

One morning she was startled by a sound at the front door. It sounded like a child crying. Opening the door, she found a little dark haired boy of about four. His face was tear stained and there was a rip in the knee of his well washed jeans.

"Mama, I want my mama," he wailed.

Picking him up in her arms, Holly tried to soothe him. "Don't cry, honey, we'll find your mama. Where did you come from?"

The tears stopped and he gave her a watery smile. "Over there."

He gestured vaguely and while she was deciding what to do with him, a young woman burst into the clearing. She had a toddler on her hip and there was a frantic expression on her face. "Paul, you little demon! How many times have I told you not to wander away? You know very well you're not allowed to go out of the yard!"

"I was just about to go looking for you," Holly told her, "but I'm glad you showed up. I hadn't the faintest idea where he came from."

"Honestly, that child is going to make me old before my time," the girl sighed. The baby was squirming in her grasp and she set him on the ground. "All right, Michael, you can get down but try not to eat any dirt." She smiled at Holly. "I'm Mary Blanchard and I'm sorry if Paul disturbed you."

Holly supplied her own name and said, "Oh, he didn't—surprised is more the word for it. Won't you come in and have some coffee?"

"I'd love a cup if it isn't too much trouble. I didn't have a chance for any this morning. Paul, don't touch anything," his mother cautioned as they entered the cabin.

"I don't think there's anything here that he can hurt himself on," Holly said.

"I was thinking more of your possessions," Mary said dryly. "Paul is a one man wrecking crew and Michael is his apprentice." She looked around speculatively. "Your place is so nice and neat. It's easy to see that you don't have any children."

Holly's face was averted as she measured out the coffee. "No, I'm not married."

"You're smart." A laugh followed the words. "I don't mean that of course. I wouldn't take a million for my two little terrors, but sometimes I think I'd *give* that amount for one whole day alone. No kids, no husband, just blessed solitude."

"That isn't all it's cracked up to be either," Holly said shortly, watching the two little boys playing happily on the floor with the deck of cards she had provided.

Why did they both have to have dark hair and light eyes? She gave them each a cookie and was rewarded with cherubic smiles.

"I guess you're right—the grass is always greener and all that. And it isn't as though I went into this with my eyes closed." An impish grin lit Mary's face. "To paraphrase Oscar Wilde, one child can be an accident, two would be downright carelessness."

Holly returned her grin. "And there is no excuse for carelessness nowadays."

"Certainly not for a bright young statistician, which is what I was before I got married."

"That sounds like an unusual job. I don't think I've ever met anyone in that field—not a woman anyway." Holly looked curiously at her guest. "It must take a lot of training—and then to give it all up. Do you ever miss it?"

Mary turned serious. "No, because I weighed all the pros and cons before I took the plunge and I decided Hank meant a lot more to me than my career. It was the right decision and I've never been sorry, but even if it hadn't worked, as least I reached out for it. The ones I feel sorry for are those poor souls who spend so much time agonizing over things that they're afraid to live."

A wail arose from the living room and Paul dashed in to announce that chubby little Michael had crawled under the couch and was unable to wiggle out again. In the ensuing commotion, he was gently eased out and placated with another cookie.

Taking a last sip of coffee, Mary announced that it was time to leave. "I've discovered that my children are like pistachio ice cream. A little is delightful, a lot is more than most people really want. Come see us if you get lonesome, Holly, we're just around the bend in the trail."

When they had gone, Holly cleared away the coffee cups thoughtfully. She put on her windbreaker and went to take her usual walk, but this time her mind was working at top speed. Mary and her brood had punctured the vacuum Holly had been living in and more than that, her words had struck home. They seemed to echo all around her in the quiet woods . . . "those poor souls who spend so much time agonizing over things that they're afraid to live."

Holly knew that she had been trying to drop out of life, but at twenty-three that wasn't very practical. Besides, it was totally foreign to her nature. She would probably always be in love with Slade. Maybe he had spoiled her for all other men and maybe she would never marry but so what? Did that mean that she was going to walk through the rest of her life like a zombie? There was a whole world out there and it was time she went back and joined it.

Packing up took only a short time and after dropping off the key to the cabin, Holly was on her way back to San Francisco. Plans swirled around in her head. First and foremost was a place to stay, because she was determined not to melt into the anonymity of another hotel room. A few phone calls to old friends would ensure her lodging for the night and tomorrow she would go job hunting.

But when the city rose up across the bridge, she decided to make one slight detour. It wouldn't hurt to go see Mac Farnsworth, her old boss, and find out what the job situation was. They had always had a cordial relationship and he might be able to save her hours of pavement pounding. He would undoubtedly ask embarrassing questions, but she was going to have to face them sooner or later. If Mac knew of any openings, at least she would have some prospects for the next day.

Holly found a parking place near the *Pleasure* Magazine offices and entered the building, determined not to think about how different her circumstances were now. But in spite of her resolve, she was assailed by uncertainties. What if Slade had blacklisted her? Almost as bad, what if Mac had already heard the story from on high and didn't want to risk getting involved with her?

There were innumerable corporate ways of giving the polite brush off. If his secretary said, "Mr. Farnsworth is in a meeting right now," or "Mr. Farnsworth says to leave your number and he will get back to you," then she would have her answer.

Holly's hands were icy as she gave her name to his secretary but her fears were groundless. Mac came out to the outer office to greet her, saying, "Holly, you're a sight for sore eyes. Come on in."

He closed the door after her and ushered her to a chair like an honored guest. "It's so good to see you again. Tell me, how was Europe?"

She moistened her lips. Now came the questions. "It . . . it was very exciting."

"I can imagine. Did you have time to do any sight-seeing?"

"Yes, I saw quite a lot."

"That's great," he beamed.

Holly looked at him warily. Was it possible he didn't know that she was no longer working for Slade? That was something she hadn't foreseen and it made things rather sticky. Sparring for time, she said, "You look like everything is going well, Mac."

He leaned back and crossed his arms behind his head. "It's like a whole new world here. I haven't been this happy in years. The pressure is off and we've turned out some in-depth articles that I think have real merit."

"I'm so happy for you," Holly said sincerely.

He smiled his thanks and said, "How about you, Holly, what are your plans?"

That could mean anything and she picked her way carefully. "I just got back in town and I'm looking for a job. Since I've been out of touch for a while, it occurred to me that you might know of an opening." She braced herself for the flood of questions that strangely enough, didn't come.

"It's strange that you should ask because your old job at the *Bulletin* happens to be open."

"How could that be?" she asked sharply. "I've been gone for weeks, surely they filled it by now."

"They did but she didn't work out." He shook his head expressively. "It looks like you turned up at just the right time."

The thought of working for Slade again was insupportable and Holly decided she would rather starve first. "That wasn't what I had in mind. Do you know of anything else?"

"Well, let's see. Times are rather tough right now, Holly, a lot of publications are folding." He looked up at the ceiling. "I did hear that the *Petaluma Times* is looking for a society editor."

"Society editor? Petaluma is a little farming community!"

He shrugged. "Maybe you'd have to double in want ads and lost and found but it is a job."

Holly was outraged. "I'm a journalist not a green kid just starting out."

"I told you it was tough. If you want my advice, you'll go back to the *Bulletin.*"

She jumped to her feet and paced the floor, scarcely conscious of what she was doing. "I can't go back there."

"Sure you can." He looked at her shrewdly. "It doesn't have to be forever. Just till things loosen up a little. Then when something better comes along you can quit."

That was true but the thought of taking Slade's money, even though she would work her ankles off for it, was galling. Still, the alternative of starting at the bottom on a little country paper was equally unacceptable. Mac watched her without comment and Holly said pleadingly, "Are you sure you don't know of anything else?"

He shook his head. "Face it, Holly, those are your two choices. This is basically a small town and we hear of all the openings."

Her shoulders sagged and she said hopelessly, "Okay, Mac, I'll think about it."

"Unfortunately, you don't have that luxury. I happen to know that they have narrowed the choice down to two people and they're going to make a decision tonight. If you want the job you'll have to get over there right away."

"You mean right now? But I couldn't . . . I mean I have to. . . ." Holly sank into a chair. "If they're that close to a decision then I don't stand a chance anyway."

"You do when you have me on your side." He pulled the telephone forward. "Get going, I'll tell them to stop the presses, Holly Holbrooke is on the way."

She gave a little laugh that almost turned into a sob. "Oh, Mac, you sound like a city editor again."

"And you're too professional to miss a deadline," he roared. "Go on, get over there!"

Mac was dialing the phone as she left the office and with a sinking heart, Holly knew she couldn't let him down. He was going out on a limb for her and the least she could do was go for the interview.

How on earth had all this happened and what was she letting herself in for? Maybe all her fears were for nothing and she wouldn't get the job. But suppose she did? What would happen if Slade found out? He would likely be furious and fire her, Holly thought resignedly.

Still, the chance of his finding out was slight. The *Bulletin* was just one drop in the vast ocean of his empire and it had already been reorganized. He wouldn't pay any attention to it for at least another year and by that time she would be long gone. Mac was right, she would be a fool to pass up this opportunity. And it wasn't as though she were shortchanging Slade. She was a topflight reporter and he would get more than his money's worth.

"I'm here to see the managing editor," she told the girl at the desk, trying to still the quiver in her voice. Why hadn't she asked Mac the man's name? It would have been more professional. Everyone was new around here now.

But the young woman smiled at her and said, "Oh, yes, Miss Holbrooke, he's expecting you. Go right in."

Entering Mac's old office was a bittersweet experience. She had been in and out of here so often, perching informally on the desk and discussing everything under the sun. Even if she got the job it would be all different now. What was the new editor like? At the moment she couldn't tell because his high-backed chair was swiveled toward the window.

Holly waited a minute and cleared her throat. When that produced no result, she said, "Um . . . I've come to apply for the job as reporter. I believe Mac Farnsworth telephoned about me." A low grunt was the only response. "Do you . . . would you like to hear my qualifications?"

"I know them by heart, Miss Holbrooke. You are

impulsive, headstrong and hot-tempered." The chair swung around and Slade was regarding her coldly.

Holly turned pale and clutched at the desk to steady herself. "You!" was all she could manage.

"Yes, me," he scowled. "Where the hell have you been? Do you know I've been going out of my mind worrying about you?"

For a moment, Holly thought she had wished him here and she couldn't stop looking at him. He was even bigger than she remembered and her heart started to thud as she gazed at the dark hair that fell across his tanned forehead and the firm mouth that had once touched hers so tenderly.

"What are you doing here?" she whispered. "You're supposed to be in Rome."

"Of course I'm supposed to be in Rome, but instead of that I've had to fly halfway across the world looking for a silly little girl who doesn't have an ounce of brains in her empty little head."

His harsh voice convinced her that she wasn't imagining things and a little color started coming back into Holly's cheeks. "Did you fly all that distance just to insult me?" she demanded.

"We'll get to that in a minute," he said ominously. "Right now I want to know where you've been all week. I've had everyone in San Francisco looking for you including a whole firm of private detectives."

Her eyes widened incredulously. "You put *detectives* on my trail? Why would you do a thing like that?" And then it came to her and she flushed angrily. "I told you I would pay back the money. You didn't have to go to those lengths."

Slade rounded the desk in a few giant strides and taking her by the shoulders, shook her until her head bobbed back and forth like a rag doll's. "Do you know what I ought to do to you for that?"

"You just did," she gasped, clutching at his shirt for support. Her hands could feel the warmth and hardness of his chest through the thin fabric and her legs began to tremble. No matter what he did to her, she couldn't fight the longing his raw masculinity aroused in her.

He brushed the tumbled hair out of her eyes with a touch that was unexpectedly gentle and cupping her chin in his palm he asked, "Why did you run away, Holly?"

Long lashes shaded turquoise-colored eyes as she resisted the impulse to put her arms around his waist and lean against him. She had forgotten how meltingly marvelous it was to be around Slade. How everything seemed to pale into insignificance except the need to touch him and hear his deep musical voice.

His breath fanned her forehead as he drew her closer. "Didn't you know I would come after you, my love?"

Tiny flames licked through her veins but Holly tried desperately to ignore them. Slade had a very slick line, but whatever had brought him back it couldn't have been her. Swallowing hard, she said, "Did Monique finish her picture, is that why you came home?"

He pulled her into his arms and tilted her face up so his hungry mouth could cover hers. There was a kind of desperation in the way he parted her lips and explored the warm inner recesses as though he wanted to devour her. His hands grasped her hips lovingly, pulling her against his hard thighs until there was no doubt about how much he wanted her.

Holly was lost in a dream world as she surrendered herself willingly to his hands, his mouth, his whole body. Waves of desire coursed from one to the other and it was finally Slade who brought them back to reality.

When he finally lifted his head it was with obvious reluctance, the molten passion still very close to the surface. Holly continued to cling to him unashamedly, unwilling to let him go, and Slade's hands tightened for a moment before he got a grip on himself.

Drawing a shaky breath, he kissed the tip of her nose and asked throatily, "Now what's all this nonsense about Monique?"

Holly descended slowly to earth. She knew Slade wanted her. There had always been this electric attraction between them but was he suggesting a relationship? And if so, did that mean she would be replacing Monique or merely getting the crumbs from her table?

Holly looked at him uncertainly. "Have you two broken up?"

"You might say that," he smiled.

"And you want me to take her place?" Holly asked tentatively. The mere thought made her shiver. Could she become Slade's mistress, knowing she would have to share him with other women? But could she say no and risk never seeing him again? It had been hard the first time but now that she had seen and touched him again, Holly knew it would be impossible.

He watched the play of emotions over her expressive face and his smile broadened as he answered her question. "You might say that too."

She still couldn't believe he wasn't playing with her, remembering that terrible night in London when she had offered herself and he had rejected her. "What made you change your mind?" she asked slowly.

"Let's just say that when you ran out of my office

with the avowed intention of marrying that little weasel Mario, which incidentally I never would have permitted, I decided it was time I took over."

Holly fiddled with a button on his shirt. "I wouldn't actually have gone through with it." And then unwillingly, "You were right about him. He was everything you said."

Slade picked her up in his arms and carried her over to the chair, holding her closely as he swiveled back and forth. "Let's don't talk about him any more." He kissed the delicate skin in back of her ear, sending shivers of delight down her spine. "Oh, Holly, you'll never know what I went through when I found you were gone. How could you leave me?"

"I didn't think you wanted me," she said simply.

"Not want you?" His arms crushed her so tightly she could hardly breathe and when he kissed her, the dominant possession left her trembling. His hands roamed gently over her body, touching, caressing, getting reacquainted, and small sparks burst into flames everywhere he lingered. "I've wanted nothing else since the first moment I set eyes on you," he murmured, nibbling on her ear.

"You had a funny way of showing it," Holly said when she got her breath back. "You spent most of your time in Rome at the film studios with Monique. How do you think that made me feel?"

"Jealous, I hope," he grinned. "But for your information, little Miss Jump to Conclusions, I was not with Monique. It was only a coincidence that she was making a movie there. Bianca Film Studios has been in financial difficulty for some time and I've been dickering to buy it."

"A *movie* studio?"

"Why not? It's a way of diversifying and we're already in the entertainment field with our movie magazines."

"But I thought—"

He gathered her back into his arms and stopped her words with a kiss. "I know what you thought. And I'm sure you thought the same thing about Marsha."

"But I wasn't wrong there was I?" Holly looked at him and then dropped her eyes. "That night in London when—" She stopped, finding that the hurt was still there. "You went to her didn't you?"

"You think I could have gone to any other woman?" He looked at her incredulously. "Do you want to know what I did?" he asked grimly. "I took a cold shower and then I went out and walked for a couple of hours."

"But *why?*"

He gave her a lopsided smile. "Because I'm an idiot. The idea of marriage scared the daylights out of me. I needed some time to get used to it."

"But I never expected you to marry me!"

"Well, you should have," he told her severely. "And if you hadn't flown out of the suite in such a rage the next morning, I would have asked you."

The thought of what she had destroyed almost crushed Holly. Slade had wanted to marry her but her temper and hurt pride had made her throw away the most precious gift he could offer.

Tears glistened on her long eyelashes and she kept her head averted. "Even though you changed your mind about marrying me, did you have to be so brutal?"

He sighed. "I know I was rotten but try to understand, honey. When I realized I'd driven you right into Alan's arms I went a little bit crazy. I had to send him away because I was afraid I might kill him. The thought of you and him. . . ." He took a deep breath. "Well, I've come to terms with that. At first I thought I couldn't take it. I wanted to be the first with you, the one to teach you about love."

"But Slade—"

"No, don't say anything," he interrupted. "It's all right. When you ran away and I didn't know what happened to you, if you were sick or if you needed me. . . ." He shuddered. "I knew then that nothing was important except finding you and making you mine. The rest doesn't matter anymore. I'm going to make such passionate constant love to you that you'll never be able to think of another man. You *will* marry me won't you, sweetheart?" he asked almost humbly.

Holly couldn't believe it—was she actually being given another chance? "Oh, Slade, *darling,* do you really mean it?" Before he could answer, she threw her arms around his neck. "Of course I'll marry you!"

He folded her in his arms and kissed her with such passion that she was shaking when he finally released her. His breathing was shallow and she could feel his heart thundering against hers as he said thickly, "Let's make it soon."

"How about tomorrow?" Holly whispered, closing her eyes as his lips trailed a line of fiery kisses down her cheek to the hidden cleft between her aching breasts.

He paused just long enough to say, "What's wrong with this afternoon?"

"That sounds even better." She gave a shiver of delight and smoothed the thick dark hair as he rested his head against her breast. "But first there is something you should know. I didn't sleep with Alan," she said softly.

He became very still for a moment and then lifted his head and gave her a small ghost of a smile. "Don't, Holly, I told you it doesn't matter."

An impish light cast sparks from her jewel-toned eyes. "I'm not too experienced in these matters, but I think you're going to find out on our wedding night that I'm telling the truth."

He cupped her face in his palms and a dawning wonder at what he found there convinced him. Crushing her in his arms, he buried his face in the scented softness of her hair and groaned, "My darling love, I don't deserve you!"

"Does that mean you're trying to get out of marrying me?" she demanded with mock severity.

The kiss he gave her more than answered her question.

Coming Next Month

Magnolia Moon by Sondra Stanford

Nicole went to New Orleans to look for a job. Instead, she found magic at the Mardi Gras. Ryan St. James was a man with everything under control—until he met Nicole. She made his blood run like a river after the storm. He made her breath race like wind through the trees. Together they challenged the very stars and wrote their love across the Southern sky.

Web Of Passion by Nancy John

The feelings Dirk Lancaster, outback lord, raised in Risa were enough to leave her aching for his every touch. In this land of torrential rains and dry spells of searing intensity, Risa could blossom into a woman open to life, ready for love, and ripe for the one man who could tame her heart and master the raging sun.

Autumn Harvest by Angel Milan

Botanist Tara Deer had plenty of plans. Then she met Kane Boland and the dreams she had once nurtured grew to include the lean Oklahoma rancher who held her heart and happiness in his hands. He could touch her with passion, then bring her to a peak of ecstasy and leave her trembling with desire. Without this man, all her dreams were but empty air.

Coming Next Month

Heartstorm by Jane Converse

Cocos Island was a land of mystery, of steaming jungles, barren rocks and pagan majesty, a land of romance with a link to the past. Here Terry Long and Dean Saunders met and clashed and came together in stormy passion beneath a canopy of trees and a golden island sun. Here they fought their way through their own misconceptions and misjudgments to greet tomorrow's dawn.

Collision Course by Carole Halston

At last the girl who had never lacked for anything had everything she wanted. Lindy Randolph met her match when she met Neil Hammonds. He was a man to dream about; the challenge was to make him dream of her. Lindy's breath caught and her heart quickened when he was near and she longed to rise with him to the heights that passion promised.

Proud Vintage by Brenna Drummond

Hurt by love, Katherine Carson was afraid to trust any man. Then, in California's Napa Valley, she met Adam Redmont, a man of pride, power and passion. Adam taught her to trust again, to express herself with a touch, a look. Together they lit a fire even time could not put out and shared the secrets that only lovers know.

READERS' COMMENTS ON SILHOUETTE SPECIAL EDITIONS:

"I just finished reading the first six Silhouette Special Edition Books and I had to take the opportunity to write you and tell you how much I enjoyed them. I enjoyed all the authors in this series. Best wishes on your Silhouette Special Editions line and many thanks."

—B.H.*, Jackson, OH

"The Special Editions are really special and I enjoyed them very much! I am looking forward to next month's books."

—R.M.W.*, Melbourne, FL

"I've just finished reading four of your first six Special Editions and I enjoyed them very much. I like the more sensual detail and longer stories. I will look forward each month to your new Special Editions."

—L.S.*, Visalia, CA

"Silhouette Special Editions are — 1.) Superb! 2.) Great! 3.) Delicious! 4.) Fantastic! . . . Did I leave anything out? These are books that an adult woman can read . . . I love them!"

—H.C.*, Monterey Park, CA

* names available on request